DATE DUE

MISS HARTWELL'S DILEMMA

MISS HARTWELL'S DILEMMA

Carola Dunn

Walker and Company
New York

First published in the United States of America in 1988 by the Walker Publishing Company, Inc.

Published simultaneously in Canada by Thomas Allen & Son Canada, Limited, Markham, Ontario.

Library of Congress Cataloging-in-Publication Data

Dunn, Carola.
    Miss Hartwell's dilemma / Carola Dunn.
    p.c.m.
    ISBN 0-8027-1041-7
    I. Title.
PR6054.U537M56   1988
823'.914--dc19   88-209
                                                   CIP

Printed in the United States of America.

10 9 8 7 6 5 4 3 2 1

=1=

MISS HARTWELL SIGHED with relief as she ruled two neat lines below the last figure in her account book. Leaning back in her chair, she gazed out of the window at the pink and yellow roses blooming in the front garden. She took off the spectacles she wore to make herself look like a schoolmistress.

It was not easy to persuade the parents of prospective students to take seriously this tall, slim, elegant redhead with no more than twenty-six years in her dish. Though she wore the plainest gowns in dreary browns and greys, long-sleeved and high to the neck, a poor fit was more than she could bring herself to sink to. And though she braided her hair, tied it in a topknot, and covered it with a spinsterish cap, copper curls were forever escaping to betray her.

Nonetheless, she had succeeded in instilling confidence in a large enough number of anxious Mamas that after six years the Castle Hedingham Academy for Young Ladies was flourishing.

Daisy, the parlour-maid, peeped round the door of her study.

"I've brung the post, miss, and a great heap there do be." She deposited the pile on the desk.

"People *will* wait until a week or two before the start of the school year to decide where to send their daughters. Oh dear, I simply cannot manage more than another two or three." Miss Hartwell sorted through the papers. "At least most of these are franked."

"There were sixpence to pay, miss, but there's a letter

from America, too, with three shilling due. I didn't have enough by me, not and get the lamb for Cook and Mrs. Vaux's needles."

"That's all right, Daisy. I shall walk down to the village myself and fetch it. Though if it is another spoiled brat used to slaves obeying her every whim, I shall most definitely not have room for her."

"I mind that young lady from Carolina, miss, her as couldn't pick up her own pocket handkerchee."

"Perhaps she has written to us. Fetch me my parasol, if you please, and tell Mrs. Vaux I am going out but shall return for luncheon. I have an appointment this afternoon."

The August morning was sultry. As she strolled up King Street, Miss Hartwell was glad of the parasol, a pale grey affair with modest, white ruffles, matching her grey muslin round dress. In Queen Street a cart loaded with aromatic hops rumbled past her, raising a cloud of dust that made her cough. She had forgotten that it was Monday, market day. The Bell Inn was bound to be crowded. She usually avoided the village centre on market days.

The vicar came through the gate of the churchyard as she passed.

"Good morning, Mr. Raeburn," she said with a smile.

He was a middle-aged, round-faced, cheerful gentleman, bespectacled, somewhat portly, and an inch or two below her in height. A faint scent of peppermint always hung about him, though he had never been seen to eat peppermint lozenges. She sometimes suspected that his adherence to Church doctrine was less than total, but he shepherded his flock with great goodwill, always ready to help those in need.

"Good morning, Miss Hartwell." He raised his hat in salute, then took a large square of blue-spotted cotton from his pocket and dabbed his forehead. A black umbrella dangled from his arm. "We are in for a storm, an I mistake not. It is hot even inside the church. I hope you have not far to walk?"

"No, just to the Bell. Do you go my way?"

He shook his head regretfully. "No, I am bound for Sheep-cote Road. I shall call in at the school on my return, if I may."

"By all means. Miss Tisdale will be delighted to see you—as will my aunt, of course." Her quizzing eye noted a slight intensification of the ruddiness of his cheeks. "Perhaps you will join us for luncheon?"

"Thank you, ma'am. I shall be happy to."

"Then I shall see you presently. Good day, Mr. Raeburn."

"Good day, Miss Hartwell." He tipped his hat again and set off the way she had just come.

As she turned the corner into St. James's Street, she paused to contemplate the busy scene. From a little beyond the Bell Inn where the street widened, as far as the green by the forge, hop growers argued price and quality with brewers' agents, harvesters haggled with farmers' wives over baskets of ripe, juicy plums and pears, a peddler hawked his trinkets, and the children of the villagers dashed about underfoot adding to the noise and confusion.

This prospect had probably not changed very much since mediaeval times, thought Miss Hartwell. If it was fated that she should be a schoolmistress, she could not ask a better place to teach history. The castle keep, brooding on its hilltop, no longer belonged to the Earls of Oxford, but the market charter granted seven hundred years ago by King John was still in force.

One day she must try to find out whether he had granted it before or after besieging the castle. It seemed odd to give such a valuable prize to one's enemy.

"Watch out, miss!" shouted a carter rounding the bend behind her at all of two miles an hour. She stepped aside, abandoned her musing, and went on into the Bell.

The long, low coffee-room with its heavy oak beams was still quiet at this hour of the morning and cool and dark after the muggy outdoors. Miss Hartwell closed her parasol as the innkeeper stepped forwards to greet her.

"Morning, miss."

"Good morning, Mr. Brown. Daisy says you have a letter for me."

"'Sright, miss. From the colonies, three shilling due. I'd of let young Daisy take it, for I knows you're good for the money, miss, but she would have it you might not want to pay that much for a letter from America."

"Daisy has a poor opinion of Americans. I'll take it, of course."

A gentleman entered the room, glanced around with a look of boredom and, ignoring the lady's presence, called "Landlord" in an imperative tone.

"I'll be with you in a moment, sir," said Mr. Brown. "'Tis on the mantel in the kitchen, Miss Hartwell. I'll fetch it this instant."

As the innkeeper bustled out, the newcomer swung round to stare at Miss Hartwell with hard eyes. She raised her chin and stared back. He was tall and dark, lean though broad-shouldered, carelessly dressed even for the country yet obviously a gentleman. He might have been handsome but for his sombre expression. In his late thirties, she decided, certainly old enough to know better than to examine her in that insolent way.

Under her scrutiny, he raised his eyebrows, bowed slightly, and turned away.

"Here we are, miss." Mr. Brown was back. "Been directed and redirected all over the country, looks like. That's why there'd be so much to pay, I daresay, for 'tis but one sheet. Thank you, miss."

Giving him the three shillings, she took the letter, dog-eared from its travels, and glanced at the address. As he said, it had been redirected at least twice, every inch of the paper covered with writing. Only one line was clearly legible. All it said was "To Miss Amaryllis Hartwell," yet she gazed at it in shock.

The line was in her father's hand. She recognised it immediately, though she had not seen that free-flowing, generous script for six years. She stared, unbelieving.

"You all right, miss?" asked the landlord with concern.

"Miss Hartwell?"

"What? Oh . . . oh yes, Mr. Brown. Thank you. Just . . . surprised. I must go."

Oblivious of the renewed interest of the stranger, she hurried out.

The heat slowed her walk, giving her time to think. She became aware that the letter was still in her hand and thrust it into her reticule. Inevitably her mind returned to the last time she had seen that handwriting, to the gay dinner on that long-ago evening, the splendid gifts, all sold long since, and the painful interview with the lawyer the next day.

Papa had unexpectedly dined with them. She thought it was for the usual reason: he had grown tired of his latest *chère amie*. To her aunt's dismay she said as much. Papa had never encouraged her to be mealymouthed, and Bertram admired her too much, or was too indolent, to protest her occasional use of unladylike language.

She shied away from the thought of Bertram.

After dinner Papa had given them each a small box, even Miss Tisdale though she was only his daughter's ex-governess. How he had enjoyed their cries of delight as they drew forth the contents: emerald and diamond earrings for his dear little Amy, an exquisite cameo pendant for his widowed sister, a necklace of carved ivory and jet beads for Tizzy. He always chose the perfect gift, and she had wondered with what monstrously expensive bauble he had dismissed his opera dancer.

Blind to the present time, she stumbled in a pothole, wrenching her ankle. The brief pain brought tears to her eyes. With an effort she blinked them back, fearful that once started she might not be able to stop weeping.

Concentrating on her steps, she reached the garden gate at last. With fierce determination she gazed at the neat white sign, its elegant black lettering proclaiming to the world that this was The Castle Hedingham Academy for Young Ladies of Good Family, Proprietor Miss A. Hartwell. Twice before, Papa had drastically disrupted her life. Whatever he was up to now, he must not be allowed to destroy her achievement here—hers and Tizzy's and Aunt Eugenia's.

Miss Hartwell looked up at the square façade of the red-brick Georgian mansion and counted along the first-floor windows until she came to their private drawing-room. Behind that window sat Miss Tisdale, doubtless refreshing her memory of some work of English literature, and Mrs. Vaux, most likely working at her endless stitchery.

Miss Hartwell hurried up the garden path between the neat rosebeds, dashed across the empty vestibule, and ran up the stairs. Pink-cheeked and panting, she burst into the drawing-room, a small room furnished with an eye to comfort rather than elegance.

" 'The race is not to the swift, nor the battle to the strong.' Ecclesiastes 9, verse 11," said Miss Tisdale, whose father and brother were both clergymen. "My dear Amaryllis, do sit down and catch your breath. Then tell us what is the matter."

"Pray do!" seconded Mrs. Vaux, looking at her niece in alarm. "It must be something quite frightful for your behaviour is usually perfectly unexceptionable, dignified even, yet you have entered the room in what I can only describe as a hoydenish manner." The widow, a still pretty though faded blonde, took very seriously her position as teacher of deportment and ladylike conduct.

Amaryllis dropped into a chair and drew the letter from her reticule. With shaking fingers she broke the seal, then thrust the paper at Miss Tisdale.

"I cannot. Do you read it, Tizzy, if you please. It is from Papa." She clenched her hands in her lap.

"Gracious heaven!" cried Mrs. Vaux, "I never thought to hear from my brother again, I vow. What does he say?"

Miss Tisdale scanned the single sheet. Her pale blue eyes widened a little, and her severe mouth twitched at the corners. Still, she spoke with perfect gravity.

"Lord Hartwell is in a fine way of business with a hardware store in Philadelphia. He hopes that if you are not perfectly comfortable in your present situation you will join him, and he remains your ever affectionate father."

"A hardware store?" Mrs. Vaux asked, puzzled.

"Ironmongery, I believe."

Amaryllis let out a whoop of laughter. "Papa an iron-monger! And his dress was always in the height of fashion, complete to a shade, even when he had not a feather to fly with. I cannot imagine it. And he wants me to join him behind the counter? Let me see, Tizzy."

"Is that all Henry says? 'Pon rep, that is somewhat brief after all these years. And not a word to his sister?" Mrs. Vaux grew pink with indignation. "Does he mention the . . . the person he ran off with?"

"He begins 'Inez and I . . . ' Aunt. I never enquired as to the name of his inamorata, but that is a Spanish name, is it not? I expect they are married long since. Oh, here is a postscript. It seems I have two brothers." She laughed again. This time there was a hysterical edge to it. "What do you suppose happens to a title when it is inherited by an American?"

" 'Lo, children are an heritage of the Lord: and the fruit of the womb is his reward.' Psalm 127, verse 3. Though why the Lord should see fit to reward his lordship I have not the least notion."

"Perhaps they are horrid children. I always wanted a brother, but not twenty years younger than myself. Tizzy, Aunt Eugenia, what am I to do?"

"Why, nothing at present, my dear," said Miss Tisdale soothingly. "When you have had time to consider the news calmly, you shall write to your Papa. How odd that his lordship ended up in America. It was 1814 when he left and we were then at war with the Americans. Yes, Daisy, what is it?"

The parlour-maid bobbed a curtsey in the doorway. "Luncheon's ready, miss, and the vicar's just come."

"Oh dear," said Amaryllis, "I quite forgot I invited him. My apologies to Cook, Daisy. Show Mr. Raeburn up and set another place at the table if you please. Though I don't believe I shall be able to swallow a mouthful," she muttered.

All three ladies strove to appear normal at the luncheon table. Mrs. Vaux succeeded because her inconsequential chatter was indistinguishable from her habitual polite commonplaces. Miss Tisdale always appeared grave but the vicar, who greatly admired her ready quotations from the Good Book allied to an irreverently ironic wit that nullified their piety, was conscious of a sense of strain.

Miss Hartwell's artificial brightness, very unlike her usual manner, was interrupted by periods of abstraction when she heard not a word addressed to her. Mr. Raeburn also noticed that her hearty appetite had failed. She refused a slice of the delicious rabbit pie and after peeling a pear ate only two bites.

The terrace at the back of the house was in the shade by the time they had finished, so they repaired thither to drink tea. Miss Hartwell left the others after a few minutes. She had an appointment with a prospective parent. As she disappeared through the French doors, Mr. Raeburn turned to his remaining companions.

"Well, ladies," he said encouragingly, "are you going to tell me what is troubling you?"

"Oh Vicar, how did you guess?" squeaked Mrs. Vaux. "I'm sure I did not speak a word of it."

"Amaryllis has received a letter from Lord Hartwell," said Miss Tisdale in a grim voice.

"Lord Hartwell?"

"Her father."

"Lord Hartwell her father? Bless my soul. Of course she is clearly a lady, but her father a peer. What in the world is she doing running a seminary for young ladies?"

" 'Thereby hangs a tale.' Hamlet, act 2, scene 5," said Miss Tisdale, who had no objection to Shakespeare if an apposite Biblical quotation did not spring to her lips. "It is not mine to tell, but if Mrs. Vaux has no objection I believe you should hear it. Perhaps you will be able to advise us."

"My brother, the viscount, was prodigious extravagant," said the widow dolefully. "Or perhaps I should say he *is*, though if he has a thriving business in Philadelphia perhaps he is not anymore."

"Your brother?" asked Mr. Raeburn, understandably confused.

"Lord Hartwell. He brought an abbey to a grange and then rented it out."

"His lordship was forced by pecuniary embarrassment to let his country house to a rear admiral," explained Miss Tisdale. "Amaryllis was very much shocked to have to leave her beloved home."

"Gambling?" ventured the vicar.

The ladies looked at each other and nodded. Mrs. Vaux took the plunge.

"No. At least, he did gamble, of course, but he was by no means addicted to gaming." She looked around nervously and then, with a significant look, whispered, "Muslin company!"

The Viscount Hartwell, though approaching fifty, had been a fine figure of a man. His life of dissipation had not blurred his features, dimmed his eyes, nor slowed his step. This he readily attributed to drinking nothing but the best Burgundy and never more than a bottle at a sitting. Neither gamester nor sportsman, he had squandered his fortune on expensively casual liaisons with high flying Birds of Paradise, whom he treated with the same reckless generosity as he did his daughter.

As the vicar did not appear to be excessively shocked, the widow went on, "My sister-in-law died when Amaryllis was only five, and Henry never married again. I lost my dear Mr. Vaux soon after, so I went to live at Hart Hall. Miss Tisdale and I brought up Amaryllis."

"Her Papa was generous with money and affection, though not with his time, and she worshipped him," the ex-governess took up the story. "I believe she had a happy childhood. Certainly she was always busy and cheerful."

"A sad romp, and merry as a grig."

"Of course she had expected to go to London for the Season when she reached seventeen, but she did not expect to have to live there year round. Mrs. Vaux and I were quite worried about her."

"She pined for Hart Hall, for the country way of life. We feared she would make herself ill. Then she made her bow to Society, and she did enjoy the balls and assemblies and routs. She was always dressed in the height of fashion, quite the most elegant young female . . . "

"Thanks to your exquisite taste, ma'am," interrupted Miss Tisdale.

Mrs. Vaux beamed and blushed. " . . . but she had changed," she finished.

"Changed?" prompted Mr. Raeburn.

Miss Tisdale pondered. "She lost her enthusiasm for life," she said at last. "She enjoyed balls and routs and masquerades, but in a . . . a sort of careless way, as if it was all meaningless. 'The fashion of this world passeth away.' I Corinthians 5, verse 31, and one of my father's favourite texts. She used to sit for hours doing nothing, dreaming."

"And eating chocolate cherries. I do not know why she never grew plump. I'm sure I could not have eaten so many chocolate cherries without growing as stout as Prinny. The King, as he is now, but that does not make him less fat. Amaryllis must have been contented though, or she'd not have kept Lord Pomeroy dangling after her for two whole years after they were betrothed. Why, she could have been married to the heir to the Earl of Tatenhill and mistress of a fine country mansion had she wished!"

"Perhaps you had best not tell me about Lord Pomeroy," suggested the vicar diplomatically. "I rather think that is Miss Hartwell's personal affair. We were talking of her father?"

"His lordship dined with us one evening unexpectedly and disappeared overnight, leaving only a brief note advising Amaryllis to consult his lawyer. He had sold Hart Hall to the rear admiral. The proceeds he used to pay off all our outstanding bills, though not his own, I believe, and to run off with the daughter of the Spanish Ambassador."

"Bless my soul, the daughter of the Spanish Ambassador?" The vicar was astounded.

"Henry always preferred dark women," Mrs. Vaux explained.

"I had thought the gentlewomen of Spain most strictly bred up and guarded."

"Thus when they taste but a little freedom, they are ready to kick over the traces altogether. They have not been taught self-control since their male relatives have expected always to control them." Miss Tisdale was deeply indignant but displayed her own self-control and continued with the story. "Naturally, Amaryllis was shattered. I shall not discuss the sense of personal betrayal. She adored her father, remember. Our immediate problem was that she had little ready money, we had less, and the lease on the London house had scarce two weeks to run."

"What did she do?" Mr. Raeburn took off his spectacles and polished them vigorously on his blue-spotted handkerchief.

"She went to her godmother, Lady Mountolivet Gurnleigh, who offered her a home."

"Which was amazingly kind of Cornelia, for she is a high stickler for every observance and there was no end of scandal attached to my brother's behaviour. It almost provoked an International Incident," said Mrs. Vaux, still faintly awed at the thought.

"She did not accept the offer," presumed Mr. Raeburn.

"No indeed. The dear girl would not for the world have asked her ladyship to accommodate myself and Miss Tisdale, nor would she abandon us."

"Lady Mountolivet Gurnleigh then suggested that she should take this house, which was empty at the time, for a peppercorn rent. I believe her ladyship would have given her an allowance, and though Amaryllis refused it, we must still be profoundly grateful to Lady Mountolivet Gurnleigh."

"You see," said Mrs. Vaux, bursting with pride in her niece's ingenuity, "Amaryllis had already decided that we should open a school."

"And most successful you have been," said the vicar. He was itching with curiosity about Lord Pomeroy's absence from the end of the tale, but having prohibited all mention of his lordship, he could hardly ask. "I take it you have not heard from Lord Hartwell until this moment?"

"Not a word," chorused the ladies.

At that moment a sheet of lightning split the sky. In the ominous pause that followed they realized that while they were talking huge, anvil-shaped clouds had hidden the sky. Then a rattling tattoo crescendoed into a crash of thunder that seemed to shake the ground.

Mrs. Vaux moaned, put her hands over her ears, and scuttled into the house. Miss Tisdale and the vicar followed at a somewhat more dignified pace. They reached the music room and closed the French doors behind them just as "the windows of heaven were opened. And the rain was upon the earth." Genesis 7, verses 11 and 12.

"Fortunately," said the vicar, "I brought my umbrella."

=2=

AMARYLLIS WALKED SLOWLY up the stairs to the top floor. She had fifteen minutes before her interview with Lord Daniel Winterborne, time enough to tidy her hair and put on a fresh cap.

Her bedchamber was tiny since the larger rooms were generally occupied by her pupils. Nonetheless, it had been her refuge for six years now, and she looked round its sparse furnishings with a sense of coming home. For a moment she felt like throwing herself on the narrow bed and bursting into tears. The resolute common sense that had carried her through those years came to her aid.

What difference did it make in the end that she now knew where Papa was? She had created a life for herself and did not mean to abandon it for an uncertain future in America with a father who had deserted her.

Through the dormer window, she glanced up at the castle on its green hill. For seven hundred years it had looked out over the village, indifferent to heartbreak and rejoicing alike. Her troubles meant nothing to those grey, age-old stones, and in truth those troubles were light compared to many.

Calm and businesslike, Miss Hartwell descended to her office.

Sitting at her desk, she sorted through the letters that had arrived that morning. One was from her godmother. She opened it and was trying to decipher the heavily crossed sheet when Daisy knocked on the door.

"There's a lord to see you, miss."

"Show him in, if you please." She set the letter aside, put on her spectacles, and waited with folded hands.

The sound of Daisy's light step was followed by a firm, booted tread rarely heard in these female precincts.

"Lord Daniel Winterborne, miss," announced Daisy.

The gentleman who strode in was none other than the tall stranger who had stared at her in the inn. She noted again the coat cut for comfort, not fashion, the carelessly knotted neckcloth, and well-worn top boots. His dark eyes still held the same appraising look as he bowed curtly.

"Good afternoon, ma'am."

"Good afternoon, my lord." Miss Hartwell inclined her head with regal condescension. "Pray be seated."

"Thank you." His voice had a curiously controlled quality, as if every word were spoken with care. He pulled a chair closer to the desk and sat down. "As I explained in my letter, I am come to inspect your school to see if it will be suitable for my daughter."

"May I ask why you have chosen the Castle Hedingham Academy?"

"It suits my purpose in being close to my home, but I have not yet 'chosen' it."

"I beg your pardon." Amaryllis was beginning to take a strong dislike to this cold, unsmiling man. She suppressed the feeling and peered at him impassively over the top of her spectacles. "On what criteria do you intend to base your decision?"

"The most important is that Isabel should be happy."

Perhaps he was human after all.

"Your reputation is high in the village," he went on.

He had been spying on her!

"My sister, Lady Carrington, recommended you highly but by hearsay only. I shall require a tour of your premises and a description of the curriculum. If all is to my liking, I shall bring Isabel for a trial period at the beginning of your school term."

Miss Hartwell stood up, eyes flashing with anger at his arrogance. He rose hurriedly. His manners were gentlemanly if anything but conciliatory.

"I fear I cannot accept a pupil on such terms, my lord," she said, with careful calmness. "I am sorry your journey was for nothing."

Surprise flickered across his face, the first hint of any emotion that she had seen on those stern features.

"I shall of course pay for the full term in advance. If Isabel decides to stay, I am willing to pay double your usual rates."

"I am persuaded we shall not suit Miss Isabel, my lord."

He gazed at her searchingly, his dark eyes troubled.

"I have offended you, Miss Hartwell. I beg your pardon. Will you not be seated?" Reluctantly she sat down, and he followed her example. "Are my requests so unreasonable then?"

"I had supposed them demands rather than requests."

Frowning, he considered her statement. When he spoke, the words seemed to emerge with difficulty, as though he deeply regretted the necessity of revealing so much about himself.

"I am not a sociable man. I am to blame if my manner has vexed you. Allow me to explain the situation to you, and perhaps you will reconsider. Isabel is eleven years old, and I fear she is a lonely child. I have been her only companion, other than her nursemaid, of course. My sister has persuaded me that she is in need of friends of her own age and of the guidance of a respectable female who can teach her to conduct herself as a lady. I . . . I do not care to be parted from her by any great distance, and Castle Hedingham is the closest seminary I have been able to find, only some fifteen miles from Wimbish."

"You live at Wimbish?" asked Amaryllis absently.

His revelations intrigued her. She had just placed his name. Lord Winterborne was the heir to the Marquis of Bellingham, and this must be his brother. She had moved in the same circles as George Winterborne once. It seemed odd that he had never mentioned a younger brother who must be very near him in age. George had even been one of her flirts for a time.

She saw the resemblance now. The same tousled dark hair, the same patrician nose, sensitive lips, and broad shoulders. Lord Daniel was much thinner than her memory of George, who at thirty had a magnificent physique that was the envy of less well endowed Corinthians. He had been handsome, too. The face before her now was marked by sorrow and, she thought, bitterness. A family quarrel? She became aware that Lord Daniel had ceased speaking and was awaiting a response.

"I'm sorry," she said, annoyed with herself for letting her mind drift. "I missed what you said."

"I hope that you have reconsidered your refusal, ma'am. I shall be deeply grateful if you will accept Isabel as a pupil, but I cannot promise to force her to stay if she is unhappy."

"Of course not."

At worst the child would leave, and they would have one less to teach, one fewer mouth to feed without losing by it. It was ridiculous to let her dislike of the man influence her management of the school. Besides, she felt sorry for the poor little girl with such a sombre companion.

"Let me tell you something of our courses of study. I teach history, account keeping, sketching, and music. Miss Tisdale teaches English literature, geography with the use of the globes, French. Mrs. Vaux is in charge of deportment, domestic management, and needlework. Our vicar comes in once a week to teach Scripture, and if any of our girls are interested in learning Latin or Greek he gives them lessons. Occasionally we find one or two of the young ladies display a particular talent for music or art, in which case we have a master come in from Colchester to help them. There are no extras, as we do not believe in making a difference between those who can pay for them and those who cannot, which leads to petty pride and envy. For the same reason we do not take parlour boarders. All the girls are expected to keep their own rooms tidy and to help with such minor household tasks as arranging flowers, mending, and dusting."

Miss Hartwell rattled through this speech at a great pace,

having given it many times before. She paused, wondering if she would have to continue with Churchgoing, healthful food, and country walks. Meanwhile, Lord Daniel looked somewhat stunned.

"It sounds perfectly adequate," he assured her.

"The girls wear blue muslin in summer, blue merino in winter. I shall give you patterns to be made up. And now let me call Mrs. Vaux to show you about the house."

Before she could ring the bell, there was a tremendous rattling crash. Amaryllis glanced up at the ceiling in alarm and Lord Daniel jumped to his feet. Then they both turned sheepish as torrential rain began to drum on the window-panes. Lightning flashed, and once more thunder boomed.

"On second thoughts," said Miss Hartwell, "I shall show you myself. My aunt is terrified of thunderstorms and will have run up to hide her head under the counterpane."

She thought he smiled, but the room had grown too dark to see anything with certainty.

"On my own second thoughts," said his lordship, "I must not stay. This downpour will soon make the roads impass-able, and I ought not to keep my horses standing in it. Thank you for your time and patience, ma'am. I shall bring Isabel on the first day of term. Here is a bank draught for the fees."

"Thank you, my lord. I shall expect you on the fourth of September."

He bowed. After locking the bank draught in a drawer, she rose to show him out. He followed her to the vestibule, where they found Miss Tisdale and the vicar looking out at the rain.

"Surely you will not go out in this deluge, Mr. Raeburn," Amaryllis exclaimed, seeing the umbrella in his hand.

"Indeed I must, Miss Hartwell. As I was just saying to Miss Tisdale, my poor sister does not care for thunderstorms and I must not leave her alone. I do believe the rain has already slackened a little."

Amaryllis and Miss Tisdale exchanged a look. Miss Raeburn kept her brother under the cat's paw without ever raising her voice, by the simple means of suffering an attack of nerves whenever things did not go her way. Since things generally did go her way, she found in thunderstorms and dogfights and such incidents an excellent excuse for reminding him of her delicate sensibilities. Amaryllis was privately convinced that had it not been for his sister's opposition, the genial vicar would have long since offered for Tizzy's hand.

Lord Daniel stepped forward. "Allow me to offer you a ride, sir," he said unexpectedly.

Her opinion of him raised another notch, Amaryllis performed the introductions. She thought the vicar looked somewhat flustered when he heard his lordship's name, but the vestibule was almost as dark as her office had been. Indeed, as the gentlemen left, huddling behind raised collars as they dashed towards the waiting carriage, Daisy brought in a branch of candles.

"Beg pardon, miss," she said breathlessly, "I'da brung 'em sooner only Cook were that startled she dropped the best teapot. Smashed to smithereens, it were, and bits all over the kitchen floor. I did tell her as you won't turn her off wi'out a reference, miss, but you know how she is."

Miss Hartwell knew. Every time there was the slightest mishap in the kitchen, Cook was sure she would be dismissed without notice. She sighed.

"Tizzy, would you mind reassuring Cook, or we shan't get any dinner. I must run up to make sure Aunt Eugenia is all right."

As she mixed a glass of hartshorn and water, she pondered the unlikely romance between Mr. Raeburn and her governess. Tizzy had certainly never been pretty, with her pale blue eyes, long, narrow face, and decided chin. Her hair was a nondescript brown, now greying, and so determined to be straight that no quantity of curling papers could put the least wave in it. Besides, Tizzy's ineradicable habit of quoting the Scriptures, with chapter and verse, on all occasions was enough to dissuade most gentlemen from pursuing the acquaintance. That she quoted with a certain disdain for appropriateness and frequently followed the quotation with a witty but sceptical disclaimer must eliminate most clergymen from consideration as suitable spouses.

Amaryllis carried the restorative to her aunt's chamber. Mrs. Vaux was curled up on her pink, frilly counterpane with the pillow over her head and pressed to her ears. She peeped out as her niece sat down on the edge of the bed, then cautiously emerged.

"There is only a faint, distant rumble now and then," Amaryllis reassured her. "Come, drink this hartshorn and you will soon feel more the thing."

"I am sorry to be such a fool," said the widow faintly but with dignity. "Only it does give me such a megrim." She swallowed the potion.

"And of course you are not frightened in the least," teased Amaryllis. "I confess that first thunderclap terrified me as well. I looked up expecting to see the chimneys crash through the ceiling, and Lord Daniel jumped from his seat like a scalded cat."

"It was very loud, was it not? And so sudden! Yet Miss Tisdale scarce even blinked, I vow."

"She has more backbone than any half-dozen gentlemen of my acquaintance. I wanted to talk to you about her if your headache is abated."

"It is nearly gone, my love, thanks to the hartshorn."

"And to the retreat of the storm." She plumped the pillows behind her aunt and moved to a chair. "I should like to see Tizzy married."

"To the vicar?" said Mrs. Vaux doubtfully. "I cannot think she will like to live with Augusta Raeburn."

"Precisely. Nor will Mr. Raeburn ever brave his sister's vapours to pop the question."

"I wish you will not use such vulgar expressions, Amaryllis."

"You know I guard my tongue in front of the girls and their parents. I have decided that we must dispose of Miss Raeburn."

"Surely you do not mean to murder her!" gasped Mrs. Vaux. "I cannot think that justified, however cross-grained she may be."

"What an odd opinion you have of me, Aunt Eugenia. No, I shall not stoop to murder unless all else fails. She must have other relatives on whom she might inflict her presence. I believe the vicar has mentioned a brother in London."

"But what should we do if Miss Tisdale did marry? We cannot run the school without her. I never did perfectly understand the use of the globes."

"Nor I."

"Are you . . . Are you going to close the school and go to America?" The widow's lips trembled and she looked suddenly old and frail.

Amaryllis hugged her and laughed. "No, indeed. I had a thousand times rather teach—even the use of the globes—than sell nails and whatever else ironmongers sell. If we manage to install Tizzy in the vicarage, I expect she will not be too grand to help us still. And if she has not the time, why, I daresay there must be dozens of unemployed governesses who would jump at the chance."

"Oh yes. I am sure you are right. But I do think it very noble of you, my love, to promote Miss Tisdale's happiness when you rely on her so."

"Fustian, aunt. I rely on both of you, but I hope I shall not stand in your way when you choose to look about you for a second husband. Now I will leave you to rest, for I have a hundred things to do." She went to the window, flung up the sash, and breathed deep. "I do believe we shall have a fine evening after all. The air is fresh and clear as a mountain spring, and Ned is out already tying up the plants the rain battered down."

Amaryllis went downstairs with a slow step. It was true that she relied on Tizzy. There was a hollow space under her ribs when she thought of losing her. Her enforced departure from Hart Hall had come just at the moment when she might be thought to have outgrown the need of a governess, but she remembered with a shiver the anguish with which she had begged her father to let Tizzy stay. Of course, dear Papa had laughed and agreed without the slightest argument.

London would not have been bearable without Tizzy. She loved her aunt and realised with gratitude that Mrs. Vaux had not only guided her through the pitfalls of Society without a misstep but succeeded in turning a country miss into an elegant young lady. Yet it was to her governess she had turned when troubled or unhappy. She owed her more than could ever be repaid, and if she cared for Mr. Raeburn she should have him.

Miss Hartwell spent the next two hours dealing with her correspondence. It was gratifying to be able to turn down so many requests for places in her school. Had there been room in the house, she might easily have employed another teacher.

They dined, as usual, at six. Cook, having recovered her composure and being anxious to make amends for the teapot, had done wonders with the lamb. Ned, the gardener and handyman, had provided fresh, tender runner beans and a baby vegetable marrow. Ned preferred to let his vegetables grow as large as possible before he picked them, however tough or bitter they became, but the storm had torn his vines to pieces so the ladies profited by the destruction.

After dinner, Amaryllis took a pruning knife and went into the front garden to tidy the rain-battered rosebushes. The setting sun caught the scattered petals in its golden glow and turned them into a carpet finer than any out of Turkey. Pink, crimson, yellow, and a dozen shades of green, all the colours in the garden seemed exceptionally vivid. Amaryllis concentrated on her task, carefully cutting off the petal-less heads, breathing the mingled scents of flowers and rich brown earth.

"Miss Hartwell."

"Ouch!" Startled, she stabbed herself on a thorn, and

turned to greet the vicar with a finger in her mouth. "Mr. Raeburn, it is most ungentlemanly in you to surprise a lady who is surrounded by rose thorns. Did you wish to see Miss Tisdale?"

"No, no, I have only a moment. Augusta expects me back for dinner. I hope you will not think me interfering, Miss Hartwell, but I feel I must warn you."

"If you mean to warn me against pruning rosebushes, you are too late."

"More serious than that, I fear," he said with an unwontedly agitated look. "I greatly dislike speaking evil of anyone, but I cannot reconcile it with my conscience to leave you in ignorance."

"In ignorance, sir? You must not accuse a schoolmistress of ignorance, you know."

"It pleases you to tease, ma'am. I well know your playful humour, but I beg you will be serious. What do you know of Lord Daniel Winterborne?"

"Little enough. Only that he is, as I surmise, the son of Lord Bellingham and that he means to send his daughter to the Castle Hedingham Academy."

"He is a rake, Miss Hartwell. I have known him by reputation for many years though I have never met him before today. I have heard tales of him that I cannot repeat to a young lady of gentle birth."

"I thank you for your warning, Mr. Raeburn, but do pray be easy. It is my intention to teach his daughter, not to flirt with him. Besides, I did not like him above half. I am surprised to hear that he has the least success with females of any sort, since his manners are far from ingratiating. He was, in fact, abominably rude."

So, she thought as she watched him trudge down the muddy lane in his galoshes, Lord Daniel is a rake. She had best keep an eye on the older girls when he came to visit Miss Isabel.

===3===

WITH TWO WEEKS to go before the beginning of term, Mrs. Vaux set in motion her last-minute preparations.

Several women were hired from the village, in addition to the two regulars, to clean the house from top to bottom. Sheets were counted, darned, 'sides-to-middled,' replaced, hemmed, and re-counted. Vast quantities of coal and candles were ordered and delivered and arrangements made with a local farmer to supply almost equally vast quantities of milk, butter, and eggs. Two housemaids and a kitchen maid returned from spending the summer with their families and set to with a will polishing silver and furniture.

One fine day, Miss Hartwell and Miss Tisdale escaped from the excessive domesticity by hiring a gig and driving into Colchester. Amaryllis enjoyed her rare opportunities to take the ribbons, even though the Bell's plodding nag could not have been more different from the matched greys she used to drive in Hyde Park. She did not miss them near as much as she did her favourite riding mare, but she had not ridden in six years. She sometimes wondered if she ever would again.

Miss Tisdale visited every bookshop in Colchester and returned to the gig, stabled at the Red Lion, followed by two boys laden with weighty packages. Miss Hartwell went straight to her banker and, after a half hour's consultation, emerged smiling. She proceeded to the best dressmaker in town, spending there considerably more time than she had with her banker and again smiling when she left. She was followed to the gig by a single boy—not that she had any fewer packages, but they did not weigh so heavy.

The ladies treated themselves to a late luncheon at the Red Lion. Miss Hartwell ordered cold chicken and bread and butter. Miss Tisdale, as usual, insisted on having half a dozen oysters because they were a local specialty, although she did not care for them in the least. She was swallowing the last of these, with a wry face, when Amaryllis made an announcement in a portentous voice.

"Tizzy dear, I have been extravagant."

Miss Tisdale choked. Red-faced, tears in her eyes, she coughed and spluttered, then reached for her cup of tea and recovered her breath.

"Oh dear," she said guiltily, "so have I."

Amaryllis was sceptical. The governess's ideas of extravagance were unlikely to break the bank. "What have you bought?" she asked.

"Five novels! And then I saw a copy of *Tom Jones*, and I fear I simply could not resist it. It is a classic in its way, you know, though quite unsuitable for the girls."

"How wicked you are! I hope you mean to let me read it? I am no longer your pupil, after all."

" 'Strong meat belongeth to them that are of full age.' Hebrews 5, verse 14. If you promise not to tell Mr. Raeburn I have purchased it, I will lend it to you."

"I promise. He would be excessively shocked, I wager. Oh, don't look so troubled, Tizzy. I am roasting you. I daresay he would not care a rush, for he is not at all sanctimonious. I have bought . . . But no, I believe *my* revelation shall wait until we are at home."

"Tell me at once, Amaryllis. It is most unfair, when I have confessed already." Her pale eyes sparkled with amused indignation.

"Think how unfair it will be to my aunt if I tell you first. No, you must wait."

"Then let us leave at once. I cannot imagine what extravagance you have committed."

When they reached home, Ned came out with a gloomy

face beneath his ancient cap surrounded by its fringe of snow-white hair. A small, weatherbeaten man of indeterminate age, he was the only male in the establishment and tended to be the butt of the pranks of the livelier damsels. He was never so happy as when they all left for the summer. The prospect of their return was responsible for his present, long-suffering air.

He carried the parcels up to the private drawing-room, muttering about lumbago on the fourth trip up the stairs. Amaryllis tipped him a half crown.

Still in a teasing mood, she insisted on saving three mystery packages for last. Mrs. Vaux scarce glanced at the piles of histories, plays, and poetry as they appeared but pounced on the novels. She considered them the only literature fit for a lady of fashion, unlike Miss Tisdale, who read them with guiltily defiant enjoyment.

The room filled with brown paper and tangles of string as they unwrapped their new but practical and dull winter dresses of brown, black, and grey wool. At last Amaryllis relented.

"This is for you, Tizzy," she said. "I decided we had more than enough saved in our emergency fund, so I bought something impractical for once."

"Quickly, open it," urged Mrs. Vaux, handing her the scissors as she struggled with a knot. "We have enough string saved, too. Do cut it."

The rustling paper parted to reveal a shimmer of lavender silk.

"Oh no," said Miss Tisdale, "you have given me the wrong parcel."

"No, that is yours," Amaryllis assured her. "I stood in the middle of the shop with my eyes closed, picturing you in it. Hold it up and let us see if I was right."

"But I have not worn colours in twenty years!" Half reluctant, she drew it out and stroked it with apprehensive fingers. "Lavender!"

"The colour is perfect," said Mrs. Vaux decidedly. As arbiter of taste for the household, she always had the last word on such subjects.

"How well you taught me, Aunt. Here is your reward."

Mrs. Vaux's new gown was deep blue with a light blue stripe, and Amaryllis had chosen a rich moss green for herself. As they were ready-made, none of them fit perfectly, but Mrs. Vaux vowed that the necessary alterations would be no trouble at all.

"But when shall we wear them?" she wailed. "They are not at all suitable for school."

"You know Mr. Majendie always invites us to his Christmas assembly at the castle," Amaryllis reminded her. "This time we shall be properly dressed for a festive occasion. We shall positively dazzle our neighbours."

The widow looked up at her, caught her eye, and glanced at Miss Tisdale, who was still stroking the silk with reverent hands, her face dreamy.

"The vicar," she breathed silently. "Of course."

Miss Tisdale stood up, hugging the gown to her flat bosom. " 'Vanity of vanities, all is vanity,' " she said. "Ecclesiastes 1, verse 2. But I do not care. Thank you, dear Amaryllis, it is simply beautiful!"

As she lay in bed that evening, gazing through her open window at the moon-bathed castle, Amaryllis wondered if it would go on forever, this life so drab that a new dress was a great event, a party still four months in the future a cause of excitement.

All the same, she decided, it was probably better than going to Philadelphia to sell nails and . . . whatever else ironmongers sell.

The next day she wrote to her father. She was delighted to hear from him, glad he was doing well, and grateful for his invitation. However, she was too busy at present running a select seminary for young ladies of good family to consider joining him in America. She sent greetings to her Stepmama and her half-brothers and hoped to hear from him again before another six years had passed.

As she sealed it, she realised dejectedly that she might as

well be writing to a stranger. The only thing she had in common with the Philadelphia ironmonger was the past.

The next day, she was distracted from her blue devils when Mr. Majendie's groom brought in a bundle containing the past two weeks' issues of the *Morning Post*. The owner of the castle, an elderly gentleman both kind and learned, he had encouraged the school from the start. He sent his newspapers to keep them in touch with the doings of the Fashionable World. That, he was wont to say with a twinkle in his eye, was surely the most important part of any young lady's education.

The *Morning Post* was full of reports of the proceedings in the House of Lords over the Bill of Pains and Penalties against Queen Caroline. George III had died in January. The Prince Regent, now George IV, was desperately anxious that his estranged wife, whom he loathed, should not be crowned at his side. If the Bill passed in both Lords and Commons, she would forfeit her rights as Queen and be divorced into the bargain.

Mrs. Vaux pored over the sordid details with unabashed fascination. This was undoubtedly the sole topic of conversation among the ton and, though exiled for six years, she had spent most of her life in that world and still felt a part of it.

Miss Tisdale was clearly revolted by the testimony of the Queen's Italian servants who revealed, under close questioning the state of dress, or undress, in which they had seen her and her 'chamberlain,' Pergami, on various occasions. Tizzy blenched when she read that Her Royal Highness's hand 'was in the small clothes of Mr. Pergami,' but she read on. This was history in the making, and it was the duty of any instructress worthy of the name to be fully informed.

Amaryllis had mixed feelings. Chief among these was outrage. George had taken countless mistresses over the years, not to mention his deceitful marriage with Mrs. Fitzherbert. Many of the Lords now sitting in judgment had reputations that would bear no scrutiny. How dared they condemn Queen Caroline? Yet she had, it was clear, deliberately set out to embarrass her husband and cause a scandal by rampaging about Europe in black wig and short skirts and without doubt having an affair with her chamberlain. Papa's running off with the daughter of the Spanish Ambassador seemed a minor disgrace in comparison.

The day before school started, Amaryllis carefully locked up every newspaper in a cupboard in the private drawing-room. Stained sheets and hands upon private parts had no place in the curriculum of her young ladies.

After that there was no time to feel blue-devilled. Carriage after carriage rolled up to the gate, and the house filled with gay, chattering voices as the girls unpacked their trunks and valises and bandboxes.

There were five new pupils. Two had older sisters and a third, a fifteen year old, already knew several of the girls. Miss Hartwell had received a note from Lady Carfax saying that her daughter Louise would arrive a few days late owing to a sprained ankle. Thus Miss Isabel Winterborne was the only one with whom Amaryllis need particularly concern herself.

She had not been greatly disturbed to hear from the vicar that Daniel Winterborne was a rake. After all, the Viscount Hartwell had been a rake himself, judging by his endless pursuit and conquest of women. During her years on the town she had been protected by her social position from the attentions of libertines. Now she was armoured in her concealing cap and her dark brown worsted dress. The most persistent of womanisers was hardly likely to make a respectable schoolmistress the object of his illicit affections.

Lord Daniel appeared shortly after three in the afternoon accompanied by a pale, thin child with ginger hair and huge dark eyes in a solemn face under her Leghorn bonnet. Her blue woolen dress was a size too large about her middle and much too warm for the day, which had turned hot after an early autumnal chill.

Ushered into Miss Hartwell's office, Isabel released her

father's hand just long enough to bob a clumsy curtsey and whisper "How do you do," then clutched it again. Her father looked equally anxious.

"How do you do, Miss Winterborne," said Miss Hartwell, coming forwards with a smile. "Why don't you take off your bonnet and sit down, and we shall have some lemonade before I show you the rest of the school."

The child fumbled with her bonnet strings. Before Miss Hartwell could go to her aid, Lord Daniel was on his knees beside her untying them.

Daisy brought in a tray with a glass of lemonade, a pot of tea, and some biscuits.

"Will you take a glass of wine, my lord?" Miss Hartwell asked.

"Thank you, no. Tea will do very well, ma'am." He stood protectively beside his daughter, his hand on her shoulder, his face set.

"For all the world as if he was leaving her in the lion's den," Daisy reported to the kitchen.

"Pray be seated, sir. Miss Winterborne, I should like to ask you some questions. You can read?"

"Yes, ma'am. Papa taught me."

"Do you like to read?"

"Oh yes, ma'am! I often read to Papa in the evenings. We have read *Robinson Crusoe* and *Macbeth* and *Childe Harold* and *Tom Jones* . . ."

Lord Daniel flushed and scowled as Miss Hartwell looked at him with her eyebrows raised in disapproval.

"An interesting variety," she responded, hoping that the little girl had not understood the half of what she had read. "And can you sew?"

"I hemmed a handkerchief for Papa. He carries it always with him."

His lordship's hand went to his breast-pocket as if in confirmation.

"Embroidery?"

"No, ma'am. My Nan only knows plain stitching," confessed Miss Winterborne worriedly.

Miss Hartwell's gentle questioning continued. As she had begun to suspect, the child was well versed in such subjects as might interest a gentleman. Otherwise, she was ignorant of all except the little she had picked up from her nursemaid.

Meanwhile, Lord Daniel was growing visibly impatient. "Enough of this interrogation!" he broke in roughly.

She looked at him coldly. "We must not keep you, my lord. I am sure Miss Isabel is over her first shyness and will do very well on her own now."

"Isabel." There was pain in his voice.

She rose and went to stand in front of him.

"I must learn to be a lady, Papa," she said gravely.

He hugged her close.

"I promise you, my lord, I shall neither eat her nor beat her." Miss Hartwell intended to make her tone light, but it came out sarcastic.

"Beat her!" He jumped to his feet, outraged.

"I said I shall *not*. I really think it is time you left, sir, before we come to cuffs. Miss Isabel is perfectly safe in my charge, I assure you."

"I shall be here to see her on Sunday," he said grimly, "and she shall return home immediately if she is not happy."

"As we agreed." Miss Hartwell turned to fiddle with the papers on her desk, giving them a little privacy for their farewells. She heard the sound of his boots, then the door opening and closing again. He had gone without taking his leave of her.

She turned back to the girl. "I am sorry to disagree with your Papa," she said gently. "He is only concerned for you welfare, I know."

Isabel's lips trembled. "It is not your fault. Papa has quarrelled with all the neighbours and his family, too. Nan says he carries on like a bear with a sore head. He will be so lonely without me," she added desolately.

Miss Hartwell put her arm round the thin shoulders. She was fond of all her pupils, but for some reason she was particularly drawn to this brave child with the swimming eyes.

"He will miss you, I daresay, but gentlemen always have a great deal of business to take care of, so he will not have time to grieve. You will be busy too and will soon make friends. Come, let us go to the window, and you shall wave to him."

As she expected, his lordship gazed towards the house before climbing into his carriage. He saw his daughter and waved back. Then the coachman urged on the horses, and soon they were out of sight.

Miss Hartwell took Isabel up to her bedchamber and introduced her to two of the girls she was to share with. They were sisters, one her own age, the other sixteen and in her last year at school. Isabel was polite, solemn, and uncommunicative, and the others soon stopped trying to draw her out. After making sure the eldest was helping her to unpack and put her clothes away, Miss Hartwell left them.

As she closed the door, she heard the younger sister whisper, giggling, "She has red hair!"

"Hush," said the older repressively. "Miss Hartwell has red hair, too. I have seen her without her cap and it is monstrous becoming, I assure you."

So much for eavesdroppers hearing no good of themselves, thought Amaryllis. As she passed the door of another chamber, she heard the voice of the fifteen-year-old new girl.

"Tell me again about the teachers. Now I have met them I shall know who you are talking about."

Guiltily but irresistibly, Amaryllis halted and stayed to listen.

"Miss Tisdale, that's Tizzy, is shockingly strict. Mrs. Vaux is a dear. We call her Gardens because of Vauxhall Gardens, but she is the one who should be called Tizzy because she gets in a terrible tizzy if something goes wrong. Miss Tisdale stays calm through anything. Then Miss Hartwell, she is sort of aloof, if you know what I mean. But she's kind, they are all kind. If I was in trouble like, oh if I had broke my leg or something, I would go to Tizzy."

"If you had a broken leg, you would not go anywhere."

"Well then, if you broke *your* leg. Tizzy would know what to do. But if I was really in the briars—if I was really unhappy—I should go to Miss Hartwell because I think she has been unhappy herself and she would understand."

Miss Hartwell continued down the stair with a thoughtful expression. Aloof, but kind and understanding—not a verdict she could quarrel with. A perceptive young woman, though her mode of expression had been far from elegant. Mrs. Vaux—Gardens—must set her some extra exercises in polite conversation.

For the next couple of days, Amaryllis was busy working out a schedule of classes as they gradually sorted the girls into groups with comparable abilities in various subjects. By Thursday all was running smoothly.

That morning she was in the music room, teaching Isabel Winterborne her first notes on the piano. The room ran the length of the house on the ground floor, with tall windows and French doors opening onto the back garden. Besides the pianoforte, it contained a harp, a couple of cabinets to hold music, and a large number of straight chairs.

Isabel was picking out a five-note tune when Daisy knocked and came in.

"It's Miss Louise Carfax, miss. Her uncle just brung her, that's Lord . . ." she peered at the card in her hand.

A large figure appeared behind her and plucked the card from her hand.

"That's quite all right, m'dear," said a deep, lazy voice. "I'll announce m'self."

"I axed your lordship to wait below," said the parlour-maid indignantly.

"M'niece is waiting below, and you," he pointed at Isabel, "may go and keep her company, miss, if you please. I want a word with Miss Hartwell, alone."

Isabel looked up at her teacher to find her gaping in stunned wonder, as if the large, fair gentleman were a ghost, while he held the door for her in a polite but definitely insistent manner. She slipped off the stool and left the room with all the dignity she could muster.

As the door closed firmly behind her, Miss Hartwell found her voice.

"Bertram!" she gasped.

=4=

"MY DEAR GIRL, you are as white as a sheet.' Lord Pomeroy's long stride took him to Amaryllis's side in a couple of paces. "Here, put your head down."

"Don't be ridiculous, Bertram, I have never fainted in my life," she responded with indignation. "And what an odiously unromantic thing to say, after all this time."

"If I had a romantic bone in my body, we'd have been married all this time. I'd never have let you put off our wedding again and again, waiting patiently so that you could enjoy your freedom before being tied to a husband." He gazed down from beside her with a quizzical expression.

"Do stop towering over me. Please, sit."

"I will sit if you will take off that old-maidish cap. There, that is better." He threw the offending garment on top of the piano, then pulled up a chair and sat down, taking one of her hands in his. "Why did you do it?"

"Why did I keep postponing our wedding?" She made no move to pull her hand from his clasp.

"That, yes, and why did you write me that letter breaking it all off, and then disappear without leaving me word where to find you?"

"You must have received the letter at least a week before I left town. Why did you not come in time?"

"I did *not* receive it in time. I was angry, Amaryllis. You remember that afternoon, the second anniversary of our betrothal. I felt I had waited long enough. My parents were pressing me to name a day, to settle down. They were very fond of you, you know."

"I know. I don't know why I refused you again. It was not that I so greatly enjoyed my freedom. There was a sort of inertia, an unwillingness to change anything in my life. The last change had been so painful, like going into exile. There were Tizzy and Aunt Eugenia to consider, also. I was afraid of taking on the responsibilities of being your wife and more afraid of seeing you grow indifferent once we were wed. I had seen so many marriages where husband and wife scarce spoke to each other. I was in love with you, Bertram. I could not bear that that should happen to us."

He captured her other hand. "I was angry. I decided to go away, not to see you for a month. I went to stay with a friend in Hampshire for a fortnight and then on to Tatenhill to my parents. There I found your letter releasing me from our engagement."

"I had to do it. You must see that. The scandal attached to Papa's behaviour was such that it would have been the outside of enough to keep you tied to the betrothal. Besides, there was not a penny left of my dowry."

"And of course I was marrying you for your money. Little goose!" His voice was loving. "I was still in shock from your letter when my father summoned me. He gave me an ultimatum. My frivolous, here-and-therian life was a disgrace to the family. He had obtained a position for me in Vienna at the Congress. I was to leave in two weeks with or without you, or he would make my life deuced uncomfortable. Not given to idle threats, m'father. I posted straight back to town, drove all night, but you were already gone."

"The lease on the house was up. It was that very evening, the day I last saw you, that Papa dined with us, and the next day he was gone. He had paid all our bills. He was so proud of that. Still, we had very little money. We had to go. Besides, once we had decided what to do, as Tizzy said, 'If it were done, when 'tis done, then 'twere well it were done quickly.' "

"*Macbeth*. Miss Tisdale is still with you?"

"Oh yes. I could not have managed, still could not

manage, without her."

"This house, how did you find it?"

"It is Godmama's. She lets it to us for a peppercorn rent, and since Godmama is a very literal-minded lady, she comes to visit once a year to receive her peppercorn."

He laughed but spoke seriously. "I have a bone to pick with Lady Mountolivet Gurnleigh. She refused to tell me where you had gone, and no one else knew. I have been abroad so much of the time since that I have had no opportunity to set enquiries in motion. It is entirely her fault that I did not find you sooner."

"I told her I must make a clean break, that I did not want to see anyone at all. Unless, of course, they wished to confide a daughter to my care. She referred any number of pupils to the school until we had built up a reputation for ourselves. I wish you will not quarrel with her, Bertram. She offered me a home, only I could not accept. Several people cut me dead in the street after Papa left. I could not subject her to such distress. But tell me, how is it you have found me at last?"

"I was staying a few days with my sister Caroline. When I heard the name of the schoolmistress to whom she was sending m'niece, I insisted on escorting the little baggage here myself. I must warn you, Amaryllis, Caroline says the chit is a sad romp but if you ask me I'd call her a veritable hoyden. I beg you will not ask what she was doing to sprain her ankle."

"I have every sympathy with the child," said Amaryllis with a laugh. "Aunt Eugenia used to call me a sad romp, you know. Heavens, look at the time. My history class will be waiting."

She jumped to her feet, pulling her hands from Lord Pomeroy's clasp. "Will you . . . Are you staying in the area?" she asked shyly.

"If you will recommend the best inn in the village, I shall put up there."

"Oh no, that would never do. You have no idea how news

spreads through the village, and I am a respectable school-mistress. I cannot afford tattle. You had best go into Halstead."

"I am at your orders, ma'am. When can I see you again?"

She thought for a moment. "I believe I shall take a walk by the Colne this evening at dusk," she said, blushing. "With luck no one will see us, and if they do perhaps they will think it a chance meeting."

"Respectable schoolmistress, ha!" he grinned. "I'll take my leave of Louise and be off. Until this evening." He kissed her hand and strode out.

Feeling somewhat flustered, Miss Hartwell hurriedly put on her cap and followed him downstairs. She was in time to see his back disappear through the front door. She noted that his coat of blue superfine was as superbly cut as ever, his fawn pantaloons still moulded to the strong limbs of a Corinthian though he was now, it seemed, a diplomat. His boots shone with the unmistakable gloss that announced champagne in the blacking.

Isabel Winterborne was absorbed in conversation with a sturdy, blonde girl of her own age but an inch or two taller who was tidying her hair in a mirror. They turned as they heard Miss Hartwell's footsteps.

"This is Louis Carfax, ma'am," said Isabel, adding wor-riedly, "I'm sorry I left my lesson. I did not know what to do."

"That's quite all right, Isabel. How do you do, Miss Car-fax. I am Miss Hartwell."

Miss Carfax performed a careful curtsey. "How do you do, ma'am," she said with a grin that reminded Miss Hartwell strongly of Lord Pomeroy. She swung her bonnet in one hand. "My uncle mussed my hair. that is why I am in such a sorry state."

One blonde braid was half undone, its ribbon missing. The other had been pinned precariously in a loop that threatened to descend at any moment. It seemed unlikely that Lord Pomeroy could have visited such depredations on her appearance without dragging her backwards through a bush.

"Daisy shall take you upstairs to tidy yourself. Then ask her to bring you straight to me." Miss Hartwell rang the bell. "Isabel, you are in my history class at this hour, are you not? Come."

Fifteen minutes later, Louise, now perfectly tidy, trotted into the classroom where seven young ladies were studying the Roman invasions of Britain with various degrees of attention. Isabel at once made room for her.

"You can share my book," she whispered.

"Ugh, history!" Louise whispered back.

Miss Hartwell introduced her to the other girls. "I have just explained," she went on, "that we shall spend a week on the Roman occupation. Next Wednesday, I shall hire a chaise and those of you who have studied diligently shall go to Colchester to see the Roman remains. There is an excellent confectioner's near the Roman walls, where we shall take a nuncheon."

"Famous!" exclaimed Louise. "My uncle said he is going to stay near here for a few days. I shall persuade him to go with us and treat us all to cream cakes."

"The purpose of the visit," Miss Hartwell reminded her severely as possible, considering that she was unable to hide a smile, "is to inspect the Roman ruins, not to gorge on cream cakes."

"I expect Uncle Bertram knows all about the Romans," said the irrepressible Louise. "He has been to Italy, after all. Besides, in case all of us are to go, he can take some up in his curricle so you will only need to hire a single chaise."

"True," mused Miss Hartwell. "You may ask him then, but do not pester him. Now, back to our books, or no one will be going."

Between describing in thrilling detail Queen Boadicea's sack of Colchester and going upstairs to change for dinner some six hours later, Amaryllis had little leisure for thought. Wearily, she slipped off her shoes, unbuttoned her dress, and pulled it over her head with a shiver. There was more than a hint of autumn in the chill, September afternoon.

Wrapping a green Paisley shawl, a remnant of her former extensive wardrobe, about her shoulders, she lay back on the bed to put her feet up for a few minutes. Each year it took a week or two to reaccustom herself to the demands of her profession. She was really too tired to walk by the river this evening, and the weather was not inviting. However, she had made the assignation and must keep it. She and Bertram still had a great deal to discuss.

Perhaps she had been unwise to allow Louise to approach him about the trip to Colchester. What an enterprising minx the child was. But he might wish to be gone long before then. It was natural that he should have wanted to see her, to explain what had happened six years ago; but that did not mean he was still interested in marrying her.

She remembered the feel of his hands holding hers, his kiss on her fingers and shivered again. Getting up, she dressed quickly and went downstairs. The candles were already lit. Outside the light was fading fast. She had forgotten how early it grew dark now.

Miss Tisdale was in the common drawing-room, presiding over those girls who had already come down. Unlike the private drawing-room, this was a large chamber furnished in the best taste, though somewhat shabby from constant use. Mrs. Vaux considered it her duty to train her pupils in the choice of elegant furnishings and had insisted on purchasing the best they could afford. Miss Hartwell went to Miss Tisdale and drew her aside.

"Bertram was here," she said.

"So I have heard, my dear. 'Bring hither the fatted calf.' Luke 15, verse 23. Hardly appropriate, perhaps, since 'was lost and is found' applies to you better than to his lordship, and no one could say you have wasted your substance with riotous living."

"Nor am I hungry enough for a fatted calf. I fact, I am not hungry at all. I believe I shall go for a walk instead of joining you for dinner."

Miss Tisdale nodded, her shrewd eyes concerned. "I shall make your excuses," she said briefly.

Impulsively, Amaryllis kissed her cheek.

Booted, cloaked, and hooded, she walked briskly down Queen Street to the Colne, a pretty stream that flowed peaceably through green meadows. In summer the grass was scattered with yellow kingcups and pink lady's smock, a delightful place to stroll. Now, in the chilly dusk, the muddy path was uninviting, trampled by the hooves of cattle. Amaryllis contemplated it with dismay.

"You were all about in your head to suggest such a dismal rendezvous," said an amused voice behind her. She turned to see Lord Pomeroy, larger than ever in his caped greatcoat. "Come, we shall drive back to Halstead and sit in comfort in my private parlour. It is nearly dark. No one will see you."

"They will see me at the inn," she pointed out. "I dare not."

"Hen-hearted wench. Then we must drive about in the dark, for I'll not keep my team standing in this weather."

"Of course not, You are right, I was crazy to suggest this meeting. Bertram, I cannot see you during the week. I simply do not have the time. Will you come and visit Louise on Sunday? I shall say I must discuss her education with you."

"Her misdeeds, rather. Very well, m'dear. Sunday let it be. But if you do not make time for me then, I shall lay siege to your wretched school. I give you due warning. Allow me to drive you back now."

"It is but a step, and they will hear the carriage wheels."

"I shall walk with you then," he said firmly and tucked her gloved hand under his arm.

They walked in silence to the corner of King Street, neither wishing to broach a subject that they had not time to deal with thoroughly. Amaryllis stopped at the corner.

"Go back to your horses now," she said. "They will take a chill."

"Till Sunday then." He turned to go, then swung back. "Amaryllis, do you still have my ring?"

"I sold it," she said bluntly.

After a pause, he said softly, "Do you know, I find that my disposition is more romantic than I had thought." He strode off into the night.

Amaryllis stared after him, hands clenched, a cold weight settling over her heart. Anger came to her rescue.

If she had distressed him, why did he not say so and let her explain? She had not dared entrust the valuable ring to the post and had kept it to return to him at a later date. Then they had needed money desperately—more desperately than Bertram, with his wide estates and generous allowance, could ever understand. He might have let her try to explain.

As she trudged up King Street, she remembered other occasions when he had gone off looking hurt, so unwilling to quarrel with her that he would not demand an explanation of whatever troubled him. And he always accepted her every suggestion without a murmur, even when it was a matter of putting off their meeting for three days or their wedding for two years.

He had been a buck of the first stare, a leader of the Corinthian set. Yet in his dealings with her he was something more like a milksop. Was that why she had postponed the marriage time after time? Of course, she had no wish to be ridden over roughshod . . . nor did she desire to rule the roost.

She had always taken his complaisance for granted. Now it struck her that he must have loved her very much, more than she could imagine, to put up with her whims for so long. Did he still love her?

Entering the house, she heard the sound of voices from the dining room. The rest of the household was still at dinner, the young ladies doubtless practising their company manners and polite conversation under Mrs. Vaux's benevolent eye.

Miss Hartwell took off her cloak, hung it on the row of hooks among a couple of dozen others, and shivered. It was not much warmer in the vestibule than outside, but with the shocking price of coals they could not possibly light fires everywhere in September.

Daisy came out of the dining room bearing a tray, so Amaryllis called to her and asked for a bowl of soup to be brought to the common drawing-room. Fortunately, her aunt had ordered a fire made up in there. Warming her hands at the flickering flames, Amaryllis gazed into the glowing embers and imagined herself in sunny Italy with Bertram. She could have travelled all over Europe as Lady Pomeroy instead of slaving to build a school in an obscure corner of Essex.

One of the housemaids brought her soup and built up the fire. Soon after, the girls tripped in, chattering like a flock of exotic birds in their evening gowns of pink and primrose and white. Suddenly Amaryllis was glad she had created this little community. It was something to be proud of, hardly a distasteful task she had been forced to perform unwillingly. This school had not only provided the three of them with a home but also, she hoped, educated a few young ladies to have something more in their pretty heads than clothes and dancing and the hunt for a husband.

Isabel Winterborne and Louise Carfax came in together, their heads close, whispering to each other. Miss Hartwell was glad to see that Louise had settled in so quickly and that the timid Isabel had at last found a friend. She watched them for a moment. Then one of the older girls approached her with a gay request to listen to a couple of songs she had practised over the holidays. Amaryllis went with a group to the music room and spent a delightful evening singing ballads and folk songs, though one or two, learned from brothers, had to be censored.

Friday passed with the usual classes, but Saturday was given over to fashionable pursuits.

Miss Hartwell taught dancing in the music room, demonstrating the steps and then going to the piano to play as they tried them. She enjoyed watching them hop and twirl, those taking the man's part bowing gravely, the ladies fluttering their eyelashes provocatively. If she married Bertram, she would go to balls again, dance till the early hours of the morning instead of retiring at ten to rise early.

Miss Tisdale relaxed her strict standards of literature to discuss the latest novels with the older young ladies. After all, they must be able to converse about them when they entered Society, and it was best to teach them to discriminate between those they might admit to having read and those that ought not to be mentioned in public.

Mrs. Vaux brought out a lifetime collection of magazines from which the young ladies learned the history of fashion—how they giggled at the powdered wigs and hooped skirts—and to choose the styles and colours that would suit them best. Weekday lessons might or might not instill an inclination towards serious thought. However, it was thanks to these Saturdays that only last year an ex-pupil of the Castle Hedingham Academy had been declared an Incomparable and brought a duke's son up to scratch in her first season.

On Sunday, Miss Hartwell took the younger girls to the early service at St. Nicholas. It was shorter than the later morning service, easier to sit through without fidgeting, and there were fewer parishioners to be disturbed. Today this proved just as well, as Miss Carfax was constitutionally incapable of sitting still with her mouth shut for more than five minutes. Her inseparable companion, Miss Winterborne, while perfectly self-disciplined, had clearly never been to church before and had not the least notion when to kneel or sit or stand. Miss Hartwell vowed silently to arrange a special session for the pair with Mr. Raeburn before next Sunday.

The vicar had not yet met the new pupils, since he taught at the school on Mondays, his least busy day. The girls who knew him curtseyed at the door as they passed out into the churchyard. Miss Hartwell introduced the others, noting with irritation that he stared curiously at Isabel Winterborne on hearing her name. He was of course too gentlemanly and too kind to say anything, but she knew he was marking her as the child of a rake.

Her mind at once flew back to carefully suppressed memories of her debut in town, when she had more than once overheard whispers pointing her out as a daughter of a libertine. Lord Hartwell had been far too popular for the stigma to interfere with her success, but it had hurt. Ruthlessly she suppressed the memories again while promising herself that Isabel should never suffer for that reason while in her charge.

She invited Mr. Raeburn to dine at the school on Monday and he beamed at her. "I shall be delighted, Miss Hartwell. If my sister is well, that is. Shall I see Miss Tisdale this morning? And Mrs. Vaux, of course?"

She assured him that they would both attend church and walked her column of young ladies two by two back to the school, her attention now occupied by the problem of persuading Miss Augusta Raeburn to remove from the vicarage.

=5=

In spite of the fifteen-mile drive, Lord Daniel arrived before luncheon while half the girls were still at church. Daisy went up to the common-room to announce him.

Isabel jumped up, her thin face radiant. Her cheeks had more colour than a week earlier, and Mrs. Vaux had altered her dresses to fit. She looked much less like a bewildered waif.

"Papa is come! May I go down to him, ma'am?"

Miss Hartwell nodded. The child flew from the room, followed at a more sedate pace by her teacher. Lord Daniel was standing by a window, looking out. Hearing footsteps on the stair, he turned. Amaryllis watched his face as he saw his daughter racing down to meet him. A smile of heartfelt joy and relief lightened his habitually sombre expression to such an extent that she could scarce believe it was the same man. He looked ten years younger, scarcely older than she was herself. She felt her own lips turn up in an involuntary echo.

Isabel flung herself at him. He caught her with his left arm, hugging her close, his right hand stroking her hair. Amaryllis continued down the stairs and he looked up, his face resuming its watchful harshness.

"Good day, my lord."

"Good day, ma'am."

"You wish to take Miss Isabel out?"

"Such is my intention."

"She must return by five o'clock, if you please, to change for dinner."

"If she returns at all. If not, I shall send later for her box."

"I beg you will inform me, my lord, if you decide to take her with you." Miss Hartwell ignored his unseemly lack of ordinary courtesy. Indeed, she was growing quite accustomed to it. "I cannot so easily accept the disappearance of one of my girls."

He unbent a little. "Of course, Miss Hartwell, I understand your concern. I shall not take her home without conveying a message to you." That settled, he returned his attention to Isabel. "Have you a cloak, love? It is warm at present but may grow chilly later."

Isabel fetched her cloak from the row of hooks by the front door, and without another word they left.

Miss Hartwell stared after them in exasperation. It was no use expecting better manners from the child when she had learned what she knew from her father. If she came back, Mrs. Vaux must coach her in the common proprieties that most girls absorbed without effort from their female relatives. All the same, it hurt that Isabel had left without the slightest farewell.

The carriage, a light barouche, was moving off down the street. Amaryllis noted with some surprise that Lord Daniel had brought his coachman rather than driving himself on such an informal and personal occasion. Then she heard a giggle from the top of the stairs and saw three or four girls leaning on the bannisters. Doubtless they had been peering over to catch a glimpse of Isabel's father. As Amaryllis went upstairs they scampered towards the common-room, except for Louise, who waited for her teacher.

"My Papa never looked at me so," said Louise companionably but with a trace of envy as they followed the others. "He generally looks angry when I see him, for I scarcely ever see him when I am not in a scrape."

"You have not been in any serious scrape since you came here, and so I shall tell your uncle."

"Uncle Bertram will not care. He only laughs at me. Besides, if I have not been in trouble here it is because my brothers are not here. Usually I fall in the briars because I do something they are doing and it turns out to be *un-ladylike*." She grimaced. "It is not at all fair that boys are allowed to do so many things girls are not."

Miss Hartwell distracted her from her grievance by enquiring as to the names and ages of the unjustly favoured brothers, and she very soon heard a great deal more about them than she had any desire to know.

Mrs. Vaux and Miss Tisdale had brought their charges back from church and luncheon had been eaten before Lord Pomeroy put in an appearance. Amaryllis had Daisy show him to her office and joined him there.

"Still a late riser, I see," she greeted him with a smile.

"How can you say so, when I delivered Louise to you at an ungodly hour of the morning the other day."

"It was quite eleven o'clock, and Miss Louise has revealed that you spent the night with friends near Braintree and travelled no more than ten miles on Thursday."

"Little tattletale."

"However do you manage on your diplomatic missions? I do not remember that you were ever used to rise before noon."

"I am not the only diplomat to abhor early rising, I assure you. All meetings are scheduled in the afternoon, and in any case most of the business is carried out at parties in the evening."

"Are you a good diplomat?" she asked with considerable curiosity.

"Fair to middling. My forte is talking people into compromises. I should never have been a great one because I am too lazy to work hard at it. However, I have had to resign because m'father is ill and wants me at home to take over running things. I am to be given a seat in the Commons too, which is a deuced nuisance." He grimaced, looking so like his niece that Amaryllis laughed.

She sobered immediately. "I am sorry to hear that Lord Tatenhill is unwell."

"He is well enough to attend Queen Caroline's trial or at

47

least to risk a large fine if he did not. He is also ill enough to want to see me married, and preferably with an heir, before he dies. Amaryllis, I can get a special licence tomorrow. We could be married by Wednesday. My feelings have not changed." He looked straight at her. "I was never sure of yours."

"I was in love with you," she said, rather breathlessly. "But how can I know so soon what I feel now? I have been too busy to think calmly."

"I do not want you to think calmly. I want you to tell me now that you will marry me at once."

"I cannot leave the school at such short notice, Bertram. Surely you can understand that."

"The school? To the devil with the school! Let them find someone to take your place," he said impatiently.

She gazed at him in shock. "It is *my* school," she cried. "I am not employed here to walk out when I feel like it. I created it from nothing."

He sighed and shrugged. "How long then? This time I shall not let you put me off indefinitely."

"We are no longer engaged, Bertram," she said quietly. "I have not yet agreed to marry you. If I do, I promise I shall give you a date and stick to it, but I will not tie you down until I know my own feelings better."

"I am tied to you, whether either of us likes it or not."

"Do not be so melodramatic, my dear." Amaryllis hid her impatience behind a smile. "You have been abroad all these years. I daresay there are a dozen beauties newly come on the Marriage Mart who will suit you as well as, or better, than I. Go look about you."

"What, go through all that circus again? Never. Well, since you will not give me yea or nay, I had best go and take that little imp of mischief my niece out for a drive."

With a reproachful look he raised her hand to his lips and departed. Amaryllis was left with the hollow feeling that his devotion to her might well be as much a result of his indolent unwillingness to look for another bride as of his indubitable affection.

Since the sun was shining, Miss Hartwell, Mrs. Vaux, and Miss Tisdale divided the rest of their pupils into three groups according to their enthusiasm for country walks. Mrs. Vaux took those who considered a mild stroll sufficient exercise for a saunter down the lane. Miss Tisdale led the next group, the largest, for a walk through the village and down Nunnery Street to the river. They carried baskets, since their route passed a thicket of brambles and the blackberries would be ripe.

Miss Hartwell set off across the fields with five energetic young ladies. The hedgerows were laden with scarlet rosehips, crimson haws and the pink and orange fruit of the spindle tree; a hare darted through the stubble fields at their approach, chased by the shadows of puffy clouds racing across the sky. She returned to the house two hours later tousled and pink-cheeked, the gusty wind having blown away her megrims.

Daisy met her at the door with the news that Lord Daniel and Miss Winterborne had returned and were awaiting her in the office. Miss Hartwell was delighted. She put off her bonnet and pelisse and with no thought for her appearance went straight to see them. Lord Daniel was sitting in a chair with Isabel perched on the arm. She smiled at the charming picture they made. He rose to greet her, smiling in return.

"I hope I have not kept you waiting long," she said, suddenly breathless.

"Not at all, ma'am. A few minutes. I see you have been out walking. The exercise suits you."

"Oh dear, am I so windswept?" She consulted a mirror and patted uselessly at her copper locks. "Heavens, positively dishevelled! I do beg your pardon, my lord. Still, I daresay you will not wish me to go away now and tidy myself. Isabel has decided to stay with us?"

"If you please, ma'am," Isabel confirmed anxiously.

"Of course you shall. We are very happy to have you."

"Now come and kiss me good-bye, love, for I must have

a few words with Miss Hartwell. I shall come again next Sunday, without fail."

She put her arms round his neck, kissed him on both cheeks, and whispered, "I love you, Papa, and I do miss you, but it is such fun here and very interesting besides."

He hugged her with one arm and kissed her forehead. She curtseyed to Miss Hartwell, her curtsey already much improved, before closing the door carefully behind her.

"I miss her abominably," confessed Lord Daniel, "but I gather she already has a new friend. You will not object to telling me a little about this Louise, whom she quotes endlessly?"

"Louise is the daughter of Lord Carfax. It is a perfectly unexceptionable friendship and I believe it is doing Isabel a great deal of good. She is a somewhat retiring child, as I am sure you have realised, while Louise is a merry, outgoing creature."

"Thank you, you have set my mind at rest. All that remains, then, is to give you this." He handed her a piece of paper.

It was a bank draught, drawn in the amount of one term's school fees.

"Oh no, my lord," she exclaimed, "you have already paid in full."

"I told you I should double the sum if Isabel decided to stay."

"That was not why I decided to accept her. I hope you do not think that you could buy my compliance with your conditions!"

"It has been my experience that most things can be bought. I shall leave it with you to do with as you please," he said with utter indifference, then turned on his heel and walked out.

That odious wretch, fumed Miss Hartwell. Just when she was at last feeling in charity with him he chose to insult her. She nearly ran after him to force the draught on him, but that would certainly lead to a public and undignified scene. She was about to tear it into little pieces. Instead she locked it in her drawer. She would return it next time she saw him. Otherwise, he might never notice that it had not been cashed, and he would continue to suppose her a mercenary female just like his unfortunate lightskirts. For that, she felt sure, was what he had meant, and it was unthinkable that she should not disabuse him of the notion.

Shortly thereafter, Lord Pomeroy brought his niece back to school. It was a little after five o'clock, so Miss Hartwell told Louise to run upstairs and change for dinner.

"I will," she answered gaily, "but I shall not eat a thing. Uncle Bertram gave me tea at the Falcon and he has promised to treat us all in Colchester on Wednesday so I shall study very hard to be sure of going!"

"I see she can twist you round her little finger," Amaryllis told his lordship.

"Like you, she is difficult to refuse. But she did not have to tease very hard, for I wager it will be the only opportunity I shall have to see you before next Sunday," he said ruefully.

"I am sorry, Bertram, truly I am. I wish you will not kick your heels in Halstead all week. Have you no friends nearby whom you might visit?"

"I know Ashurst Majendie of Hedingham Castle, but not well. Certainly not well enough to drive up and tell him I've come to stay indefinitely because I am courting the village schoolmistress. Besides, I doubt he is there at present, and I am not acquainted with his father."

"What of the friends you stayed with near Braintree?"

"Friends of Caroline's. I daresay I could spend a couple of days there. At least I could take a gun out for partridge."

"An excellent idea. Much better than sitting around the inn."

"That reminds me. At the inn here in the village, where I took Louise—what was it called?"

"The Falcon. It is on the site where the castle mews stood in mediaeval times."

"Never mind that. There was a fellow in there—dark, swarthy young man with an accent I would wager to be

Spanish. He was asking all sorts of questions about the school."

Amaryllis frowned. "A gentleman?"

"Of sorts. Dressed like a popinjay, jewels everywhere, and a shocking waistcoat." His lordship looked down with complacency at his own neat blue and grey striped waistcoat with its single fob. "Wearing a sword, too. But there, I expect fashions are different in Spain as they are in most of Europe. Foppish bunch, foreigners."

"Bertram, you do not suppose he could be connected with . . . with the Spanish Ambassador's daughter? I mean a brother or something come for revenge?"

"Dash it, Amaryllis, after six years? Not but what those hidalgos have long memories and they do go in for family feuds, I believe."

"Hidalgos?"

"The petty nobility. Complicated code of honour, great pride of family, and not much common sense. I met a few in Vienna."

"You are most reassuring! Still, I expect he is merely interested in providing his daughter with an English education. I must go and change my dress now," she added as the clock struck the quarter. "I shall see you on Wednesday."

"Dash it, Amaryllis, you were used to be quite the most restful female of my acquaintance and now you will not stand still for more than five minutes before you mush dash off hither and thither."

She stood on tiptoe and kissed his cheek. "I am a working woman, my dear. Now I really must run."

He watched her until she reached the top of the stairs, then turned to leave, muttering disgustedly, "If ever I received a brotherly kiss, that was one."

He might have been cheered had he known that, as she changed, Amaryllis was comparing him with Lord Daniel Winterborne. The comparison could only be in his favour. His excellent style, easy manners, and superior address threw Lord Daniel's brusqueness into strong relief. Yet for quite thirty seconds Lord Daniel had been almost charming, and how that smile had changed his appearance. He could not be much older than thirty, especially as his brother George must be no more than five or six and thirty by now. Isabel was eleven, though. Had he married so young?

Or was Isabel a love-child?

That would certainly explain the lack of a respectable female in the household. On the other hand, Lord Daniel had said that his sister advised him to send Isabel to school, and surely his sister would not care a fig for the upbringing of a love-child. Isabel had told her that her father had quarrelled with his relations. Yet he was in communication with at least one and took her advice. Thoroughly intrigued by her speculations, Miss Hartwell hurried down to dinner.

After dinner on Sundays, the older girls were left in charge of the younger. The three ladies retired to their private drawing room, taking it in turns to check the common-room occasionally. Sipping tea from the best Crown Derby porcelain cups, half a dozen of which Mrs. Vaux had saved when the Hartwell possessions were sold up, they discussed the past week and made plans for the coming week.

Amaryllis found herself avoiding all mention of Bertram's visit, and her aunt and governess tactfully made no enquiries. She was no more willing to talk about Lord Daniel, though she did tell them that Isabel would be staying. Also, she felt obliged to pass on Mr. Raeburn's warning about his rakish reputation, which had Mrs. Vaux in a tizzy until Tizzy pointed out calmly that he was unlikely to make any attempt on the virtue of his daughter's companions.

Mrs. Vaux waited until her niece had left the room before she confided that she was afraid his lordship might attempt to make Amaryllis the object of his affections.

"She has no male relative to protect her," she said. "I daresay by the time we could get a reply from Philadelphia it would be too late."

"She has a great deal of common sense to protect her," soothed Miss Tisdale. "Nor do I suppose that Lord Daniel is any more likely to seduce his daughter's teacher than her friends. Besides, I cannot but think that Lord Pomeroy would have something to say to that."

Mrs. Vaux was reassured. Miss Tisdale was more dubious of her own reasoning. She had a low opinion of men, always excepting Mr. Raeburn, and she doubted that a gentleman already known as a libertine would be given pause by his daughter's situation if his fancy should happen to alight upon her preceptress.

Amaryllis returned to report that all was quiet and decorous in the common-room. The conversation turned to the possible hiring of a chambermaid to assist the housemaids so that one of the housemaids might assist Daisy, who was run off her feet now that there were twenty-four young ladies in residence.

"We are sufficiently beforehand with the world to afford it," Amaryllis assured her aunt after some discussion. "One of the housemaids will be able to help Daisy serve at table. Do you have someone in mind already? If you could hire her tomorrow we might impress the vicar when he dines here tomorrow evening."

"He mentioned that you had invited him when I spoke to him after church," said Miss Tisdale, slightly flushed. "Of course he will not be able to come if Miss Raeburn is unwell. Ah, it is nine o'clock, and my turn to see the children to bed, is it not? 'I will both lay me down in peace and sleep.' Psalms 4, verse 8."

There was silence until she had closed the door behind her, then Amaryllis said, "I believe I shall make it a standing invitation for every Monday. Then he can tell his sister that it is part of his clerical duties to ensure that his pupils say grace and behave with propriety at table."

"An excellent notion. Augusta interferes only with his pleasures, not with his duties," approved Mrs. Vaux.

"Augusta?"

"Yes, we are on Christian-name terms! I called in this afternoon after my walk and stayed quite half an hour."

"Splendid! I see you are a first-rate fellow conspirator."

"I have already discovered that she does indeed have a brother in London, and that he lives in Chapel Street, which is an excessively fashionable address," said Mrs. Vaux with pardonable pride. "Perhaps it is not quite fair to pretend to seek her friendship, but for Miss Tisdale's sake I will do it."

"Yet you always address Tizzy so formally. You are not on Christian-name terms with her after all these years."

"I asked Miss Tisdale several years ago to call me Eugenia, but she maintained that she would not be comfortable addressing thus the sister of her ex-employer. I would not for the world so demean her as to call her Melpomene if she will not reciprocate."

Amaryllis giggled. "If my name were Melpomene," she admitted, "I should prefer that no one used it. It is bad enough to be called after a Greek shepherdess. I cannot think what her parents were about to name her for the muse of Tragedy."

"I hope you have a plan in mind," her aunt went on. "It is prodigious unpleasant to have to listen to Augusta complaining for thirty minutes at a time, I vow."

"I need more information before I can contrive a successful scheme. Try to find out why she does not choose to live with the tonnish brother, and as many things that give her the vapours as you can."

Preparing for bed later that evening, Amaryllis realised she had not told her aunt or Tizzy of the inquisitive Spaniard. Still, there was no need to alarm them. No doubt he would turn up in a day or two to enroll a daughter in the school, or perhaps he wanted to give Spanish lessons. As Bertram had said, it was not likely that some relative of the Spanish Ambassador should have tracked her down with revenge in mind after all these years. All the same, it was not only the chilly sheets that made her shiver as she climbed into bed.

= 6 =

MONDAY MORNING BROUGHT rain, blowing in wintry drifts across the village and dashing against the windowpanes with a rattle like a snare drum. September or no, Mrs. Vaux ordered fires lit in every room that would be used during the day.

Mr. Raeburn arrived at the school with his greatcoat soaked through, his umbrella having turned inside out within a few steps of the vicarage. One of the housemaids hurried the dripping garment to the kitchen, while Daisy ushered the vicar into the small, cosy parlour where he would spend the day attempting to inculcate the tenets of Christianity into four or five young ladies at a time.

Patient and genial, Mr. Raeburn had no opinion of preachers of hellfire. He had the greatest difficulty in checking his tendency to expatiate upon charity and compassion at the expense of more abstract virtues. His greatest joy was when, as happened not infrequently, one of the girls would bashfully hand him a portion of her pin money with a request to see to the comfort of some parishioner whose troubles he had mentioned. They all loved him, and not a few considered the inexplicable peppermint scent that imbued his presence to be synonymous with the odour of sanctity.

It was still pouring with rain at four o'clock when he had finished his lessons. Miss Hartwell asked him to rake Louise Carfax over the coals for her behaviour in church, and then to explain the service to Isabel Winterborne so that she would be less confused next Sunday.

Louise emerged from her scolding utterly unabashed. "Don't be frightened," she whispered to Isabel, who was nervously awaiting her turn. "He's nice."

By the time Isabel came out to confirm that, excepting her Papa, the vicar was the nicest man she knew, it was too late for him to return to the vicarage before dinner. Miss Augusta might have hysterics if she wished, he would know nothing about it. Thus, Amaryllis sent Tizzy to entertain him with a glass of Madeira until dinnertime.

" 'Wine that maketh glad the heart of man,' " said Miss Tisdale. "Psalm 104, verse 15. I do not believe my father ever used it for a sermon, but he was wont to quote it after dinner."

The meal was greatly enlivened when Daisy poured a glass of water for Mrs. Vaux and a frog leaped out of the pitcher in a shower of droplets. Several girls jumped up onto their chairs, squealing, though how that would save them was unclear as the frog was hopping about the table. The unfortunate creature sprang for shelter and landed in a dish of salad. Louise grabbed the offending beast as it scrambled out, trailing greenery and leaving oil-and-vinegar footprints on the white tablecloth.

"Shall I put him outside, Miss Hartwell?" she enquired, trying hard to suppress a look of unholy glee.

"If you please," Amaryllis answered, the corners of her lips twitching. "And you will see me in my office immediately after dinner." So much for her theory that Mr. Raeburn's presence would be conducive to superior decorum.

"Yes, ma'am." Eyes sparkling, Louise whispered, "It was worth it!" in Isabel's ear as she passed.

" 'A merry heart doeth good like a medicine,' " opined Miss Tisdale. "Proverbs 17, verse 22. But take away that salad, if you please, Daisy."

"I hope you will not punish Miss Carfax too severely," begged Mr. Raeburn, who had been surprised into a most unclerical guffaw. "Bless my soul, I have not so enjoyed a meal in many a long day." When he plodded out into the rain some time later, he was still chuckling at the memory.

Miss Hartwell had half a mind to ban Louise from the outing to Colchester. However, that hardly seemed fair since she had studied hard. Besides, there would be no excuse for Bertram to join them if his niece was not to be of the party. Instead she had her write an essay on cruelty to animals. The frog had certainly been much more alarmed than anyone else.

On Tuesday afternoon it was still raining, and the trip to Colchester was in doubt. After school, Louise and Isabel were found doing a most extraordinary dance in the vestibule. It involved a lot of stamping, gyrating, and waving of arms. Louise explained.

"My brother learned a rain dance from an American boy at Eton. It is what the Redskins do to make it rain when there is a drought. So we are doing it backwards to make it stop."

Apparently the theory was valid, since by five thirty it was clearing. Wednesday dawned sunny and by breakfast time promised to be warm.

"It's called an Indian summer," said Louise with satisfaction.

At nine o'clock the chaise from the Bell Inn was waiting at the gate, and a few minutes later Lord Pomeroy's smart curricle drew up. He had his own chestnuts harnessed and his equipage altogether took the shine out of the hired carriage.

There was some squabbling before Louise, Isabel, and one other girl squeezed into the curricle with his lordship and the disappointed four climbed into the aged chaise with Miss Hartwell. Lord Pomeroy looked as if he was inclined to join in the squabble when he saw her disappear inside with her charges.

The curricle could have reached Colchester in half the time but, to Louise's vociferous disapproval, her uncle chose to remain close to the chaise all the way. With a noted whip behind him, the Bell's ostler pushed his horses all the way. They arrived before noon.

The confectioner, warned in advance of their coming, provided a cold collation, which was barely touched, and a great many cream cakes, all of which disappeared. Lord Pomeroy paid the reckoning and was enthusiastically thanked by his niece and her friends. It was with a certain torpor that they repaired to the ruins of the Roman city.

Miss Hartwell had made this excursion twice before and was well primed with facts for their edification. Before she could begin her lecture, she found herself drawn off along a secluded path by his lordship. As soon as they were out of sight, he pulled her into his arms and kissed her, instantly dispelling the notion that indolence was responsible for his attachment.

"Bertram, you must not!" she gasped as he released her, and she put up her hands to straighten her bonnet.

"Did you dislike it?" he asked with a glint in his eye. "I did not notice that you tried to kick my shins."

"How could you ask such a question?" she said severely. "Of course I disliked it excessively. I am not accustomed to being *mauled* by those I had considered gentlemen."

He smiled. "It's my belief I should have tried it years ago. It does not pay to be too much the gentleman. However, I beg your pardon, and I promise not to do it again. This afternoon. Unless you tempt me beyond bearing."

"I must go back to the girls at once."

"All right, I promise. No conditions. Let me have you to myself just for an hour," he coaxed. "They cannot get into a great deal of mischief in a single hour."

"What makes you think that? With Louise among them, five minutes will suffice." Nonetheless she allowed herself to be persuaded and they wandered on while she told him about the frog in the water pitcher.

She enjoyed the afternoon, and to her relief the worst trouble she found when they rejoined the young ladies was a torn ruffle. To be sure they had not learned much history, but as Bertram said, the ancient Romans were not a common topic of conversation in the best society.

That evening she lay in bed, thinking back over the day.

Bertram was excellent company, and she was looking forward to his promised visit on Sunday. It was delightful to be with someone who saw her as a beautiful woman and a member of the Haut Ton, not as a dowdy schoolmistress. Yet his kiss had disarranged her bonnet more than her composure. Judging by the novels she had read, a lover's kiss ought to thrill and agitate a maiden even to swooning. She was not given to swooning and hesitated to put her trust in the emotional accuracy of a novel, yet surely she should have felt more than surprise.

Perhaps she had known him too long to experience excitement at his touch. She knew that when they were married he would be a gentle and considerate partner. Yes, she would marry him, next summer when the school year came to an end. She would marry Bertram, she thought sleepily, and Tizzy would marry Mr. Raeburn, and Aunt Eugenia . . . Brother! What about Aunt Eugenia? Before Amaryllis could tackle that problem she fell asleep.

The next day the skies were blue again. As soon as the morning sun had dried the dew from the lawn, Miss Hartwell took several girls out into the back garden to sketch. There was a huge old oak, its leaves now beginning to yellow after the first frosts, which made an excellent subject. Later she would have them draw it leafless, with gnarled skeleton exposed, then in the spring, clad in fresh golden-green.

Ned trudged up the garden and came to her side.

"Would 'ee come look at the brollycolly, miss," he urged with an extraordinary series of winks, gestures, and shrugs.

"At the broccoli, Ned?" said Miss Hartwell in surprise. The old countryman considered the vegetable in the light of a sinister foreign plot and had baulked at being requested to grow it, but he had never before asked for advice on its cultivation.

He jerked his head, winked again, and waved his arms at the young ladies. "Aye, miss, and the serrely too."

"Have the rabbits been at it again?"

"Jis' come see!" begged Ned.

Mystified, Miss Hartwell followed him down to the kitchen garden and gazed at the celery bed. A mistle thrush was pecking at a snail, and an orange-breasted robin perched on the handle of the gardener's fork and sang a few liquid notes to her.

"Arr, 'e be awaitin' for I to dig 'is dinner fer en," Ned explained.

"He is charming. Is that what you wanted me to see?"

"'Nay, then. Din't want to fright the young leddies, did I."

"Fright the young ladies? Pray tell me what this is all about, Ned. What is wrong with the celery?"

"Nowt, miss. Best serrely I iver growed. 'Tis the furriner I mun tell 'ee of."

"A foreigner! Not a Spaniard?"

"Dunno 'bout thet. Dark, 'e wor, and dressed up fit to kill. Flash cove. 'E wor axin' 'bout the school and the young leddies. Din't tell en nowt, did I."

"He spoke English?"

Ned cackled. "Better nor I, miss, better nor I. 'Ceptin' when 'e swore at I, 'twere in some furrin lingo." The memory amused him so much that he bent double with laughter and tears came to his eyes.

"Thank you, Ned, for telling me, and for not telling him, and for not frighting the young ladies. You will be sure to let me know if you see him again?"

"Aye, miss," gasped the old man. He touched his ancient cloth cap and hobbled off, still snickering.

Momentarily distracted from her worry by the question of whether the cap was ever removed from that hoary head, a matter of perennial interest among her pupils, Miss Hartwell walked slowly back to her class.

The Spaniard again. There could not be two dark-visaged foreigners making enquiries about the school. Six years since Papa had absconded with the Spanish Ambassador's daughter. Could it possible have taken six years for a vengeful relative to find her? It had taken Bertram six years, she reminded herself. The thought brought no comfort, since it implied that Bertram had not tried very hard, and that the mysterious foreigner might indeed be on her trail. If he was seen again, she had best warn Tizzy and Aunt Eugenia to be on their guard.

By Sunday, there had been no further reports of the Spaniard. Amaryllis decided she had been making a mountain of a molehill and went off to early service in a cheerful mood. Today she would return the bank draught to Lord Daniel. Let him dare to look at her with that cynical expression after that! When she reached home, she left word with Daisy to tell his lordship that she desired a word with him. Shortly after ten, the parlour-maid appeared at the common-room door and announced that he was waiting in her office.

Isabel bounced up.

"May I go down, Miss Hartwell?" she asked eagerly.

"You may come down to the vestibule and wait there, but I wish to speak to your father before you go out with him."

The bright eyes clouded. "Have I done something wrong?" she whispered.

Miss Hartwell gave her a quick hug. "Not at all. You are an excellent student and I was proud of your improvement in church this morning. I have business with Lord Daniel."

"Pray do not let him make you angry," begged the child, her solemn face still worried.

"Miss Tisdale says he that is slow to anger is better than the mighty," announced Louise.

"Thank you, Miss Carfax, I shall bear that in mind," said Miss Hartwell drily. "Come, Isabel, let us go down."

Lord Daniel was pacing the office like a caged panther, his dark hair ruffled, a frown creasing his broad forehead. He swung round as she entered and strode towards her.

"Is something wrong with Isabel?" he demanded.

"No, nothing. I merely wished to return this to you." She moved past him to the desk and took out the draught. "I told you I should not accept it," she said, handing it to him.

He looked down at the paper, then at her with surprise in his eyes.

"I cannot suppose that the school brings in enough for you to turn down such a windfall," he said harshly but with some confusion.

Her chin went up. "We do well enough to make it unnecessary to accept bribes, my lord." He did seem to have a genius for destroying her composure.

"My apologies, Miss Hartwell. It must be gratifying to see the success of an establishment you have built from nothing."

There was warm admiration in his tone, and it was her turn to be surprised. Before she could respond he spoke again, as if he regretted the lapse in his hostility.

"Is Isabel ready to go out?"

"She is waiting for you in the vestibule."

He bowed and was gone. Shaking her head in amused exasperation, Amaryllis watched through the window as he and his daughter went down the garden path and into the waiting carriage. In spite of his unmannerly exit, he left her feeling that he understood her pride in the school. She recalled Bertram's impatience when she had told him that she could not leave at a moment's notice. He seemed almost to regard it as a joke that she was a schoolmistress. When she was married to him and a countess, would she look back on these six years as if they had been a mere aberration in her life?

The arrival of the object of her musing put an end to her reflections. He sauntered into the office and bowed gracefully over her hand. "Daisy told me you were in here," he explained. "I said she need not announce me."

It was typical of his charm that he should already have learned the parlour-maid's name. She was probably ready to eat out of his hand.

"All the same, Bertram, it will not do to let the whole world know upon what terms we stand," she said severely. "As the uncle of one of my pupils, it is proper that you wait to be announced."

"Fustian, my dear! Now go get your bonnet and let us be

off."

"Bertram, I wish you will listen to me and understand my position. We are not in London now, where it is perfectly proper for a gentleman to drive a young lady in Hyde Park in an open carriage. I cannot go out with you."

"We shall take Louise along for chaperone."

"Even if Louise were sufficient chaperone, which she is not, I have five or six girls expecting to go walking with me this afternoon. We do not get so many fine days at this season that we can afford to miss the opportunity for exercise."

"Surely Miss Tisdale or Mrs. Vaux might take them."

"They have duties of their own."

Lord Pomeroy inspected his glossy, spotless Hessians and sighed. "I daresay it is not out of reason muddy where you intend to go?" he asked hopefully. "I shall come with you. In fact," he cheered up, "this will do much better than taking that inquisitive little brat with us. The others will serve to keep her out of our hair."

"I fear," said Miss Hartwell, "that Louise is not one of our more vigorous walkers. She will not be among the group, and since you are come ostensibly to see her, it will not do."

"Not a vigorous walker, eh?" said his lordship grimly. "I've never seen a child with as much energy in my life. Let me have but one word with her and we shall see if she is not a vigorous walker."

Laughing, Amaryllis gave in. Nor did Louise put up much of a fight, when told that Uncle Bertram would take her into the village for luncheon first.

When word spread that Miss Hartwell's group was to have a dashing male escort, its numbers doubled instantly. For the first quarter mile across the flat, green meadows Lord Pomeroy was inundated with blushes and giggles, but he had a decade of experience in damping the pretensions of schoolroom misses. They soon gave up and left him in peace.

With the girls walking ahead, his lordship made several efforts to draw Amaryllis away from the path they had

taken. She avoided this as neatly as he had avoided the
snares of her charges, and they all returned together to the
village some two hours later. Suffering from varying
degrees of weariness, they ambled through the narrow,
winding streets between pastel-washed cottages of wattle
and daub, the larger brick houses of the merchants, crooked
black-and-white Tudor buildings, until the party came to
the tiny triangle of open space known inaccurately as Falcon Square.

Lord Pomeroy took one look at the façade of the Falcon
Inn, one of the oldest and crookedest of the timber-framed
buildings, another look at Louise's hot face, and suggested
tea all round. His popularity instantly restored, he led the
way into the cool, dim interior. Bowing, he invited the
young ladies to seat themselves and went to consult the
landlady.

Pots of tea and pitchers of lemonade appeared, followed
by platters piled high with scones and cream cakes. Bertram
sat down with Amaryllis at a small table to one side, took
a deep draught from his tankard of ale, and leaned back in
his chair to watch the devastation.

"You must starve them," he exclaimed.

"Not at all, only we do not have cream cakes on the menu
unless someone has a birthday. We give them healthy foods
like brollycolly." Half against her will, she told him about
her interview with Ned.

"That settles it," he said firmly. "I shall move to Castle
Hedingham this very evening and propriety be damned."

"Then you think it likely that the Spaniard will create
some sort of mischief?"

"Not at all likely," he grinned, "but it gives me an excellent excuse to see you every day."

She was unable to dissuade him, though she tried once
more when they returned to the school. In spite of herself,
she was relieved to have him nearby, so she felt doubly guil-
ty when she realised she had not told him she would marry
him.

It was too late for today. He had gone back to Halstead

to arrange the removal of his gear, his valet, and his groom to the Blue Boar. By spreading his largesse among the various hostelries, he hoped to win to his side the innkeepers who were probably the village's greatest gossips. With luck they might scotch any scandal for fear of losing his custom.

Not that he cared if the yokels talked about Amaryllis. It could not make the slightest difference to his intention to marry her. But it would make her uncomfortable and so was best avoided, just as long as the avoidance did not cause him any inconvenience.

=7=

MISS HARTWELL, FEELING unaccountably tired, went upstairs with the intention of lying down on her bed until it was time to change for dinner. She was halfway up the last flight when Daisy called to her from the landing below.

"Miss, miss, it's Miss Isabel's Pa asking to see you."

"Drat!" said Miss Hartwell in an unaccustomed outburst of vulgarity. "What ails the man now?" The thought of going all the way down to the ground floor, and later climbing all the way back, made her legs ache. "Where are Miss Tisdale and Mrs. Vaux, Daisy?"

"Miss is in the common-room, and Madam is laid down on her bed, miss."

"Then pray show Lord Daniel to the private drawing-room. We shall not be disturbed there."

A fire had been laid in the drawing-room, but not yet lit. Though the afternoon had been warm, autumn announced itself in the chill of approaching evening. Miss Hartwell sank onto a comfortably overstuffed sofa and wished she could put her feet up. A moment later Daisy ushered in Lord Daniel.

"Will I light the fire, miss?" she enquired.

"Not on my account," said his lordship. "I shall not stay more than a moment."

"Light a pair of candles, Daisy, if you please. Pray be seated, my lord, even if it is for two minutes, because I am tired and I do not wish to have to crane my neck to see you."

He laughed and sat down. Again she wondered at the change wrought in his face by the alteration of expression.

His laugh sounded rusty from disuse, and she was glad to have provoked it.

"What a charming room this is," he said, glancing around.

Surprised, she followed his gaze. She had grown so accustomed to the furnishings she scarcely noticed them. The flowered chintzes and apple-green carpet, though faded, were certainly cheerful; and the pale yellow walls made it seem sunny on even the dreariest days. How odd in him to comment on it. She looked at him with suspicion. Was he trying to turn her up sweet? She dismissed the possibility. From what she had seen of his character, it was more that he was simply making an unwonted effort to be pleasant.

"Thank you," she said hurriedly, in some confusion. "It is our favourite room, though we do not often have time to sit here during the school year. What can I do for you, sir?"

"I think it proper to inform you that I am sending Isabel's pony over to be stabled in the village. She greatly misses her daily ride. Naturally, you cannot be expected to provide mounts for your pupils."

"Nor do I have time to accompany her. You will not wish your daughter to ride unsupervised."

"No. I had not thought. However, one of my grooms may ride over to take her out."

Amaryllis phrased her next words carefully. He was obviously in a conciliatory mood and she had no desire to offend him.

"I am sorry, my lord, but I believe I should be wrong to permit this. I told you at our first meeting that we do not have extras or parlour boarders. Isabel is already favoured in that you visit her weekly. Some of the girls receive no visitors at all. I cannot think it fair that Isabel should be especially privileged, and I do not care to see her singled out as an object for envy and spite." Seeing that he was bewildered, she added gently, "I know that you love her very deeply and want only the best for her. It is not always easy to know what is best. I admire your willingness to send her to school. I hope you will agree with me that her relationship with the other girls is more important than her riding."

The bitter look was back on his face. For a moment, remembering what Isabel had said of his quarrels with neighbours and relatives, she wondered if he would tell her riding was more important than friendship. However, he assented without demur.

"Is Isabel a good student?" he asked hesitantly.

"Excellent. She reads extremely well for her age, and what is more significant in the long run, she is interested in everything and studies hard. Her manners are also much improved."

He flushed, but nonetheless looked proud.

"And she has made friends? You described her as a retiring child, I remember."

"She is still quiet, but she is on good terms with the other girls. One cannot expect her to suddenly become sociable when she has been used to solitude. However, Louise Carfax is still her bosom-bow. Indeed, you would have thought me to have windmills in my head to call her retiring had you seen the pair of them the other day." She described the anti-rain dance. To her delight, it drew another laugh from him.

"Miss Carfax sounds like an enterprising young lady," he remarked, then added thoughtfully, "You say that some girls receive no visits? Should you object if I asked Isabel to invite a few of her friends to Wimbish for the day?"

"What a kind notion," exclaimed Amaryllis in amazement.

"I can send the carriage over early," he went on, oblivious to her relief or her surprise. "The apples are ripening in the orchard. Perhaps they will like to pick some to bring back to school. I daresay you will wish to chaperone them?"

"Someone must go with them. Miss Tisdale, or perhaps Mrs. Vaux . . ."

"I hope you will choose to come yourself. You are Isabel's favourite teacher."

"I . . . Thank you . . . that will be delightful." To her annoyance she felt herself blushing, which was utterly unjustified by his tone. He had sounded detached, as if he did not care who went except insofar as it affected his daughter. Not that there was the least reason to suppose that he had any other motive.

He stood up, an ironic gleam in his eye. "Next Sunday then. Will half past nine suit you?"

"Y—yes. Yes, that will do very well."

He bowed and took his leave.

Windmills in the head indeed! Amaryllis scolded herself. How could she have allowed a noted rake to talk her into accompanying a group of young ladies to his lair? She must at least make sure that Isabel invited the youngest possible, though she had heard alarming tales of libertines with a taste for little girls. Had not the notorious Harriette Wilson and her sisters joined the muslin company at an amazingly early age? She must keep her wits about her and not let any of them out of her sight. Yet apple picking sounded a thoroughly innocent pastime . . .

Heavens! she thought suddenly, sitting bolt upright, Bertram expected to see her next Sunday. What on earth would he think when he learned that instead of spending the day with him, she was going to traipse off across the county to call upon another gentleman? And that gentleman a notorious rake!

The moment had come, she decided as she once more climbed the stair to her chamber, to consult Tizzy and her aunt. Immediately after dinner, she hurried them up to the drawing-room.

"I cannot imagine why you are in such a rush," complained Mrs. Vaux as she settled into a chair by the fire. "I did not have time for a dish of apple charlotte, and you know it is my favourite. Cook makes a very fine apple charlotte."

"I'm sorry, Aunt Eugenia." Amaryllis hugged her. "I will ask Daisy to fetch you some when she brings the tea. I have a great deal to discuss with you."

" 'Nothing is secret which shall not be made manifest.' Luke 8, verse 17. I expect Lord Pomeroy still wishes to marry you?"

"Yes, he does. How did you guess, Tizzy? Though I suppose it is unlikely that he should have stayed in the neighbourhood only to see Louise."

"Highly unlikely," observed Miss Tisdale drily.

"Bertram has offered for your hand again? How splendid!" Mrs. Vaux clapped her hands. "At last I shall see you Lady Pomeroy, with your own house and carriage and no duns at the door. Lord Tatenhill is as warm a man as any peer in the country, I daresay, and he is no nipcheese. La! You will have more pin money than we spend in a year."

"If I marry him, the world will call it creampot love," said her niece slowly. "I had not thought of that. And the scandalmongers will all be raking over Papa's conduct."

"If? Never say you have not accepted, Amaryllis? Indeed you must not play fast and loose with him again. A gentleman cannot be expected to come up to scratch time after time."

"What is the sticking point?" asked Miss Tisdale. "The old scandal? If his lordship does not regard it I am sure you need not. Or is it concern for myself and your aunt? There are always governesses in want of employment, my dear, and now that you have everything running smoothly we may easily find someone to take your place, though naturally we should miss you."

Since Amaryllis had urged this to her aunt when they were discussing Tizzy marrying the vicar, she could hardly demur.

"Those objections are not so easily dismissed," she said with a frown. "However, the main problem is that I am not at all sure I wish to be married to Bertram!"

"Nonsense!" Mrs. Vaux was now near tears with vexation. "He is charming and good-looking and wealthy and complaisant and he loves you to distraction. What more can you possible ask for in a husband? If I ever heard anything so chuckleheaded."

"It is indeed difficult to argue against such a list of virtues, Aunt. Perhaps I am being goosish. But I have promised that this time, if I accept his hand, I shall immediately set the date and not tease him with delays. It would be the outside of enough to throw my cap over the windmill while I have doubts."

"You have been long too independent to decide easily to commit yourself to the care of another," agreed Miss Tisdale. "I am sure you will do what is best. Is Lord Pomeroy fixed in the country indefinitely?"

"That he is willing to bear the tedium for my sake ought to be enough to persuade me," said Amaryllis gloomily. "However, he has insisted upon removing from Halstead to Castle Hedingham, so I expect I shall see him more often."

Mrs. Vaux brightened. She caught herself just in time not to blurt out that there would be no end of gossip. Amaryllis would have to marry him in the end to foil the gossipmongers, and though she would miss her niece quite dreadfully, it was her dearest wish to see her happily wed.

"Another thing I must tell you about," Amaryllis went on, "is the reason he is come to the village, which is not merely impatience to be near me." She explained how both his lordship and Ned had seen a mysterious Spaniard making enquiries about the school.

Mrs. Vaux emitted a faint shriek.

"Your Papa will be the death of me yet," she wailed. "Perhaps if we tell the man that Henry is in Philadelphia, he will go off to America and leave us in peace?"

"I cannot suppose, ma'am, that there is the slightest connection," said Miss Tisdale firmly, looking daggers at Amaryllis.

"Oh no, Aunt Eugenia," she said shamefaced. "I did not mean to alarm you. It is vastly unlikely after six years. Only Bertram has taken a bee in his bonnet and uses it as an excuse to hover over me. Which is most unfortunate at this precise moment, because I have accepted an invitation."

"An invitation?" Miss Tisdale glanced at the clock. "Your life grows hourly more entangled, but I beg you will save this story until I return from checking the common-room." She stalked out with a rustle of skirts, shaking her head in amused dismay.

Seeing that Mrs. Vaux was inclined to dwell on the sinister Spaniard, Amaryllis asked whether she had visited Augusta Raeburn that afternoon.

"I spent quite half an hour with her and she offered me tea, though I could not stay for it," said the widow triumphantly.

"It is three years since the Raeburns came here. Is she not suspicious at your sudden friendliness?"

"Not in the least. She is too occupied by far with her own feelings to wonder about the motives of others."

"And did you discover anything that might be of use to us?"

"Travelling makes her ill, but I cannot see that that will help us."

Amaryllis shook her head regretfully. "Hinder us rather."

"And she cannot abide the smell of cheese and will not have it in the house."

"Then we must be sure to have a good cheese on the table for the vicar on Monday evenings. However, unless we can persuade a cheesemaker to move in next door to the vicarage, that is not very helpful either."

"I shall persevere. Only if both you and Miss Tisdale are to marry, I doubt I can run the school by myself, Amaryllis, had I ever so many governesses to help me."

"Dear aunt, you cannot suppose that Bertram and I should abandon you in such a situation. Now hush, here is Tizzy."

"Louise Carfax has been telling fortunes by melting lead in a spoon over a candle," announced Miss Tisdale, "and dropping it into cold water. Where she came by the lead I cannot say. Unfortunately, the handkerchief wrapped about the handle of the spoon caught fire, but the girl holding it at the time dropped it before she was burned."

"Is the carpet much damaged?" asked Mrs. Vaux anxiously.

"Louise was performing the experiment over the hearth, so there is no damage. A sensible child in her own peculiar way. Now, Amaryllis, what is this invitation?"

At that moment Daisy came in with the tea tray. Amaryllis asked her to send up some apple charlotte for Mrs. Vaux, and busied herself making tea. One of the housemaids brought up the dessert, and they all settled about the fire sipping from the elegant china.

"Oh dear," said Mrs. Vaux at last, setting aside the empty dish with a contented sigh, "I ought not to have eaten that, I know. I shall have to let out my gowns. Now, tell us about your invitation."

"It is not precisely *my* invitation."

Feeling her cheeks grow warm, Amaryllis gazed into the flickering flames in the hope that any unusual colour in her face would be laid to their account. She explained Lord Daniel's proposal for the outing on the following Sunday, stressing that it was planned as a treat for the girls. The older ladies exchanged glances.

"An obliging notion," commented Miss Tisdale.

"That is what is so odd. In general he is one of the most disobliging men I have ever met. I can scarce exchange a word with him without quarrelling."

"Then I had better go with the girls," suggested Mrs. Vaux uneasily. "It will not do to be quarrelling with your host and the parent of a pupil, and there is no need to fear that he will have designs against my virtue."

Amaryllis looked up with a smile. "How can you say so, Aunt? You are as pretty as ever and have only to put on your new silk dress to be a worthy object of any man's attention, whatever his intentions."

It was the widow's turn to blush, but she asserted firmly that she had never so much as glanced at a man since dear Mr. Vaux's death and she did not mean to begin now.

"As to Lord Daniel having designs against anyone's virtue," Amaryllis went on, suppressing her own unease, "he must be the greatest mooncalf in nature to wish for an intimate association with such a contrary female as he perceives me to be. And I shall not wear my new silk dress, so he will continue to think me a dowdy as well. Papa always liked his . . . his fancy pieces to be dressed in the height of fashion."

"You are determined to go then?" asked Miss Tisdale.

"He took me by surprise with the request and I accepted. I do not think it proper to withdraw now. As Aunt Eugenia says, he is the parent of a pupil and not to be offended gratuitously."

Avoiding their eyes, she went to make sure the common-room had not been set ablaze, though after Tizzy raked them over the coals it was unlikely that any of the young ladies would dare so much as touch a candle for a week.

As Amaryllis closed the door behind her, Mrs. Vaux grew suddenly agitated.

"It has just come to me!" she announced in a shocked voice. "Lord Daniel Winterborne—I knew the name was familiar. His wife—it was far worse than poor Henry's scandal, I vow."

"I do not care to hear," said Miss Tisdale firmly.

"But ought I to tell Amaryllis?"

" 'Let the dead bury their dead.' Matthew 8, verse 22. Though the old proverb says it better: Let sleeping dogs lie."

Mrs. Vaux shook her head worriedly but agreed not to disclose Lord Daniel's scandal unless his future actions should warrant it.

Amaryllis came back. "They are as quiet as mice," she said gaily. "Whatever did you say to them, Tizzy?"

Amaryllis turned the conversation to school matters. Nothing more was said that evening of Lord Pomeroy, Lord Daniel Winterborne, or the ominous Spaniard. It was raining when she went up to bed. She closed the curtains tight against the night and lay wakeful, listening to the mournful sounds of dripping eaves, an owl hooting in the distance, the church clock striking midnight. Her dreams were haunted by faces: Bertram's fair, genial, and Daniel Winterborne's dark and moody.

By morning she had come to two decisions. She would confess to Bertram about her plans for Sunday as soon as possible, stressing that it was purely a business occasion. And she would try to find out from Isabel just how seriously Lord Daniel had fallen out with his family. For some reason, it was a great relief that he was still in contact at least with a sister and not so depraved as to be cut off completely.

=8=

ON MONDAY, WHEN Daisy went into the village to pick up the post at the Bell, Amaryllis gave her a note to deliver to the Blue Boar. She wanted to see Bertram, and more particularly did not want to risk his turning up at the school and asking for her.

A light drizzle was falling, making the world damp and grey and cold. Reluctantly, she asked him to meet her at the Bell at four. It was bound to give rise to gossip, but they had already been seen together at the Falcon, though surrounded by schoolgirls, and he was now known at the Blue Boar.

Daisy came back with her billet intact and reported that his lordship was not staying at the Blue Boar. Vexed, Amaryllis wondered if he had settled on one of the other inns for some reason, or if he had suddenly decided he did not wish to marry her after all and had shabbed off without a word.

She managed to laugh at herself. The notion of Lord Pomeroy doing anything so ungentlemanly was absurd.

The mystery was solved a few hours later, when Mr. Majendie's groom appeared with a fresh bundle of newspapers and a brief scrawl from Bertram. A quick look disclosed that Queen Caroline's trial was still the chief subject of the news. She locked the papers away and turned to the letter.

Bertram had met Ashurst Majendie in Halstead on Sunday evening and had been invited to stay at his father's house for as long as his business kept him fixed in the district. He suggested that she should ask Mr. Majendie to allow her to bring her history class to study the castle ruins as they had the Roman ruins in Colchester. That, he averred, had been a splendid excursion.

Since she had in any case intended to do so, though not for a few weeks, Amaryllis quickly wrote the request and gave it to the groom. She took several groups of young ladies up the hill each year and was sure Mr. Majendie would oblige.

At four o'clock, Amaryllis left the classroom and, having ascertained that Mr. Raeburn would be delighted to stay to dine, repaired to her office. No more than two minutes later, Bertram sauntered into the room. He was dressed in riding breeches and top boots, his hair curling damply.

"I bring a message from Mr. Majendie," he said in a deliberately loud voice.

Amaryllis saw Daisy hovering in the doorway behind him.

"His lordship *would* come in, miss," she said indignantly.

His lordship grinned and flipped a shilling to her with an accuracy that would have astonished anyone unacquainted with his reputation as a crack shot. She caught it niftily and curtsied, but did not budge an inch.

"That's all right, Daisy," Amaryllis told her. "As you hear, Lord Pomeroy has brought a message from the castle. You were quite correct, though, to attempt to announce his arrival before showing him in.

The maid shook her head reprovingly at his unrepentant lordship, curtseyed again, and departed. In spite of her disapproval, she tactfully closed the door behind her.

"I went riding this afternoon," Bertram said, "so I left my horse at the Bell and walked over. I really do bear a message though. Mr. Majendie will be pleased to allow you to explore the castle on Wednesday. If you go to the house, his housekeeper will give you the keys. He's a nice old boy."

"Lewis Majendie is a well-known agriculturalist, a member of several Learned Societies, and author of a paper on the history of Hedingham Castle for the Society of Antiquaries," corrected Amaryllis. "But you are right, he is a nice old boy, and a highly regarded Lord of the Manor. It is a pity, though, that the castle passed out of the hands of the Earls of Oxford after being in the de Vere family since the Norman Conquest."

"Are you about to give me a history lesson?" he asked suspiciously. "I am not one of your pupils, you know."

"Not now. If, as I suppose, you intend to join us on Wednesday, we shall cover six centuries or so in the course of a few hours."

His lordship groaned.

They chatted for a few minutes, then Amaryllis said that she must go up to the common-room to see to Mr. Raeburn's comfort.

"Daisy will think it an excessively lengthy message if we are closeted together any longer," she pointed out. "However, as a guest of Mr. Majendie it will be perfectly proper for you to request an introduction to the local vicar. Come up with me."

"Must I? I am not over fond of the clergy. An uncle of mine is a bishop—devilish chap."

"Of course you need not, though I must. We shall meet on Wednesday, after all, unless William the Conqueror frightens you off. By the way, I shall be unable to see you on Sunday, I fear. A matter of business."

"Business on the Sabbath? Shocking! You must put it off. Sundays are the only time I can spend with you."

"I cannot. I must chaperone some of the girls on a visit."

"Where to? Can I not go? I am sure by now they are coming to expect my escort."

"To Wimbish. It is a small village some fifteen miles from here." She found herself ridiculously reluctant to pronounce the name of their host, but he might hear it from someone else and wonder why she had not mentioned it. "It is the home of one of our girls, Isabel Winterborne. Her father, Lord Daniel, has permitted her to invite her friends to spend the day there."

"Lord Daniel Winterborne," he mused. "The name sounds

familiar. One of Bellingham's sons?"

"So I assume, though he has not mentioned the connection."

"You remember George? I've not seen him since Vienna. He was at the Congress. I heard he was in Italy last winter, but I never caught up with him. Don't believe I ever met Daniel, though. Come to think of it, wasn't he with the army in Spain?"

"Was he?"

"Yes, now I remember! He . . . But that's no tale to tell a gently bred female. You must have been in the schoolroom yourself at the time."

"At what time, Bertram? You cannot leave me in suspense like this!"

He was adamant. Many gentlemen of the Haut Monde were as eager to pass on on-dits and tidbits of scandal as any society matron, but Lord Pomeroy considered it vulgar. He looked at Amaryllis consideringly, as if wondering whether to warn her to be on her guard. However, he dropped the subject, stood up, and offered her his arm.

"Lead me to the vicar," he said with resignation.

She complied, with a backward glance at the account book and correspondence that would have to be dealt with tomorrow. They found Mr. Raeburn talking to Miss Tisdale by the fire in the common-room. There were only three girls there, reading in a corner. The others would be scattered about the house, studying, drawing, practising their music. A few hardy souls were probably taking the air in the garden, well wrapped against the weather. Mrs. Vaux would be laid down on her bed.

She introduced Lord Pomeroy to the vicar, knowing that in spite of his professed dislike of churchmen he would be impeccably polite and probably charming. They soon discovered that they both, along with Miss Tisdale's father and brother, had been students at Magdalene College. Miss Tisdale had heard so much about it that she was able to join in their reminiscences, giving Amaryllis leisure to consider Bertram's words.

It seemed he knew something to Lord Daniel's discredit, yet he did not think her in danger from him. Was it because he still saw her as a member of the Ton, beyond the reach of any but a thorough-going blackguard? At least that meant he did not thus stigmatise Lord Daniel. More likely he simply thought her too dowdy by far to attract the attention of a rake. That was what she had decided herself, but all the same it was a lowering reflection!

Miss Tisdale took it upon herself to invite Lord Pomeroy to dinner. He looked down deprecatingly at his riding clothes and mud-splashed boots, but she hurried to assure him that he need not regard his inability to change.

If he thought that dining with three schoolmistresses, a clergyman, and a horde of giggling girls was bound to prove sadly flat, no hint of it appeared in his face or voice as he accepted. Amaryllis was sorely tempted to test his patience by seating him between chattering Louise, who was after all his niece, and silent Isabel. She resisted that temptation, succumbed to another, and placed him beside herself, though with Louise on his other side.

Lord Pomeroy behaved throughout the meal with perfect propriety, his composure threatened only when Daisy offered him a choice of lemonade or milk.

"Milk!" he exclaimed, outraged.

"It is good for you, Uncle Bertram," his niece reproved him.

"Lemonade, please, Daisy," he requested meekly.

Mrs. Vaux had warned him to stay behind with the vicar at the end of the meal, in order to give the girls an opportunity to practise withdrawing from the room and leaving the gentlemen with their port. This was accomplished in good order. His lordship was rewarded when Amaryllis returned to the dining room with a bottle of brandy, kept strictly for medicinal purposes.

Nothing could persuade him to go up with Mr. Raeburn to the common-room.

"Mr. Majendie is expecting me," he pointed out smugly.

"Then wait while I put on my boots," said Amaryllis. "It

has stopped raining. I will walk with you as far as the corner."

The clouds had blown over, leaving a starry sky. The air was mild and fresh, more like spring than autumn, though drifts of fallen leaves under the trees were a reminder of coming winter. Her hand tucked under Bertram's arm, Amaryllis savoured the mingled scents of woodsmoke and wet grass as they strolled down King Street.

"Was dinner so very bad?" she asked, a laugh in her voice.

"Not at all. I wish the food at Eton had been half so good. And as for the company, I have had worse at many a diplomatic banquet."

"There speaks a diplomat. I must turn back now. I shall see you on Wednesday?"

"I am looking forward to my history lesson. Goodnight, my dear." He kissed her wrist between glove and sleeve, watched as she walked back until she turned in at the gate, and then strode on into the village.

She was still very dear to him, though she had changed over those six missing years. She was still the only woman he had ever wanted to make his wife. He did not want to press her for a decision, yet he must have an answer soon, for his father was suddenly growing old and his dearest wish was to see his heir married and settled.

Still, if she refused him, he could do little to search for a bride until the new Season began in March, when every eligible damsel in the kingdom would be paraded for his edification. All the matchmaking Mamas in town would seek out the wealthy heir to an earldom. The thought, as usual, appalled him. All he wanted was Amaryllis, and he must spend the months until March proving and reproving his devotion so that when the time came for him to insist on an answer, she would have no doubt that he loved her. He looked back, but the night had swallowed even the white blur of the proud sign announcing the school's presence.

Amaryllis opened the gate and lingered a moment with her hand on it, reading the sign by memory since the starlight was too dim to make out the letters. The expected feeling of achievement eluded her. The thought of going up to face her four and twenty pupils was disagreeable. Bertram's reappearance had made her dissatisfied with her lot. Why had she not told him she would wed him? Was there a lingering sense that it would be unfair to marry only to escape?

But I love him, she thought in sudden panic. Don't I?

A rustling sound drew her attention. She peered towards the group of silver birches on her right in the corner of the garden. Their ghostly trunks stood out clear, making the shadows behind them the blacker.

It could be a hunting cat, perhaps a hedgehog or even a badger. A twig snapped with a sharp crack. An explosive sneeze followed, then what might have been a muffled curse.

"Who is there?" Amaryllis demanded. "Ned! Bertram!" She had no hope that they would hear her, but perhaps her shout would give the intruder pause.

A figure muffled in a dark cloak rushed towards her. As she stepped back, raising her hands protectively, a swinging arm caught her a glancing blow and knocked her sideways to the ground. Her assailant leaped over her prone body, dashed through the gateway, and disappeared into the night.

For a few moments Amaryllis lay perfectly still listening. All she heard was her own heart beating madly. She became aware of her bruised hip and arm and shoulder, and the dampness seeping through her cloak from the ground. Cautiously she raised herself and looked around.

On the path beside her was a white handkerchief. She picked it up, stood up, and put it in her pocket. Trying not to make a sound, she moved to the gate, looked both ways into the blackness of the lane, then carefully closed the gate making sure it did not click. Then her nerve broke and she fled up the path to the front door. Locking and bolting the door behind her, she rang for Daisy.

"I slipped on the path and fell," she explained. "My cloak

83

is all muddy. Can you clean it?"

"Oh miss, I hope you didn't hurt yoursel'!"

"No, I am just a little shaken. Pray do not mention it to anyone, for I do not want a fuss."

Taking the cloak and folding it over her arm, Daisy felt in the pockets.

"Here's your handkercher, miss."

Amaryllis took it and put it in the pocket of her gown, then hurried up to the common-room, glad for the nonce of the reassuring presence of so many people.

When she went to bed, she looked at the handkerchief. It was certainly not one of her own, being a square of fine linen too large to belong to a lady. In one corner was an embroidered rose, crimson with green leaves and stem and vicious-looking thorns. She could not recall ever seeing the thorns represented in embroidery before.

She folded it and tucked it away in the back of her drawer. It seemed likely that the intruder had been the mysterious Spaniard. She would be more careful in future not to go out alone in the dark, but she saw no reason to further alarm Aunt Eugenia by reporting the incident. She would mention it to Bertram, though she could not think of anything he could do about it. Judging by the enormous sneeze, the man ought to take to his bed for a while anyway.

The sky turned cloudy overnight, but the weather continued mild and dry, if grey. On Wednesday afternoon, Miss Hartwell assembled her beginning history class and they set off for the castle. They crossed Falcon Square, made their way up Castle Lane and over Bailey Street, where once a wall protected the outer bailey of the castle. From here only the tower on the top of the keep was visible, the rest hidden by trees now gold, bronze, and russet in their autumnal glory.

In mediaeval times the hillside had been carefully cleared of any growth tall enough to hide a man. The hill was not high but it dominated the surrounding plain and an attacking army must have been visible miles away. Even before the invading Normans took it from its Saxon lord, in ancient British days, this place had been defended by ditch and earthen wall.

As they walked up the steepening slope, Miss Hartwell described the scene as it must have appeared when King John besieged the castle. The Earl of Oxford's archers in coats of mail stood guard on the concentric walls circling the hill; men in armour, their surcoats emblazoned in red and blue and yellow, prepared for sorties, their weapons clashing, their shouts filling the air. In the fields below, where now cattle grazed, King John's soldiers rode among tents and pavilions bright with pennants.

"What were they fighting about, ma'am?" asked Louise Carfax. "They were all English, were they not? They ought to have been fighting the French." She had frequently joined her brothers in refighting the battles of the Napoleonic Wars.

Miss Hartwell sighed and explained Magna Carta for the third or fourth time. "When King John took the castle," she said, "the barons invited the Dauphin of France, the heir to the French throne, to help them win it back. More often than not, throughout history, England has been at war with France, but not quite all the time."

"King John was fighting the French," Louise pointed out. "I beg your pardon, ma'am, but it's true, is it not?"

"But King John was a bad king!" said Isabel, shocked.

Foreseeing the beginning of another civil war, Miss Hartwell hastened through time to Henry VII. The then Earl of Oxford had aided Henry Tudor throughout the Wars of the Roses, enduring exile for the Lancastrian cause. Safe on his throne at last, King Henry graciously paid a visit to Hedingham Castle. The earl had gathered all his retainers and dressed them in his livery, red and yellow with white star and blue boar. To honour the king on his departure, they lined the route from the castle, that very track where they were now walking.

"My lord," said the king, "I have heard much of your hospitality, but I see that it is greater than the speech. These handsome gentlemen and yeomen which I see on both sides of me are sure your menial servants?"

"If it may please your Grace," answered the earl, "that were not for mine ease; they are most of them my retainers, that are come to do me service at such a time as this, and chiefly to see your Grace."

"By my faith, my lord," said the king, "I thank you for your good cheer, but I may not have my laws broken in my sight. My attorney must speak with you."

"And he fined him fifteen thousand marks," said Miss Hartwell, "which was a very large fortune then.'"

"That was not fair," cried Isabel indignantly, "after the earl helped him win the throne!"

"You see, Henry Tudor had seen the private armies of the noblemen overthrow Richard III in his favour, and he had no intention of being deposed likewise. He made a law saying no one might have more than a certain number of armed followers in livery."

"Very sensible," approved Louise. "Only think, they might have gone on fighting each other forever, instead of the French."

Miss Hartwell could not help but wonder what would happen when she taught these two about the Civil War between Parliament and the Royalists.

They had reached the brow of the hill. On their left, a beautiful brick bridge, built in Tudor times to replace the drawbridge, crossed the dry moat. On the right stood the mansion raised a mere century ago by Robert Ashurst, who bought the castle when the de Vere line died out.

As they approached, the front door opened and Lord Pomeroy emerged, swinging a bunch of keys in one hand.

"I saw you coming," he explained as he joined them. "Mr.

Majendie has been telling me some tales of the castle's history in preparation. Did you know that Henry VIII . . ."

" . . . fined the earl fifteen thousand marks for having too many soldiers," interrupted Louise. "Was not that famous, Uncle Bertram?"

"Brat," said his lordship. "You have spoiled my best story."

"You can blame me," Amaryllis confessed, laughing. "I had hoped to dispose of at least part of the history lesson before you joined us. At least that is one little bit of history Louise will not forget in a hurry."

She and Bertram led the way across the bridge past the brick gatehouse. The girls gasped as they caught their first unobstructed view of the keep. It was an impressive sight, the smooth grey stone rising sheer for seventy-five feet, broken only by a few narrow windows. Louise's attention was immediately drawn by the square indentations that pockmarked the wall at regular intervals.

"Cannonball holes!" she cried with ghoulish glee.

"I think they would be round," frowned Isabel, "and not so . . . so *precise*."

"They would have smashed the wall to bits," agreed one of the older girls.

"Quite right," approved Miss Hartwell. "The castle was never attacked after the invention of gunpowder, and those that emerged from battle were indeed 'smashed to bits.' Can anyone guess what the holes were for?"

Even Lord Pomeroy looked blank.

"Mr. Majendie did not tell me that," he complained.

"They supported the scaffolding when the castle was built. Come, let us go round the other side to the entrance."

The keep stood near the centre of a roughly circular grassy area. Only overgrown hillocks showed where the other buildings of the inner bailey had been, and the once-proud curtain wall was now an encircling mound, easily crossed by the cattle that grazed where men-at-arms had gathered for war. A stone staircase rose from the ground to the keep's arched entrance door on the first floor. They climbed up it to a landing just outside the door. Below them was a square, walled enclosure, windowless and doorless.

"There was a tower here to protect the door," Miss Hartwell explained. "Its ground floor, below us, was an oubliette."

Again her pupils looked blank, but this time his lordship knew the answer.

"If you please, ma'am," he said with a grin, "was that not a dungeon entered only by a trapdoor in the ceiling?"

The girls crowded to the rail and looked down with wide eyes. A heap of blown leaves covered half the floor. Over the centuries since the roof had gone, dirt had accumulated and now supported a few straggling ragwort plants, their yellow heads bright in contradiction to the grim purpose of the rough walls.

"I'll wager ghosts frequent this spot," said Lord Pomeroy with a grin.

"There are periodic reports of villagers seeing things, but no story of consistent haunting," said Miss Hartwell with a shudder. "Let us go in." Pausing in the doorway, she pointed out the slot in the twelve-foot-thick wall where the portcullis had been lowered from above as an extra precaution.

"I cannot imagine how King John ever captured the place," exclaimed Louise.

They went down the wide spiral stair to the ground floor. Since there were no windows the only light came from the stairway, but to Louise's disappointment the gloom concealed only storage space. Back up they traipsed to the entrance floor, where the soldiers had lived. The windows were mere slits, enough to let in light and air and doubtless howling winter gales, but too narrow to admit missiles from outside. Miss Hartwell, expecting some pertinent comment from Louise, looked around to find she had disappeared, and Isabel with her.

"Drat the child!" she said, vexed. "Bertram . . . My lord, where is your niece?"

"If I know Louise, she is back at the dungeon," he said. "I'd wager on it. Do you go on upstairs, I shall fetch her."

The next floor, the Banqueting Hall, was two storeys high. A huge arch in the middle supported the timbered ceiling over twenty feet above. Double windows admitted enough light to see easily the richly carved stonework, the huge fireplace, and the minstrels' gallery tunnelled into the thickness of the walls half way up between floor and ceiling.

It was in this magnificent chamber that Mr. Lewis Majendie continued the hospitable tradition of Christmas banquets and merrymaking.

Here Louise disappeared only as far as the gallery, which she declared to be "beyond anything great." She wished Papa might be persuaded to put one in the dining-room at home.

"Can you imagine what she and her brothers would get up to?" asked Lord Pomeroy with a groan. "Fortunately there is not the least likelihood of such a thing, or I should never dine there again."

The top floor was dull in comparison. Here the de Vere family and their nobler guests had retired from the hubbub of the room below, to converse, to sleep, and probably to plot. The many curtained-off alcoves and niches provided private corners for the ladies. From the windows could be seen mile after mile of countryside, chequered green and brown, though much of the village was hidden by the nearby trees.

Turning from the view, Miss Hartwell discovered that Louise and Isabel were missing again.

"They went back to the dungeon," reported one of the girls. "I heard them whispering."

Heaving a sigh, Miss Hartwell gathered the rest of her small flock. Lord Pomeroy gallantly offered his arm, and laying her hand upon it she started down the stair. By the time they reached the first floor, dizzy from going round and round the spiral, she was glad of the support. Only one small figure stood at the rail outside the door, leaning over in an attitude of alarm.

With an oath, his lordship strode to Isabel's side. "What

the devil do you think you are doing?" he demanded of the pit, heedless of his feminine company. "Amaryllis, the little shatterbrain is down in the dungeon!"

Miss Hartwell giggled. "The very place," she exclaimed. "I wonder I did not think of it."

"I wanted to see what it was like," explained Louise composedly from below. "It was easy. I just climbed over the rail and lowered myself and dropped. Only I cannot see how to climb out."

"That," said her uncle wrathfully, "is the purpose of a dungeon!"

"What shall we do?" asked Isabel, frightened.

Miss Hartwell put her arm round the child's thin shoulders and hugged her. "Don't worry, goosecap. Lord Pomeroy will go and find one of Mr. Majendie's gardeners and bring a ladder."

"Lord Pomeroy may indeed do so," said that gentleman. "However, Lord Pomeroy has a very good mind to take everyone else out to tea first."

Louise gazed at him in horror. "Uncle Bertram, you would not. You could not be so . . . so *inhuman*! At the Falcon?"

"It is tempting. But Mr. Majendie's housekeeper has invited you all to tea at the house, so I believe after all I shall merely see the rest safely bestowed before I rescue you."

"And then I may have tea?"

His lordship looked at his erring niece with raised eyebrows.

"I'm very sorry, Miss Hartwell, to have caused so much trouble. *Please* may I have tea?" Louise begged and apologised in one breath.

"Please, ma'am?" Isabel added her voice.

Miss Hartwell laughed. "You would be very well served to have broke your leg," she admonished, "but since you did not, I see no reason to starve you. Come, girls, let us get out of this cold wind."

"I shall wait here with Louise," declared Isabel stoutly. "Please, ma'am?"

Amaryllis looked at her with surprised approval. Little Miss Winterborne was gaining self-confidence at last.

"If you will," she said with a smile. "Though I beg you will not feel it necessary to join her in the dungeon to show your sympathy."

═══9═══

SOLEMNLY PERSEVERING, THE tip of her tongue caught between her teeth, Isabel played the scale of C upon the pianoforte. Plink, plink, plink up the keyboard and plink, plink, plink back down to middle C. With a sigh of relief she raised her gaze to her teacher's face.

"Bravo," said Miss Hartwell, clapping.

Isabel beamed. "My aunt will be happy to hear that I am learning to play," she said.

"Your Papa mentioned that your aunt had advised him to send you to school." Amaryllis seized the opening. "Is that his sister?"

"Yes, my Aunt Mary. Lady Mary Carrington. She comes to see us sometimes, but not very often. She told Papa that I must learn to be a lady, and he could not teach me himself because he is a gentleman. I heard her say that she would like to have me learn with my cousins, but Sir Archibald would not hear of it. Sir Archibald is Aunt Mary's husband."

"Perhaps your Papa had a disagreement with him. You told me once he had fallen out with all his relatives. I am glad that your aunt does not take offence."

"Yes, and Uncle George comes to visit us sometimes, too. More often than Aunt Mary. Only I should like to know my cousins, and my grandfather. Nearly all the girls here have Grandpapas, and cousins and brothers and sisters, and I have not even a Mama."

Amaryllis was ready to expire with curiosity about the missing Mama, but looking down at the doleful little face she realised that this was not the moment to enquire. With her arm around Isabel, she brushed aside the gingery curls and kissed her forehead.

"Your Papa loves you enough for any number of relatives," she assured her. "And I am sure your uncle and aunt are fond of you."

"Uncle George sits me on his knee and gives me sugarplums to eat."

"Then I am perfectly certain that he holds you in great affection," laughed Amaryllis, trying to reconcile that picture with the top-o'-the trees Corinthian she had known. "Now back to work. I have a little tune for you to play to celebrate your scale of C."

The music lesson finished, she was on her way to her history class when Daisy called to her. Mr. Majendie's groom had delivered a note.

"'Tis from Lord Pomeroy, miss," said the maid, suppressing a grin.

She took it with a conscious look, impatiently thrust it into her pocket and hurried on. No doubt Bertram was proposing some quite ineligible rendezvous. Yesterday afternoon's junketing at the castle had been enough to give rise to any amount of gossip, and she could not afford to provide further food for speculation. He simply did not realise that a schoolmistress could not behave with the freedom of a viscount's daughter, nor how important the school was to her.

Pens sharpened, her pupils settled down to write an account of the history of Hedingham Castle. Judging by experience, Amaryllis knew a fascinating variety of misconceptions would surface, but for the moment all was peace. She took out Bertram's letter.

A messenger from London, from his father, had just arrived. A number of urgent matters needed attention at Tatenhill, and though the Queen's trial was in recess, the earl was not well enough to travel there and back. Bertram had already left for Tatenhill and did not know when he would be able to return. He begged her to believe that his sentiments remained unchanged, and that at a word from her he would send for her to come to Tatenhill where they might be married quietly at a moment's notice.

Amaryllis stared blindly at the paper, disappointment, sympathy, and relief warring within her. Before she could analyse her feelings, a whisper caught her attention.

"Psst, Isabel! How do you spell 'dungeon'?"

She smiled to herself. Louise was probably inventing marvellous stories about the unfortunate prisoners in the oubliette.

She turned to her preparations for the next lesson.

That evening, she wished she could share with Bertram his niece's version of history. King John was a Bad Man, even though he fought the French, which was a good thing to do. He took the castle from the Earl of Oxford and threw the earl's retainers in the 'dungyon'—apparently Isabel's spelling was not to be relied upon—and they were never seen again. When the earl recaptured his castle he threw King John's retainers in the dungyon, and they were never seen again. Later on, King Henry threw some of the earl's retainers in the dungyon because he had too many, but since it was the earl's dungyon he rescued them with a ladder and gave King Henry all his money instead. Somehow, Louise had managed to connect to the dungyon even Queen Matilda's death at the castle and Queen Elizabeth's visit, four hundred years later.

Isabel's essay, on the other hand, demonstrated a clear abhorrence of violence and sympathy for the underdog. Amaryllis wondered whether she had acquired her ideas from her father, or whether they arose from an instinctive revulsion against his harshness, though it never turned against her.

How little Amaryllis knew of the man. On Sunday she had the opportunity to learn more about him, even before she saw him. His carriage, drawn by two dapple-grey and two sorrel horses, arrived at the school promptly at nine when she was scarce returned from church.

"I am sorry you should have been called so early from

your bed on the sabbath," she exclaimed to the coachman as Isabel's chosen guests climbed into the vehicle.

"Nay, miss," responded the thickset, middle-aged man, his eyes twinkling under bushy brows as he saluted her in a military manner, "though I'd a bin happy to for Miss Isabel. The master sent me over last night to put up at the inn, for he bain't one to overwork man nor beast. He sent both pair o' cattle to shorten the journey for the young ladies, so I'll be staying again this night to rest 'em."

Having safely bestowed her friends, Isabel came up.

"Thank you for coming to fetch me, Grayson," she said, craning her neck to look up at his perch.

He beamed and saluted again. "Any time, Miss Isabel."

They joined the others inside. The carriage was comfortable and commodious, though decidedly crowded since Isabel had invited as many friends as she thought could be squeezed in. Miss Hartwell sat with three girls facing the horses, and five more had piled themselves, giggling, onto the opposite seat. Skirts were crushed and bonnets knocked awry, but in view of the occasion everyone was good-humoured.

The grey, mild weather had continued, but that morning a wind had arisen. By the time they reached the halfway point, at Finchingfield, the clouds were gone and the sun shone in a pale blue sky.

Unexpectedly the carriage stopped, and Grayson called down, "I brung some bread, miss."

"Oh please, Miss Hartwell, may we feed the ducks?" cried Isabel hopefully.

On receiving a surprised affirmative, the girls scrambled out. Amaryllis descended in a more dignified manner, accepting Grayson's proffered arm. A charming scene awaited her. Before her spread a village green, with a large pond of clear brown water, sparking in the sun, where floated a multitude of ducks. Beyond, the cottages of Finchingfield straggled up the hill to the half-timbered Guildhall and the square Norman tower of the church at the top.

Grayson passed out three loaves of stale bread, and the

young ladies advanced on the pond. As if repelling an attack, the ducks swam frantically for the shore, quacking loudly, struggled out of the water, and flocked towards the invaders. White domestic ducks with yellow bills, handsome brown mallards with glossy green heads and white-ringed necks, a solitary grey goose, they all squawked with joy as they recognised in eight young ladies a source of free food.

"Lots o' folks feeds 'em," Grayson explained to Miss Hartwell. "They reckernise a loaf a mile off, I reckon."

"What a delightful place," she said. "And to think I have lived so close for six years without ever seeing it."

Very soon the ducks were squabbling over the last crusts and everyone climbed reluctantly into the carriage. They set off up the hill.

"The goose bit me," said Louise in great indignation, waving her ungloved hand. "There was a duck eating out of my hand, and then the goose came up and chased it off and bit me."

Two of her fingers had red marks on them, but there was no real damage. Amaryllis could only wonder why the goose had chosen Louise to bite. She seemed to attract trouble as much as she sought it out.

They drove on for some time by way of country lanes and small villages. Just when the journey grew tedious, Isabel announced that the land to the left of the road belonged to her father. She sat forward on her seat to point out landmarks, and Amaryllis looked about with interest. The gentle slopes of the low, rounded hills were mostly covered with wheat stubble, already being plowed under in places. Well-kept hedges divided the wide fields from each other, and here and there spinneys provided further protection against the wind, though this was not wooded country. Huge solitary oaks, beginning to lose their yellow-brown leaves, lent variety to the landscape.

Amaryllis noted that the hedgerows, alive with fluttering, chirping birds, were weighed down with hips and haws and hazel nuts. According to country lore, such a bountiful harvest predicted a cold winter. They rolled through the hamlet of Radwinter, and half a mile beyond turned left between gateposts of weathered brick. There were no gates and no gatehouse.

"We're home," crowed Isabel.

To either side stretched more harvested fields rather than the parkland to be expected of a gentleman's residence, but the drive was gravelled and in good repair. It wound round the side of a hill, where, sheltered from the north winds, stood a rambling manor house built of oaken beams and richly red local brick. The tile roof sprouted a profusion of ornate Tudor chimney stacks. They lent the place an air of extravagant gaiety vastly at odds with what Amaryllis had discovered of its owner's disposition. The carriage rounded a circular sweep and pulled up before the front door. A pair of golden Sussex spaniels, snoozing on the brick steps, raised their heads and gazed at the carriage with liquid, expectant eyes.

"Juno! Jupiter!" called Isabel, struggling to open the carriage door in her hurry to get out. The dogs pricked up their floppy ears. "Juno, it's me!"

They gambolled up, stubby tails switching madly, as she half fell out. She flung an arm round each silky neck and submitted to having her face washed by two loving tongues. Amaryllis blinked tears away as the sight revived a painful memory. She had to leave her dogs behind when she removed from Hart Hall to London. Lord Hartwell had given her a lapdog but it was not the same, and she had soon made a present of it to an admiring friend. She followed girls and dogs up the steps. The front door had opened by now, and a flustered, untidy elderly woman stood there.

"Heavens above, Miss Isabel, how many have you brought with you?" she cried.

"My father said I might bring as many as I pleased, Prosser," the child answered with dignity.

"Well, it's not my place to complain," complained the housekeeper, "but if his lordship expected more than two or three it's more than I bargained for, I must say. However, least said, soonest mended. You'll be wanting to tidy yourselves, I'll be bound, so if you'll be pleased to follow me, miss and young ladies, I'll show you the way."

About to step over the threshold, Amaryllis was struck by a sudden, inexplicable agitation. Had she been wrong to come? Trying to regain her composure, she turned and gazed around. The circle of lawn surrounded by the drive was neatly mowed but barren of the flowerbeds she would have planted there. Beyond stood an orchard with rosy apples peeking through the yellowing leaves and horses grazing beneath the boughs. The carriage was disappearing round the east wing of the house, where doubtless the stables were located.

A little hand slipped confidingly into hers. "Do you like it, ma'am?" asked Isabel anxiously.

She smiled down at three hopeful faces. "It is very pleasant," she told the child, and scratched the dogs behind the ears.

"Won't you come in? The others have gone above-stairs but I must go and see Papa first. He is in the library."

They stepped into the centre of a long, high-ceilinged hall with a fireplace at one end and a carved wooden staircase, age-darkened, rising at the other.

"I had best go and tidy myself as your housekeeper suggested," said Amaryllis, taking off her gloves.

"Papa will not mind if you are not tidy. I shall take you up to my own chamber afterwards. Please come."

Amaryllis let herself be urged towards a door to one side of the stairs. Isabel opened it, tugged her through, then abandoned her to fling herself at Lord Daniel. Just rising from his chair, he was abruptly thrust back into it as his daughter landed in his arms. While they exchanged greetings, Amaryllis looked about the room. It was large, well lit by tall, mullioned windows, and every inch of the walls was hidden by books. There was a desk to one side and several comfortable-looking chairs, some by the windows, others near the fireplace. She moved to the nearest bookshelf to study the titles.

"An eclectic collection, Miss Hartwell," said Lord Daniel drily. He had extricated himself and stood up, and as she turned he bowed politely. "As you will recollect, I told you that I am not a sociable man. Literature absorbs a considerable portion of my time, especially since Isabel is no longer with me."

"Your farms are in good heart, my lord. I am sure you must expend some time on them also."

"I have good tenants and a good bailiff, but you are right, I take care that everything is done properly," he admitted with surprise. "Tell me, what does a schoolmistress know of the land?"

"I was not always a schoolmistress," she said shortly. "Isabel, if you will show me where to go, I had as lief take off my bonnet."

He stepped forward and took her hand. A tingling shock ran up her arm, making her heart jump, and she scarcely heard his words.

"I beg your pardon, ma'am. I did not mean to offend you." He spoke softly, and his dark eyes searched her face. "I had hoped that this would be a holiday for you as well as for Isabel's friends. Forgive me."

"Of course, I mean, there is nothing to forgive. It was a perfectly natural question." Amaryllis heard herself babbling like the sort of featherheaded widgeon she had always despised. "Pray excuse me, sir, I really must go and see what my girls are doing."

Isabel took her upstairs to a sparsely furnished bedchamber where a ewer of rapidly cooling water awaited her.

"Do you have everything you need?" she asked. "Ring the bell if you want anything else. I shall be next door with the others."

She skipped out. Amaryllis sank down onto the bed and removed her bonnet. For several minutes she sat there, trying to understand what on earth had come over her down in the library. At last, shaking her head uncomprehendingly, she got up and washed her face in the lukewarm water. A brush and comb lay on the dressing table. She unpinned her hair, brushed it slowly, and put it up again, severely restraining the copper curls. Gazing at herself in the mirror, she wondered how she could feel so strange when she looked no different from usual.

Deliberately, she set herself to examine her surroundings. Isabel's bedchamber confirmed the vague impression she had received from what she had seen of the rest of the house. In its concentration upon the necessary and lack of the decorative, it was a thoroughly male environment. There was dust in the corners and on the mantel. The brass doorknobs needed polishing. The bed hangings were threadbare and the windowpanes grimy. Mrs. Vaux, a most particular housekeeper, would have thrown up her hands in disgust. This house was sadly in need of a mistress.

Appalled at the direction her thoughts had taken, Amaryllis jumped up. She realised that the chatter of young voices in the next room had ceased some time since. When she went out into the hallway the door was open, the chamber empty. Isabel must have taken them all somewhere. Listening in the hope of hearing their whereabouts, Amaryllis descended the stair. Lord Daniel was lounging in the doorway to the library, obviously watching for her.

"Isabel is giving her friends a Grand Tour," he said with a smile. "They will come to no harm. I have ordered tea. Will you sit with me in the library?"

The invitation sounded much too intimate, but she could think of no way to refuse that was not churlish. Sternly she reminded herself that she was his daughter's teacher and doubtless he wished to discuss Isabel's progress. It was entirely her own fault she was feeling like a green girl meeting a personable gentleman for the first time—and that he was both personable and charming, in this mood, she could not deny.

Somehow she found herself seated in a remarkably comfortable leather armchair near a window with his lordship opposite her. Between them stood a small table bearing a tea urn, pot, and two cups.

"Pray do the honours, Miss Hartwell. I am unhandy."

She made the tea and poured a cup. "Milk and sugar, my lord?"

"Thank you, no."

He took the cup and saucer with his right hand. His arm jerked and for a moment it seemed the hot tea would spill in his lap, but he quickly righted it with his left hand and set it down carefully. Puzzled, Amaryllis noticed that he used only his left hand to pick up the cup thereafter. The brooding look had returned to his face. To distract him from his embarrassment, she asked him what was his favourite reading.

"Gothic novels," he said provocatively, a glint in his eye.

"Indeed! Then may I recommend Miss Austen's *Northanger Abbey*? After reading it you will be quite unable to appreciate a Gothic novel ever again."

He laughed. "I have read it, ma'am, and must agree that it is a cure. No, as I told you, my tastes are eclectic. You will find in this room everything from Miss Austen's works to the classics—in translation, that is, for I am no scholar. If you care to look around, perhaps you will find something you would like to borrow."

"Thank you, you are very kind, but I have little time to indulge in reading for pleasure. Much as I enjoy history, it is tedious to read nothing else for months on end, though my pupils do their best to make it interesting." She described Louise Carfax's version of the history of Hedingham Castle.

He laughed again and asked her a question or two about teaching history. They went on to discuss the school in general, and time passed unnoticed until the housekeeper appeared to announce that luncheon was ready.

The girls were already in the dining room, flocking like starlings about a cold collation set out on a long sideboard. Here again the masculine influence was apparent: cold roast beef, a ham, pigeon pie, with no sight of the kickshaws and sweetmeats a thoughtful hostess would have provided for her female guests' delectation. Nonetheless, the young ladies ate heartily, and Miss Hartwell, supplied by her host with a generous plateful, surprised herself by displaying a most unladylike appetite.

Afterwards, Lord Daniel provided baskets and they all went to the orchard to pick apples, accompanied by the spaniels. The sun was still shining, though the breeze was cool. As the girls scattered between the trees, chattering as they searched out the sweetest fruit, Isabel came up to Amaryllis and took her hand.

"Please, will you come and meet Pegasus?" she asked. "Look, he has seen me."

A sturdy Welsh pony was trotting towards them. Amaryllis bent down and picked up a windfall. Holding it on her flattened hand, she offered it to Pegasus, who took it gently with a whuffle of his soft lips. She rubbed his nose.

"He likes you," said Isabel in a satisfied voice. "Papa, may I ride?"

Lord Daniel was watching Amaryllis. He started at his daughter's question.

"Ride? Why, I suppose so. At least, what do you say, ma'am? The young ladies may all take turns on Pegasus if they wish, and I have a mare who would suite you very well, I daresay, if you care to join them."

"Thank you, my lord, but we are none of us dressed for riding."

He looked at her in dismay. "No, of course not. You will think me very stupid," he added ruefully. "I am unaccustomed to considering the dictates of female fashion."

"It is not merely a matter of fashion, but of comfort and convenience. These dresses are cut quite wrong for sitting in the saddle. However, I expect Isabel has a habit in the house and I see no reason why she should not take Pegasus out, if she promises not to fly away."

"He does not really fly. No, I shall not ride if my friends cannot ride too. I had not thought. I shall go and find Louise and pick some apples." Retrieving her basket she disappeared among the trees.

"What a thoroughly good-natured child," exclaimed

Amaryllis.

"Unlike her father," Lord Daniel responded with a sardonic quirk to his lips.

"*I* did not say so. You have been all that is complaisant—today. I wish I was able to accept your offer of a ride. It is all of ten years since I enjoyed a good gallop." She sighed.

"Ten years! You are not half old enough to have been running a school for ten years."

"I lived in London for several years, and I am sure you are aware that to gallop in Hyde Park would put one quite beyond the pale."

"I did not know. I go to London only on business."

That explained why she had never met him in the society his birth entitled him to frequent, though not why he avoided it.

"It is so, I assure you. Indeed, the highest sticklers frown upon a modest canter."

"You have not yet explained how you recognised my land to be in good heart."

"Simple enough. I lived in the country all my life before removing to London. My father took no great interest in the estate, and I was too young to try to remedy the lack, but I was aware that all was going to rack and ruin." She tried to speak lightly.

As if recognising her emotion, he turned the subject back to horses.

"Should you like to see my stables? I lay claim to no superior cattle, since I am more interested in their abilities than their looks, but it will take us out of this devilish wind."

She accepted, grateful for his tact. As they strolled around the side of the house, she noticed that he was careful to stay on her right side. If she needed to take his arm, it would be the left one that he offered.

It was warm in the stableyard, sheltered from the breeze but catching the sun. They spent a pleasant half hour treating the horses to windfall apples, of which he had collected a pocketful.

A distant clock struck three.

"Heavens, is it so late?" exclaimed Amaryllis. "We must go, or we shall not be back before dark."

"I shall order the carriage," he said at once. "While Grayson is putting the horses to, one of the men shall collect all the apples your girls have picked and put them in a box to take with you. You shall come into the house and drink tea till all is ready. I warned Prosser to keep water on the boil."

She laughed. "Ignorant as you may be of female fashion in clothes, I see you understand the female need for tea at all hours. Thank you."

Half an hour later, the coach with the box of apples tied on the roof and nine passengers squeezed inside rolled down the drive and out between the gateposts. Everyone was tired and a little sleepy. They talked quietly or drowsed, leaving Amaryllis to her thoughts. These were confused. She had seen Lord Daniel in an entirely new light and a flattering one. That did not explain her own extraordinary reactions to him. She had fluttered like a Bath miss, and she had never been a fluttering female, even in her first Season. She almost hoped it might be the early, light-headed symptoms of an attack of the grippe.

It was dusk when the carriage pulled up in front of the school. With Isabel and Louise, she went to thank Grayson while the other girls straggled into the house. While Isabel gave him some message for her father, Amaryllis turned to Louise.

"Congratulations," she said gaily. "You have not fallen into a bumblebath all day."

Louise's face was alarmingly pale. "Yes, I have," she contradicted hollowly. "I think I ate too many green apples. I have the most dreadful pain in my middle."

=10=

IN ORDER TO escape describing her day at Wimbish to her
aunt and Tizzy, Amaryllis pleaded exhaustion and retired
to bed early. She was nearly as tired as she claimed, and
did not lie awake long.

As usual, she was too busy during the week to brood, and
on Friday a letter arrived that drove all else from her head.
She went so far as to summon Mrs. Vaux and Miss Tisdale
from their classrooms.

"Aunt Eugenia! Tizzy!" she cried as they arrived together
in her office. "Godmama is coming here tomorrow, and
since she does not travel on Sundays, she wishes to stay
until Monday!"

Lady Mountolivet Gurnleigh, owner of the house they occupied, had always visited at the end of June before, on her
way home after the London Season. At that time she would
collect her peppercorn rent. Amaryllis had never been able
to persuade her that term was a metaphor for a small
amount, so every year she handed over a peppercorn. Cook
had enough in the larder to pay the rent for a hundred years.

At the end of June, all the young ladies had generally
gone home. Her ladyship had never seen her house actually in use as a school, and there was no guessing what she
would think of it. She had taken a notion to look in on the
Queen's trial, which was due to resume next week. Since
she took the rule against travelling on the sabbath as literal-
ly as everything else, it suited her very well to spend that
day with her goddaughter. Amaryllis was fond of her godmother, and excessively grateful, but the thought of trying

to entertain that toplofty matron for a whole day in such a situation appalled her.

" 'The Sabbath was made for man, and not man for the Sabbath.' Mark 2, verse 27," said Tizzy unhelpfully.

"Oh dear," said Mrs. Vaux. "You know it is quite impossible to keep the house immaculate with two dozen girls running about. I usually have time to clean before she comes. I shall have to send at once to the village for extra help and consult Cook as to a menu, and Daisy must go and buy what is necessary, and room must be reserved at one of the inns for her coachman and outriders and stabling for her horses, and the girls must be warned to be on their best behaviour for you know what a stickler Cornelia is, and how prodigious fortunate that I have kept her chamber on the first floor free for you know we could use the space a hundred times over, I vow."

"You must have had a presentiment of this occasion," said Amaryllis with a smile as her aunt ran out of breath. "I know you will work a miracle as you always do, and everything will be perfect by the time she arrives. What can Tizzy and I do to help?"

Classes were cancelled for the rest of the day, and with the aid of two extra women from the village the house was scrubbed and polished from top to bottom until it gleamed. Girls could be found in every corner practising their curtseys on each other, and glorious odours wafted from the kitchen. Ned was on his knees in the front garden, removing every errant blade of grass from the flowerbeds and coaxing half a dozen late-blooming roses to keep their fading petals just three days longer.

Shortly after four on Saturday afternoon, a magnificent equipage with crested doors, drawn by four matched bays, pulled up in front of the school. Lady Mountolivet Gurnleigh had sent two other coaches laden with servants, luggage, linen, and plate, ahead to London with her downtrodden companion. She was travelling light, with only two trunks strapped on top and accompanied only by her dresser, her coachman, four outriders, and a footman hanging on for dear life behind. All but the dresser wore bottle-green livery and powdered wigs. The housemaid set to watch for the arrival was so flabbergasted by this apparition that she forgot to call Daisy until the footman was halfway up the garden path.

Daisy boxed her ears. "Run and tell miss her la'ship is come," she ordered, peeping through the window and seeing that the tall, spare abigail was descending from the carriage already.

The footman was as haughty as a lord, much haughtier in fact than a number of lords Daisy had met. Having ascertained that Miss Hartwell was at home, he returned to the carriage to help his mistress descend. This operation occupied both himself and the maid, since Lady Mountolivet Gurnleigh was as tall as her abigail but built on majestic lines. Daisy had seen it before, but she still watched in fascination as three purple ostrich plumes emerged followed by a mountainous figure in a purple pelerine trimmed with sable.

"My muff, Gribbins." The words floated to her as the dresser reached into the carriage and produced a sable muff the size of a spaniel. "My reticule, Gribbins." A handbag large enough to hold said spaniel.

Taking the footman's arm, the purple mountain advanced up the garden path with Miss Gribbins in her wake bearing a shawl, a bandbox, and a dressing case. As Daisy curtsied, once to my lady, once to Miss Gribbins, Miss Hartwell hurried down the stairs to greet her godmother. Amaryllis was enveloped in a vast embrace, then her ladyship released her and examined her with some severity.

"You are pale. I trust you are not wearing yourself to a shadow with this seminary of yours?"

Since Lady Mountolivet Gurnleigh's alarmingly high colour clashed abominably with her purple draperies, and she always thought everyone else pale, Amaryllis ignored this criticism.

"How delightful to see you, Godmama! Won't you come

upstairs and take off your hat? The usual chamber, Gribbins," she added to the dresser.

Miss Gribbins, a Friday-faced woman dressed in black bombazine, curtsied in a stately manner and sailed away towards the kitchen. Though she did not appear to hurry, she reached the first floor chamber before her mistress, accompanied by a housemaid bearing a jug of hot water. It would have been greatly beneath her dignity to carry the jug herself. Indeed, to be staying in a house with no butler, no housekeeper, no footmen, no servants' hall, accorded ill with her notions of what was due to her consequence. Her air of toplofty disdain cowed the school's servants so that they scarce dared open their mouths in her presence.

Lady Mountolivet Gurnleigh, enveloped in mauve satin, was at last safely installed in the private drawing-room with a glass of Madeira at her elbow. Miss Tisdale made her curtsey and withdrew. She knew well that, as a former governess, she would be considered disgracefully encroaching were she to take her share in entertaining their honoured guest. Mrs. Vaux, whose birth and breeding were unexceptionable though her present occupation was no more exalted than Miss Tisdale's, was relieved to find herself still addressed as "dear Eugenia." She settled down with her ladyship to a comfortable cose.

Amaryllis listened with half an ear to their gossip of the doings of the Upper Ten Thousand. Everything her godmother said was undoubtedly true, since she had no opinion whatever of rumourmongers and never repeated on-dits. However, the world they were discussing seemed so far off and irrelevant that Amaryllis found it uninteresting. Time enough when she married Bertram to concern herself once again with the shocking news that Lord X's youngest daughter had run off with Sir Y to Gretna Green.

It occurred to her that her ladyship probably knew all there was to know about Lord Daniel Winterborne. Though she scorned rumour, few facts about the Polite World escaped her eagle eye, and her memory for scandal was nothing short of phenomenal. Open enquiry would arouse her suspicions, but there must be a way to inveigle her into revealing all. Amaryllis set her mind to the problem.

It was out of the question to subject Lady Mountolivet Gurnleigh to dining with twenty-four schoolroom misses, even had the prospect of conveying her below-stairs and back up again not been daunting. A small table was set up in the drawing room, and after changing her dress, Mrs. Vaux rejoined her there. Amaryllis, in the face of disapproval, maintained that she must dine with her pupils, but afterwards she left them to Tizzy in the common-room and repaired to the drawing-room.

Her ladyship graciously conveyed her compliments to the cook, and then asked in somewhat waspish accents whether her goddaughter was now able to spare her a little time. Mrs. Vaux slipped out, promising to return to take tea with "dear Cornelia." Lady Mountolivet Gurnleigh at once turned to the attack.

"Tatenhill's heir is back in England and still unmarried," she announced. "I observed your request not to tell him your whereabouts after Hartwell's disgraceful behaviour, but if he has worn the willow for you these six years, it would be foolish beyond permission to continue to avoid him. If he applies to me, I shall inform him."

"Lord Pomeroy has found me out, ma'am," said Amaryllis, her face crimson. "He has done me the honour to renew his suit, and I suppose I shall have him."

"Suppose!" Her ladyship was outraged. "Where are your wits wandering, miss? For two years you played fast and loose with him, and now he is nodcock enough to return to your apron strings you say you *suppose* you will have him! Do you expect me to believe that you prefer playing schoolmistress to marrying one of the best catches on the Marriage Mart and becoming the mistress of Tatenhill? Let me tell you that if you throw away this chance to return to respectability, you need expect no further help from me."

With difficulty, Amaryllis suppressed her anger. "I have not yet revealed to Bertram that my father is now an ironmonger in America," she said, outwardly calm. "It is possible that he may cry off when I tell him."

"An ironmonger? Viscount Hartwell an ironmonger!"

"Yes, ma'am. Papa married the . . . the lady he ran off with, and they own a hardware store in Philadelphia. He has invited me to join them there and help in the store. I have two half-brothers, it seems."

Lady Mountolivet Gurnleigh, a stunned look in her rather protuberant eyes, struggled in silence to absorb this news. Never one to hesitate, she came to a quick decision.

"There is no need to tell Pomeroy until after you are wed. Philadelphia is three thousand miles away. What your father does there can have no conceivable effect on your life here."

"Godmama! Never did I think to hear you countenance such havey-cavey goings-on. I cannot possibly consent to concealing such a thing from my betrothed."

Her ladyship's bosom heaved as if buffeted by a North Atlantic gale. "And why, miss, have you not told him yet?" she enquired dangerously.

"I hesitated to interrupt the sweet nothings he was whispering in my ear," said Amaryllis, smiling cajolingly at the old lady. "Come, Godmama, I have said I will have him, if he will have me, so let us not brangle and brawl."

"I hope you do not teach your pupils to use such unladylike expressions." Lady Mountolivet Gurnleigh's outrage was muted. Threats having failed she turned to bribery to ensure that her much-loved goddaughter should do what was best for her. "I daresay you may be worrying about Eugenia. When you marry I shall provide for her of course. An allowance large enough for her to live in comfort, if not luxury."

Amaryllis kissed her plump cheek. "How kind you are," she said. "That does indeed relieve my mind. Now, what do you say to meeting a few of my girls?"

Her ladyship graciously expressed her willingness, and Amaryllis went off to fetch them. She had already decided who to present. That they must be particularly decorous damsels went without saying, but she also chose them for their families. She wanted her godmother to recognise immediately the names of four, so that she would be curious about the fifth—Isabel Winterborne.

It went exactly as she had planned. Lady Mountolivet Gurnleigh congratulated her on her pretty-behaved charges, and then went on, "I cannot quite place Miss Winterborne. Bellingham's heir is not married, I know though he must be six and thirty if he's a day. Never say you accept by-blows in this fine academy of yours."

"Isabel is Lord Daniel Winterborne's child, ma'am."

"Lord Daniel. Hmm. Ah, I have it. Divorced."

"Divorced?" asked Amaryllis, aware of a cold, sinking feeling.

"That's it. His wife went off with some military fellow, I believe. Bellingham pushed it through the Lords as quietly as possible, but these things cannot be hushed up. Quite disgraceful, a ramshackle business at best. It must have been just a year or two before Perceval was shot, too."

"What has the Prime Minister's assassination to do with the Winterbornes?"

"Nothing whatsoever. Only the murderer's name was Bellingham, you may remember, and the papers associated it with the Marquis's title. The shock of that, on top of the divorce, was too much for Lady Bellingham. Took to her bed and died a few weeks later."

"I have been told that Lord Daniel is something of a rake," said Amaryllis cautiously.

"Not that I know of. I daresay he has his game pullet in keeping, like the rest of them, but I should have heard if he were a downright loose fish. And do not let me hear those words on your lips, miss. When you are as old as I am you may say what you please."

"Which words, Godmama?" Amaryllis asked with an innocent face.

"You know very well, baggage," growled her ladyship.

Mrs. Vaux came in, followed by Daisy with the tea tray. Glad of the interruption, Amaryllis took her cup and went to sit a little apart, leaving the older ladies to their gossip.

She listened for a moment. To her relief, Lord Daniel's name was not mentioned.

At least his lordship was not an out-and-out libertine, she thought. Mr. Raeburn must have heard something to offend his clerical sensibilities, or perhaps offended neighbours had invented disgraceful stories. The Fashionable World considered keeping a mistress scarce even a peccadillo. She was sure Bertram must have had his barques of frailty during their long parting, and it did not disturb her in the least. He had probably frequented the muslin company even during their betrothal, in fact. She was glad she had not thought of that at the time. It might well have upset her then.

Was that why Lord Daniel's wife had left him? A young girl coming innocent to marriage might well have been shocked to learn that her new husband was visiting lightskirts—but not shocked enough, surely, to lower herself to their level by deserting home and child to go off with another man. What had driven her to such a desperate and irrevocable step?

Amaryllis remembered her first interview with Lord Daniel—his arrogant, peremptory manner, his harsh, unsmiling face. She had taken him in instant dislike. Since then she had seen another side to him. He was a loving, gentle father, could be a charming companion, and seemed to be a considerate employer. Perhaps his bride had seen the two facets of his character in reverse order—the adoring suitor transformed into a surly, morose, dictatorial tyrant. Life with him must have been unbearable to make the alternative appear acceptable.

Thoroughly depressed, Amaryllis excused herself and went to join Tizzy and the girls in the common-room. Isabel came to sit beside her.

"I was a bit frightened of Lady Mountollay," she confided.

"Lady Mountolivet Gurnleigh."

"Lady Mountolivet Gurnleigh," she repeated carefully. "She is nearly as big as her name."

"And fierce-looking too," agreed Amaryllis, trying not to

giggle, "though we should not say so, you know. Besides, her bark is worse than her bite, I promise. Do you know what that means?"

"Oh yes, just like Papa. I heard Nan say that to Prosser once when she was complaining."

"I think you are very fond of your Nan."

"Yes, I am, but I should so like to have a proper Mama," said Isabel with a sigh.

Lying in bed that night, curled up under the covers with the curtains pulled close against the cold, Amaryllis wondered whether Bertram had already found himself a new ladybird since his return to England. How odd it was that a man could court one woman while making love to another. For the first time she wondered whether her father had mistresses while her mother was still alive. Gentlemen, for all their talk of honour, really had the oddest morals.

Doubtless Lord Daniel had much more time to visit his *chère amie* since he had sent Isabel to school, Amaryllis realised. In effect, her services were allowing him to enjoy the strumpet's charms at his leisure. How dare he use her school for such a purpose! Too furious to think rationally, she lay glaring at the ceiling until she fell asleep.

Lady Mountolivet Gurnleigh insisted on struggling down the stairs and into her carriage for the brief ride to church the next day. Miss Tisdale had taken half the girls to the early service so that Amaryllis could accompany her god-mother. Thus, she was absent from the house when Lord Daniel picked up Isabel.

Her ladyship entered St. Nicholas Church like a battleship towed by a pair of tugs, Amaryllis and her aunt, and followed into harbour by a flotilla of lesser ships sailing in pairs. Massively magnificent in maroon and grey stripes, she captured every eye in the congregation, and when the organ began the first hymn, her imperious baritone captured every ear.

After the service she retired once more to the private

drawing-room, where Amaryllis and Mrs. Vaux took turns to attend her. Amaryllis found it easy to avoid meeting Lord Daniel when he brought Isabel back, but the afternoon seemed endless. By dinnertime, she was heartily glad that she had refused her godmother's kind offer of a home when her father absconded.

The evening passed no faster. Tizzy joined them in the drawing-room, sitting modestly in a corner as a governess ought and speaking only when spoken to. Amaryllis deplored this behaviour but made no protest. There was not the slightest likelihood of changing her ladyship's views.

As Tizzy herself said, " 'Can the Ethiopian change his skin, or the leopard his spots?' Jeremiah 13, verse 23."

However, Amaryllis did insist on going herself for the usual checks on the common-room. On her third visit, she opened the door to find most of the young ladies gathered about the hearth, giggling and whispering. They hushed each other at her appearance and parted as she approached. On the hearth-rug lay an extraordinary animal. Its body was plump and rather shapeless, with long, dark, glossy fur. Its eyes glinted silver in the flickering firelight, and from its head grew three tall . . . purple . . . plumes . . .

"Oh, you wicked children," gasped Miss Hartwell, collapsing with laughter into a nearby chair. "I quite thought you had discovered a new species of animal."

Louise Carfax came to stand before her, her face half-guilty, half-revelling in the success of her creation. "It was me, Miss Hartwell," she confessed. "I didn't damage them, honestly. I stuffed the muff with a pillow. The eyes are buttons. I sewed them on, but they will come off easily. And the feathers were just pinned on the hat so I can put them back."

Miss Hartwell shook her head and summoned up a frown. "You had better do so immediately," she advised, "before her ladyship's maid discovers your depredations. Off you go, quickly now, but I shall ring a peal over you tomorrow."

She went back to the drawing-room, wishing she could

tell Tizzy and Aunt Eugenia about the latest evidence of Louise's ingenuity. She had scarcely sat down when there was a knock on the door.

"Come in," she said.

Miss Gribbins marched in, towing by the ear an alarmed Louise who cradled her creature in her arms.

"My lady," she uttered in tones of absolute outrage, "I found this young person sneaking into your ladyship's chamber with *this*!" She pushed the child forward and stood with arms akimbo.

Amaryllis jumped up, but before she could intervene an unfortunate impulse caused Louise to thrust the animal towards Lady Mountolivet Gurnleigh while making a noise vaguely like a barking dog. Amaryllis raised her eyes to heaven. *Was* it ingenuity, or rather suicidal tendencies? Her ladyship's cheeks were purple and she was making gobbling noises in her throat. Louise looked aghast, as if everything had come about without the least volition on her part. Mrs. Vaux appeared puzzled, and Miss Tisdale was biting her lip in her corner, obviously doing her best not to guffaw.

Amaryllis stepped forward, removed the beast from Louise's arms, and handed it to Miss Gribbins.

"I'm certain your skills are equal to restoring all to normal," she said soothingly, pushing the abigail gently but inexorably towards the door. She turned to Louise, took her hand, and led her towards Lady Mountolivet Gurnleigh. "Godmama, allow me to present to you Miss Louise Carfax. She is Lord Pomeroy's niece, you know."

Her ladyship blinked. Her alarming colour began to fade towards her more normal carmine. She threw a glance of reproachful comprehension at her goddaughter.

"How do you do, my dear," she said to Louise with an assumption of complaisance. "I am well acquainted with your grandmother, Countess Tatenhill. Lady Caroline is your mother, I believe?"

Amaryllis breathed a sigh of relief.

=11=

WHEN LADY MOUNTOLIVET Gurnleigh's carriage drove up before the school on Monday morning, the news quickly spread. By the time she emerged from the house in her refeathered hat and bearing her once-again eyeless muff, a rabble of small boys was waiting to watch her departure. Footman, coachman, and outriders haughtily ignored this unwanted audience.

Her ladyship, seated in the coach, passed her reticule to her dresser. "Gribbins, some sixpences."

With a regal gesture she cast the silver into the crowd, rewarding the lower orders for displaying the proper awed gratitude for her presence among them. The ragamuffins stopped squabbling over the coins to cheer as the carriage rolled down the street.

Amaryllis went back to her class, feeling sadly let down. She had not exactly expected her godmother's visit to resolve all her doubts and vacillations, but it was dispiriting to find herself in just the same state of indecision. Neither threats nor promises could push her into marriage with Bertram, and, she was forced to acknowledge, learning that Lord Daniel was divorced in no way decreased his attractiveness. For her own peace of mind, she would just have to avoid him in future.

In the common-room after dinner, Isabel came to sit beside her.

"Papa said yesterday that I may take some of my friends to Wimbish again next Sunday if the weather is fine. May I?"

Amaryllis could think of no good reason to refuse. She need not go herself. Tizzy could chaperone the young ladies just as effectively.

"Very well. Who do you wish to take with you this time?"

"I shall invite different people, to make it fair, but I should like Louise to come again. Some of the girls have been out with their own visitors, so they will not mind, do you not think, ma'am?"

"I expect that they will survive the disappointment," she said gravely, hiding a smile at Isabel's certainty that the excursion was a treat worth fighting over. She was aware of a strong desire to go herself, but it would not do. "It is Miss Tisdale's turn to go with you, I believe."

Isabel looked dismayed. "Oh but Papa particularly said to ask Miss Hartwell," she said doubtfully.

Amaryllis's breath caught in her throat, but she replied with tolerable composure, "Perhaps your Papa is not acquainted with Miss Tisdale yet. It is you and your friends he wishes to see, and it would not be fair for me to have all the outings, would it?"

"No . . . but I should like you to come." The child looked up at her pleadingly. "Could you not come too?"

"No, my dear. I cannot leave Mrs. Vaux alone all day."

She was almost relieved when, towards the end of the week, the weather deteriorated to the point where any sort of travel could be undertaken only with the greatest difficulty. For three days rain fell in torrents, lashed by gale-strength winds. She was not at all surprised when, on Saturday afternoon, a sodden, mud-covered groom arrived with a message from Lord Daniel. Daisy brought the note to the music room, where Amaryllis was teaching the steps of the Sir Roger de Coverley to eight breathless young ladies.

"He says the roads are so bad it would take us five hours to get to Wimbish, if we ever did arrive," announced Isabel, scanning the damp paper. "Oh," she added, disappointed, "he will not come himself tomorrow either."

"If you was to see the sorry state the groom's in, miss,"

said Daisy, "you wouldn't be surprised. A gentleman wouldn't want to present hisself in that condition. 'Sides, there's trees down across the roads all over, by what he do say. Took him three hours a-horseback."

"See that he is fed and his clothes dried before he starts back," ordered Amaryllis.

"He's by the kitchen fire now, miss, but he won't stop. Seems his lordship said to go to one of the inns in the village, hoping as how it might be drier by morning. He'll dry hisself there and do but wait to see if miss has a message to go back."

"You will not wish to keep the poor man waiting in his wet clothes, Isabel."

"No, ma'am, but may I go and thank him for coming? I expect it is Jem, and he is a particular friend of mine."

"Be quick then. We cannot dance the Sir Roger with one missing."

Isabel scampered off, returning a few minutes later while the groom left with instructions to "give all my love to Papa."

It was still pouring the next morning, and Amaryllis decided it was impossible to take the girls to church. There were plenty of umbrellas, but they would be undoubtedly be blown inside out in no time. She sent Ned with a message to Mr. Raeburn, asking him to come to luncheon and read a few prayers or whatever he thought suitable. She had, after all, told all her young ladies' parents that regular churchgoing was part of the curriculum.

The vicar responded that, much as he would have enjoyed lunching at the school, the shrieking of the wind was making Miss Augusta vapourish and he did not like to leave her. Amaryllis exchanged a significant glance with her Aunt Eugenia and went to the music room to look out some books of hymns. Mrs. Vaux followed her.

"I have had no chance to tell you," she said, "but I managed to pop out to see Augusta for a few minutes last Sunday while you were attending Cornelia."

"Did you know this about the gales, then?"

"No, though I have frequently heard people say that high winds bring on the tic, so perhaps it is true that she is vapourish. Only how it helps to have poor Mr. Raeburn dancing attendance I cannot understand. Perhaps I ought to go to her this afternoon."

"Dearest Aunt, I cannot allow you to go out in this weather. You would certainly blow away, unless you were drowned in a puddle first. Tell me what you discovered last week."

"It is the most amazing thing, Amaryllis. Augusta is positively terrified of disease, but she cannot stop her brother visiting the sick. You know how conscientious he is. So when he comes home from a visit, she makes him wash himself and his clothes with peppermint camphor."

"That explains the odour of sanctity then. What a disappointment. However, I am sure we can exploit Miss Raeburn's fear of sickness, if I can think how."

"I have a plan," said Mrs. Vaux modestly, "only I expect it will not answer. You are much more ingenious than I, my love."

"Tell me," encouraged Amaryllis.

"I thought I might tell Augusta that we are tired of being schoolmistresses and mean to turn the house into a fever hospital instead. I daresay she will not care to live so close to a fever hospital."

"Aunt Eugenia, you would not!"

"Once she has removed to London, we need not do it," the widow pointed out.

"I never guessed you had such an imagination, or such impudence," said Amaryllis, grinning.

Mrs. Vaux blushed but went on boldly, "Or perhaps I should tell her we mean to run a Bedlam?"

Her niece regarded her in stunned silence for a moment, then shouted with laughter.

"Augusta has not mentioned specifically that she is afraid of lunatics, but many people are, you know."

"Can you imagine my godmother's face if rumour reached her that we intended to turn her house into a Bedlam?"

119

Mrs. Vaux giggled. "She would have an apoplexy," she admitted. "You do not think it a good plan, then?"

"I think it a splendid plan, only I believe I shall try to come up with something a little less drastic. There is no hurry, after all. Aunt Eugenia, Godmama told me that if . . . when I marry she will make you an allowance so that you do not have to continue at the school."

"She will? How . . . how very kind. I hope she does not mean for me to live with her?"

"No, no, do not look so alarmed. I am sure she will give you enough to rent a small house and have a companion to live with you."

"You may be certain I shall never treat a companion as Cornelia treats hers. If Tizzy does not marry after all, perhaps she will come with me. Only what will become of the school?"

"By then it will be a fever hospital, so we need not worry about it. Oh, I suppose it will close down, unless Godmama chooses to rent the house to someone who will run it. But perhaps I shall not marry Bertram. For all I know, he will cry off when he learns of Papa's new occupation."

"Fustian! He did not care before about Henry's misdeeds, so why should he now? You have not told him yet?"

"No," said Amaryllis slowly, "the moment never seemed quite right."

"Then write to him, my love," said Mrs. Vaux comfortably. "Depend upon it, that will bring him rushing to your side to reassure you."

Amaryllis immediately decided that nothing in the world should make her write to Bertram about her father.

By the following Sunday, the storms had abated, and the roads were drying out under a fine October sun. When Amaryllis woke, her windowpanes were growing a garden of frost flowers, and the grass outside was hoary white. By the time Lord Daniel's carriage drew up before the gate, an icy breeze was blowing.

"Shall you be warm enough?" she asked Tizzy anxiously.

"Perhaps I had best go instead."

"Why should you feel the cold less than I? Not that I expect to feel it in the least with nine of us in the carriage!"

They discovered that, on his lordship's orders, the coachman had provided hot bricks for the travellers' feet. Amaryllis gave in. She waved farewell and turned back towards the house, impatiently brushing away a tear.

"That wind is cold enough to make your eyes water, I vow," she said to Mrs. Vaux.

By the time the three ladies retired to the drawing-room after dinner, Amaryllis was on tenterhooks to know how Tizzy had been received. She had much ado not to demand an account immediately. Tizzy and Aunt Eugenia seemed to have endless school business to discuss, and she simply could not keep her mind on it.

"So you did not freeze to death in the coach," she said at last.

"No, indeed. I have not been in so comfortable a vehicle since your father's carriages were at our disposal."

"And when you arrived?"

Tizzy gave her an odd look, but answered readily. "His lordship came out to the front steps as we pulled up. He must have been on the lookout. Isabel ran to him. The others followed. As I was descending from the coach, he looked up with a smile of greeting, which turned to shock and then to anger. He strode down the steps towards me and said, in a sarcastic tone, 'We are not acquainted, madam. My invitation was to Miss Hartwell.' Naturally I was at a nonplus. I thought to explain that I too was a teacher at the school and quite as capable of chaperoning the young ladies. However, you know how my tongue betrays me. I said, ' "Be not forgetful to entertain strangers, for thereby some have entertained angels unawares." Hebrews 13, verse 2.' "

"Tizzy! Did you really?"

"I did. His lordship looked me up and down. 'Angels?' he said. 'Now I know where Miss Hartwell learned her wit.' After that he was perfectly obliging, though distant. He

121

offered me tea in his library, and I greatly fear I must have made my envy plain, for he invited me to stay there and read what I would. I could not resist. So after all, I proved myself less capable than Amaryllis at playing chaperone and was glad I had not boasted."

"I was not with the girls all the time I was there either," admitted Amaryllis guiltily.

"I daresay you were with his lordship," said Tizzy drily. "I should not have noticed had he abducted every one of them. 'King Solomon loved many strange women.' The first Book of Kings, I believe, though my father never used it as a text. One would not choose to hold up such an example to the congregation."

"I cannot think it in the least likely that he should abduct anyone. Indeed, Godmama told me that she has never heard that he has the reputation of a libertine, so I am sure that Mr. Raeburn exaggerated."

"I expect he misunderstood, or heard a false report," put in Mrs. Vaux quickly, seeing that Miss Tisdale seemed to be about to take up cudgels on the vicar's behalf.

"Oh dear," said Tizzy ruefully, "there's the Ten Commandments: 'Thou shalt not bear false witness against thy neighbour.' Exodus 20, verse 16. And also I Timothy 5, verse 13: 'Tattlers also and busybodies, speaking things which they ought not.' "

Amaryllis and her aunt rushed to comfort her.

"Gammon!" exclaimed Amaryllis. "He was most reluctant to speak evil of anyone, but thought it his duty to warn me."

"The commandment is surely against deliberate falsehood, and against malicious gossip. Dear Mr. Raeburn is certainly incapable of either."

"Besides, it is entirely Lord Daniel's fault if people invent Banbury tales about him. In general his manners are not such as to recommend him to any person of sensibility, and he can be excessively rude and overbearing. Even Isabel says he has affronted all his neighbours and most of his family." Knowing her words to be true, Amaryllis recalled with wistful wonder the delightful day she had spent with him.

Lost in her recollections, she scarcely noticed when Mrs. Vaux trotted out to check on the common-room. Tizzy interrupted her musing.

"I did not wish to alarm your aunt," she said in a hushed voice, "but I believe I saw the Spaniard you told us about."

"Oh no. Is he loitering about the school again?"

"That is what is so odd. He was not here but lurking in the hedgerow near Lord Daniel's house. I did not catch more than a glimpse, but he was very dark and foreign-looking, with a most un-English moustache."

Amaryllis frowned. "At Wimbish? How extraordinary. Surely it cannot be the same man. Was his dress foppish?"

"No, very plain. I gained the impression of a servant, not a gentleman, though even the most dandified exquisite must think twice before concealing himself in a ditch in all his finery."

"I daresay a Spanish gentleman skulking in the wilds of Essex might well have a servant doing likewise, but how could he have discovered that I might go to Wimbish today? No, I cannot believe that there is any connection. Whoever he is, if he continues to hide in hedgerows in this weather he will soon be carried off by a galloping consumption, I wager."

Mrs. Vaux came back into the room at that moment, and Miss Tisdale returned to their earlier conversation.

"Shall I inform the vicar tomorrow that his opinion of Lord Daniel is mistaken?" she asked.

"No," said Amaryllis decidedly. "That would lend the matter an altogether excessive importance. Well, Aunt Eugenia? What is Louise Carfax up to this evening?"

"Nothing worse than inventing the rules of chess as she goes along. Since her opponent is Isabel, who is equally ignorant, their game is peaceful if unorthodox."

"And since you have never been able to grasp the principles, dear Aunt, you were unable to set them right, I make no doubt."

That night the cold spell came to an end. A period of grey,

damp, depressing weather set in. Everything dripped, brown leaves fell sodden from the trees to lie in soggy piles beneath, and several girls came down with the grippe. Her days divided between teaching and nursing, Amaryllis dropped exhausted into bed at night and was asleep the moment her head touched the pillow. One of the sick girls developed an inflammation of the lungs. A doctor and her parents had to be sent for, and for a day or two her life was in danger.

By the end of October, Amaryllis had scarce set foot out of doors for two weeks and was looking, as the vicar informed her kindly if unflatteringly, "sadly pulled about." At this unpropitious moment, Isabel announced that Papa, though unaccountably recalcitrant, had agreed to allow another visit to Wimbish.

"Shall you come this time, ma'am?" she asked Amaryllis, her dark eyes hopeful. "Papa was quite cast into the dismals when you did not last time."

"Perhaps," said Amaryllis tiredly, though smiling a little to hear the slang she had picked up so fast. "Do not tease me, pray, there's a good girl." She had not seen Lord Daniel since the first Wimbish outing and was not sure whether she wanted to go or not.

Now that everyone was on the road to recovery, she could spare the time. Indeed, she was ready to seize any excuse to get out of the house. On the other hand, she would be cooped up in a closed carriage for hours. She felt that for her own peace of mind she ought to avoid Lord Daniel, yet she had scarcely spared him a thought in weeks, which was hardly the sign of a developing *tendre*. And if he, on his part, had found her attractive in spite of her drab apparel, to see her looking "sadly pulled about" must cure him of his infatuation.

Mrs. Vaux was a poor traveller. The jolting of a carriage made her utterly wretched, so it was out of the question that she should go. Amaryllis asked Tizzy if she should like to return to that magnificent library. An expression that in anyone else might have passed for coyness appeared on the governess's plain face, and a tinge of unwonted colour painted her high cheekbones.

"I did enjoy the library," she admitted, "and I should like to spend more time there, but Mr. Raeburn has promised to call on Sunday afternoon while your aunt is with his sister."

"My dear Tizzy, I do not know that I ought to allow you to receive your admirer in my absence."

"But he is a clergyman, Amaryllis, and the girls will be there. I shall not see him alone."

"I am roasting you, Tizzy dear. You may see him alone with my goodwill, and I hope he has the sense and resolution to pop the question."

"I do not think it at all likely," said Miss Tisdale dolefully. "His first obligation must be to his sister and I cannot suppose that she will wish to share the vicarage with me."

Amaryllis was tempted to disclose the plot to dispose of Miss Raeburn, but thought it unwise to raise any hopes that might not be fulfilled.

"If he loves you," she said bracingly, "and I am convinced that he does, then he will let nothing stand in his way. I shall go to Wimbish then, and leave you to your wooing."

=12=

BY SUNDAY AMARYLLIS was ready to change her mind about going to Wimbish. A feeling of mounting anticipation warned her that she would be unwise to see Lord Daniel, and on top of that, she felt distinctly under the weather. However, a single look at the faces of Tizzy and Isabel made her steadfastly ignore her doubts. She took her seat in his lordship's carriage, Grayson urged on the horses, and they were off.

Before they reached Finchingfield, Amaryllis wished she was at home. It was a mild day but wet, with a light drizzle falling, and the damp seemed to have invaded her bones. She closed her eyes and leaned back against the well-padded seat. One of the girls Isabel had invited had a raucous laugh, the despair of Mrs. Vaux, and was easily amused. The noise slashed through Amaryllis's aching head like a broadsword.

At last they pulled up before the old brick house. Feeling fragile, Amaryllis followed the girls out of the coach. Preceded by the excited golden spaniels, Lord Daniel was coming down the steps towards her. There was a joyous welcome in his eyes, replaced almost at once by wariness. His first remark was not encouraging.

"You do not look at all well."

"I do not feel at all well," she snapped. "I believe I must be coming down with the grippe. You had best not come near me or you will get it too."

Undeterred, he took her arm. "Come in out of the rain,"

126

he urged gently. "There is a fire in the library, and you will feel more the thing after a cup of tea."

Tears filled her eyes at his sympathetic tone. She forced them back, biting her lip. "If tea cured the grippe, I should not have been nursing half the school these three weeks," she said waspishly.

He raised his eyebrows with a quizzical look but said nothing and continued to lead her into the house. He waited while, feeling utterly miserable, she gave her cloak and bonnet to the housekeeper, then he ushered her into the library.

If possible, the room was still pleasanter on this murky day than when the sun shone beyond the windows. Beneath the marble mantelpiece a fire burned briskly in the grate, where well-polished brass andirons shone. Lamplight glowed warm on gleaming wood and glossy leather. The dankness outside emphasised the comfort within.

"Sit down." Lord Daniel indicated a chair by the fire.

Unable to summon up the energy to cavil at his peremptory manner, she sank into the chair, which was as comfortable as it looked, and closed her eyes.

"I beg your pardon, my lord," she said pettishly. "I ought not to have ripped up at you when you meant to be kind." She heard him moving about the room.

"Indeed you ought not," he responded. "I so rarely mean to be kind that I require every possible encouragement. So pray encourage me by drinking this glass of Madeira. We shall see if it is a better remedy than tea."

Amaryllis opened her eyes. He was standing before her, offering the glass of wine with a smile that made her heart turn over. She took the goblet with a murmured word of thanks, sipped at it, and set it on the table beside her.

Then, possessed by an inexplicable spirit of contrariety, she said, "But I should have liked some tea."

"I should never have put you down for a capricious female." He rang the bell. "It must be a symptom of the grippe. Prosser, some tea for Miss Hartwell."

The housekeeper had appeared so promptly that Amaryl-

127

lis suspected she had been listening at the door.

"Yes, my lord," she said, her face sour. "Will your lordship take tea also?"

Amaryllis was sure he would make some excuse to leave her and her megrims alone. That had always been Bertram's strategy when she was feeling cross-grained, and her father's also. To her surprise, Lord Daniel stayed and drank tea with her.

"Do you feel more the thing now?" he asked, regarding her critically. "Your colour is better."

"The tea was refreshing, but now I am stupidly hot. I had best move away from the fire." She struggled to rise from the enveloping chair.

He was beside her in a moment, his hand on her shoulder. "No, stay there," he ordered in his autocratic way. "I shall bring a screen to shield you from the heat."

From one corner of the room he fetched a folding screen of canvas painted with charming landscapes, carrying it under his left arm. She watched with a frown as he set it up, fumbling awkwardly with his right hand. In general his movements were quick and sure, but sometimes he seemed to lose control of his right arm.

"Is that better?" he asked, turning to her. "The devil! I believe you are running a fever." He laid his cool hand on her forehead. "Yes, you most certainly are."

"I am perfectly all right. What does a gentleman know of fevers?"

"As much as a schoolmistress knows of agriculture, or more. I nursed Isabel through all the usual childhood ailments. Here." He hooked a footstool with his toe and pulled it towards her. "Put your feet up on this, lean back, and close your eyes. I shall go and see what Isabel and your girls are doing, and I hope you will manage to sleep a little."

When she made no move to obey, he bent down, lifted her ankles, and deposited them on the stool. She felt too weak to protest, so she contented herself with glaring at him before she leaned back and closed her eyes. She heard him chuckle, and then the door closed softly. Bertram never laughed at her or ordered her about, she thought with drowsy indignation.

When she woke, the brass clock on the mantel said ten past two. On the table beside her a tray held a glass of lemonade, an apple, a pear, and two slices of chicken. Consumed with thirst, she drank the lemonade at a draught before she realised that Lord Daniel was standing near a window, watching her.

"Definitely feverish," he said, moving towards her. "I shall have several rooms made up and you shall all stay here until you are recovered. One of the grooms may take a message to Castle Hedingham."

"Quite impossible. I feel very much better."

"If you are concerned about propriety, I shall take a room at the inn in Wimbish. Now, will you eat something?"

Disarmed by his calmness, she admitted that the pear looked singularly succulent.

"Let me core it for you."

Picking up the silver fruit knife and fork, he neatly cut it into quarters. Amaryllis watched his hands, the long, strong-looking fingers with their neatly trimmed, immaculate nails. He cored one piece, and was about to start on the second when he dropped the knife with a clatter. As he tried to retrieve it, his fingers refused to obey him. For a moment he looked very young and utterly vulnerable.

"What is wrong with your arm?" Curiosity and compassion overcame Amaryllis's good breeding. A moment later she cursed herself as a painful flush mantled his lean cheeks and he scowled at her.

"That is none of your business, ma'am. The fact that I have placed my daughter in your care does not give you leave to pry into my personal affairs."

"I have no intention of prying." Knowing herself in the wrong, she spoke coldly. "I merely meant to express my sympathy."

"I have no need of your sympathy, Miss Hartwell. I beg you will keep it to yourself."

"You may be sure that in future I shall." He was detestable. She had been right to resist coming to this place. She stood up. "It is time we were leaving. May I request that you order the carriage and inform the girls that they must get ready to depart?"

"By all means, ma'am. I shall send Prosser to you immediately, and the coach will be at your disposal in fifteen minutes. Good day, ma'am." He bowed curtly and strode out of the room.

As her annoyance faded, Amaryllis shivered. It was most fortunate that they had quarrelled, she thought, or she would have been seriously tempted to accept his invitation to stay. She felt wretchedly ill, and all she wanted to do was to retire to bed and sleep forever.

However, she roused herself to speak cheerfully to the girls. She asked them what they had found to do, and half-listened as they described the bonfire they had managed to have despite the rain, the guy dressed in Lord Daniel's old clothes, the roasted chestnuts and delicious half-raw potatoes. She had forgotten it was Guy Fawkes Day.

Settling in the carriage, she braced herself to endure the journey. Grey afternoon was merging into dusk when they reached the school. As the coachman helped Amaryllis down from the carriage, she leaned heavily on his arm. He peered at her from under his bushy eyebrows.

"If ye bain't sick, miss. Here's a fine to-do! Let me help ye to the house now. Whatever possessed ye to go a-jauntering about in sich a state?"

"Thank you, Grayson." She cut off the flow of soothing words as they reached the door and fumbled in her reticule for a shilling.

He put his weather-tanned paw over her hand. "Never ye mind now, miss. Get ye inside and warmed up. Miss Isabel, fetch someone to yer teacher right smart now."

Amaryllis stumbled across the threshold and stopped short as Bertram strode into the vestibule.

"I hear you've been visiting that fellow Winterborne again," he said, his face unwontedly grim. "What the devil do you mean by it?"

Amaryllis slapped his face, burst into tears, and headed on leaden feet for the staircase.

When she woke, very late the next morning, she was much improved. Aches and fever were gone, and a huge bouquet of red rosebuds on her dressing table did a great deal for her state of mind. She assumed they were from Bertram. Where he had found them in the depths of the country in November was a mystery, but surely it meant he had forgiven her for her imprudent visit to Wimbish and her behaviour last night. There was a note propped against the vase. She started to sit up to go and get it, but a sudden dizziness overwhelmed her. She lay back lethargically and breathed the roses' perfume.

A few minutes later, Daisy peeped round the door. "Are you awake, miss? How do you feel?"

"Lazy. I should be glad of some tea, Daisy, and will you pass me that letter, if you please."

"Right, miss. You got a light dose of the grippe if you're better a'ready."

"Yes, thank Heaven." She opened the note as the maid slipped out.

Bertram offered his profound apologies for his Turkish treatment of her when she was ill. He knew very well that her visit to Wimbish had been perfectly innocent and unexceptionable, and his only wish was to remove her from a situation where her duties included such undesirable acquaintances.

Unreasonably irritated, Amaryllis tore the paper in half and dropped it on the floor.

Mrs. Vaux appeared, bearing tea and shortbread and a bowl of something she referred to as "a strengthening broth." Amaryllis drank it with docility and ate a piece of shortbread when informed that Cook had made it specially. Mrs. Vaux then went to the dressing table and brought back a box, tied with a red velvet ribbon, that Amaryllis had not noticed.

"From Bertram, my love," she said. "He was shockingly

distressed to find you absent when he arrived yesterday. He is on his way from Tatenhill to London and can stay here only a few days."

Amaryllis opened the box. It held chocolate-covered cherries. She offered them to her aunt, then popped one into her mouth. The sweet, juicy stickiness took her back to London days, to the handsome, dashing young Corinthian she had fallen in love with.

Of course she loved Bertram! She ate another bonbon, then closed the box. They were sweeter than she remembered, a trifle sickly. She drank some tea.

"Shall you allow Bertram to come and see me here, Aunt?" she asked. "I believe I shall not go down today, if you can manage without me."

"Of course we can, and of course you must stay in bed until you are perfectly recovered, and no, I shall certainly not allow Bertram to visit you in your bedchamber."

"I thought not. I should like something light to read, if you please, though I daresay I shall sleep again presently. If Bertram comes, pray give him my thanks for the flowers and the chocolates. Is Mr. Raeburn here?"

"Yes, and wearing a prodigious long face. Miss Tisdale too is not happy, I think, though it is hard to tell because she is never precisely full of fun and gig. I need not tell you that he did not come up to scratch yesterday. However, I believe I have discovered a weak spot in Augusta's armour."

"You would not have been telling a bouncer these past weeks if you gave her to suppose we had opened a fever hospital."

Mrs. Vaux brushed this aside impatiently. "No, no. I decided it was time to learn why she does not care to live with her brother in London. Amaryllis, her brother is butler to Lord Langston. I was never more shocked in my life. He is something of a black sheep in the family, for they are of gentle birth of course. Augusta is quite ashamed to have a close relative in service, even in so respectable a position."

"You must be on terms of great intimacy for her to have admitted to such a thing, which is very clever of you but I cannot see how that will help us."

"No, and I was quite cast down into the dumps when she said it, for she cannot possibly make her home with a butler. Only think what they would say in the servants' hall, even if Lord Langston were to allow it, which is not in the least likely. I daresay the brother has no more than a room or two to himself. But then I mentioned that I was well acquainted with dear Millicent, and I claimed to have noticed that her household was particularly well run. Augusta begged my pardon and asked if I was referring to Lady Langston. I saw she was impressed at my speaking so familiarly of a person of such consequence, so I went on chattering about all our London acquaintance and the people I knew when dear Mr. Vaux was alive. Her eyes grew quite round and she did not interrupt me once. She has a vastly overrated idea of the superiority and exclusiveness of the Ton, my dear, and I have raised myself several notches in her estimation simply by telling her I once spoke to the Prince Regent. The King, that is."

"I hope you have dragged Tizzy and me up behind you," said Amaryllis laughing.

"I did not mention that your papa is . . . was . . . is a viscount," said Mrs. Vaux anxiously. "You said most particularly that you did not want it known."

"Quite right. However, if Miss Raeburn is so easily overawed, I may in the end use the fact on Tizzy's behalf. We shall see. You have done a magnificent job, dear Aunt. If I were the British Government I should hire you as a spy, but right now I am going to send you away and indulge myself with a doze."

The next time Amaryllis woke she felt much of her strength restored, though she was still disinclined to dress and go below stairs. A bundle of newspapers beside her bed reminded her that she had asked for something light to read.

They were the latest numbers of the *Morning Post*, sent down by Mr. Majendie. They contained the reports of the defence phase of Queen Caroline's trial, and Amaryllis read them with interest. The witnesses for the defence were not disreputable Italian servants but respectable English people who had met the Queen and her so-called Chamberlain abroad. They all claimed that they had seen nothing to make them suspect that Pergami might be the Queen's lover.

Thomas Denman, Caroline's Solicitor General, had taken two days for his summing up. The Queen, he claimed, was innocent of any wrongdoing, all of which had originated in the depraved minds of her Majesty's degenerate Italian servants. At the end of an emotional peroration he quoted: "If no accuser can come forward to condemn thee, neither do I condemn thee: go, and sin no more."

The Tory *Morning Post* made hay of this contradiction, printing a verse it claimed was current in the capital:

> Most gracious Queen, we thee implore
> To go away and sin no more;
> Or if that effort be too great,
> To go away at any rate.

Amaryllis, in spite of her sympathy for the Queen, could not help giggling at this. She longed to know the final verdict, but that was the last of the pile of papers. She hoped the King's suit would be thrown out, except that perhaps it might comfort Lord Daniel if the King were to be divorced, as he was himself. Not that Lord Daniel's feelings meant anything to her.

Amaryllis went down to the common-room the next day, still a little shaky and well wrapped up. She reclined on a couch, feeling elegantly languid, while her pupils sat round her and read their compositions aloud. They were all touchingly happy to see her recovered, especially Isabel, who pulled her chair up close to the couch. When it was time to go to the next class, the little girl bent over her and kissed her cheek, then flushed scarlet, muttered "I am so glad you are well," and fled.

Bertram came to take lunch with her while everyone else was in the dining room. He apologised again for having cut up stiff over nothing and would not hear a word of her explanations.

"Only say you forgive me, and we shall forget it ever happened," he urged. "My only excuse is my disappointment in not finding you here as I had expected. I must be off to town tomorrow, and I doubt I shall be able to return until December. I shall say that I mean to escort Louise home for the holiday. Mr. Majendie has invited me to his Christmas assembly on the sixteenth, and I would not miss it for the world. It is six years since I danced with you."

"The sixteenth? That is earlier than usual."

"I understand he does not spend Christmas at the castle this year."

"School does not end until the fifteenth. The day after is always utter chaos, with carriages and parents and servants running in and out all day. It is hardly the day I should choose to go to a ball."

"But you will go. Your beauty is not of the sort that requires an entire day of primping and preening to appear to advantage. However, I warn you that if you intend to go in your greys and browns and wearing a cap like a spinster, I shall be forced to take matters into my own hands."

"Oh?"

"I wager you'd not accept a gown from me, but my mother will be delighted to make a present of one to her future daughter-in-law."

"That will not be necessary. I bought new gowns for all of us last summer, and we have been saving them for the Christmas party."

"Is yours green, by any chance?"

"How well you know me, Bertram." She smothered a sigh, thinking that marriage to Lord Pomeroy would be prodigious comfortable though sadly lacking in excitement.

His lordship looked complacent.

Soon Miss Hartwell's next class came in. These were the older girls, with a tendency to ogle the handsome gentleman who was so unaccountably paying court to their old maid of a schoolmistress. Lord Pomeroy quickly made his escape, saying he was going for a ride and would return at four. When he did so, Amaryllis received him in the drawing-room. Her aunt and Tizzy were there, seated discreetly as far from her as the small room allowed. After greeting his lordship they returned to their own conversation.

Bertram was looking particularly magnificent. His buckskin breeches were as closely moulded to his strong legs as was his coat to his broad shoulders. He brought a fresh breath of outside air into the room with him and sat down beside Amaryllis on the sofa. She raised her hand and smoothed his fair hair, ruffled by the wind. He caught that hand in his and kissed the palm. His lips were hot on her skin.

"When shall we be married, Amaryllis?" he demanded in a low voice.

With a shock, she recognised passion burning in his blue eyes. He had never looked at her so before. Or was it that she had not noticed, not known what she was seeing, until the thrill of Lord Daniel's touch had opened her eyes to a new sensation?

She was searching for an answer when a commotion in the passage outside saved her. Daisy's contralto scolded. A youthful soprano that sounded suspiciously like Louise Carfax kept repeating "I'm trying, honestly!" and an inarticulate rumble that could only be Ned performed the *basso continuo*.

"My niece," groaned Bertram as a knock sounded on the door. He strode towards it but before he could open it, it burst open to admit Louise, followed by Daisy and then Ned.

"I'm trying, honestly!" announced Louise once again. Clamped under her arm was a fishing rod, at the sight of which her uncle blenched. From it dangled a tangle of line. Attached to the end of that line was a peculiar brown object with which she appeared to be wrestling. It did not look like a fish of any known species. Amaryllis recalled all too clearly the last time Louise had invented a new species.

Her gaze moved on beyond Daisy, who was apologising

for allowing the disturbance to reach the drawing-room, to Ned. His head was bare—absolutely bare. Circled by the fringe of white locks, his naked pate rose pale and shining, in startling contrast to his weatherbeaten face. He looked like a singularly disreputable monk.

"I mun have me cap," he muttered in repetitive litany.

"Hush!" said Bertram. His eyes were lit with unholy glee though otherwise his good-natured face was stern.

Everyone fell silent.

"Thank you, Daisy, you may go," said Amaryllis with a curious gasp, caused by her effort not to burst with laughter. "Well, Miss Carfax?"

"I cannot get the hook out of the fabric," explained Louise. "It is barbed so that it does not slip out of the fish's mouth."

"I hardly think that is what Miss Hartwell wishes to hear," said Uncle Bertram, removing the limp brownish object from her grasp and deftly extricating the barbed hook. He handed the object to Ned.

"Her wor up in th'oak, worn't her, a-fishin' fer me cap," said the gardener indignantly, hiding the gleaming dome beneath its wonted covering.

Amaryllis set herself to soothe the old man, and Bertram slipped him a crown. He went off, still muttering, and they both turned to Louise.

By the time she left, penitent for having embarrassed a member of the lower orders but still clearly of the opinion that her jape had been worth the tongue-lashing, it was nearly five o'clock.

"What on earth possessed you to give the chit a fishing rod?" Amaryllis demanded of Bertram. "You must have guessed that angling is not on our curriculum."

"Cry pax!" he grinned. "At least acquit me of any suspicion of her intentions. I have not so much imagination. I fear I must go now, my dear. Mr. Majendie has invited guests for dinner and I promised to attend. I must be off to London first thing tomorrow. May I write to you?"

"I neither forbid it, nor expect it. Come now, Bertram, you had rather ride a hundred miles than write a single sheet, I vow."

"How well you know me," said his lordship ruefully.

=13=

Amaryllis resented not being invited to Mr. Majendie's dinner party. Her standing was high enough to ensure an invitation to the Christmas assembly, attended by the more genteel farmers and lawyers and such, but too low for a private dinner, it seemed. She chided herself for being goosish. She had never before dreamed of such an honour and to be miffed, only because Bertram was going and she was not, was idiotic. When she was Bertram's wife, the table of every nobleman in the country would be accessible, even the King's table. Not that she had the least desire to dine with that gross old man.

She soon forgot her pique in the daily round of school affairs, and as the next Sunday approached another source of discomfort arose. When Lord Daniel came to visit Isabel, Amaryllis felt obliged to see him to apologise for her inexcusable and ill-mannered churlishness. It was with mixed feelings that she greeted the news, delivered by a groom on Saturday morning, that his lordship would not be coming the next day. He was abed with the grippe.

Naturally, she was delighted to postpone humbling herself before that surly gentleman. On the other hand, it gave her one more thing to apologise for. Also she remembered all too clearly that, though her illness had been brief, the life of one of her pupils had been in danger. A healthy young man was hardly likely to succumb to the grippe, but perhaps his trouble with his arm was a sign of some constitutional weakness that might make him vulnerable. She would have liked to consult Isabel on the reason for his disability; recalling his violent reaction to her question, she did not.

On Thursday when Amaryllis looked through the post in her office after breakfast, there was a letter from him. The ostensible purpose of the letter was to request that she inform his daughter of his complete recovery. He would see Isabel on Sunday as usual. He was less certain of seeing Miss Hartwell, and as he had some small matter to impart to her he took the liberty of writing.

It was no liberty, she thought crossly. It might be improper for an unmarried lady to correspond with a gentleman, unless they were practically betrothed as she was with Bertram. For the parent of a pupil to write to her teacher was perfectly unexceptionable. She read on.

Lord Daniel blamed himself for disregarding her warning to keep his distance. She was in no wise to consider herself responsible for laying him flat on his back for a week. He understood from Isabel, to whom he had written before falling ill, that she herself had suffered for no more than two days, which he considered sadly unjust.

A smile on her lips, Amaryllis turned to the next page. His handwriting was beautiful, large and clear, but it must have cost Daisy several sixpences to retrieve the letter from the post. She ought to restrict her pupils to the daughters of peers, so that their fathers might always frank their communications.

Lord Daniel's next words brought a frown to her face. Having now experienced the grippe himself, he wrote, he forgave her for having been so cross-grained.

It was one thing to beg pardon, quite another to be condescendingly forgiven for a fault one had not yet acknowledged. Cross-grained, was she? Bertram was by far too gentlemanly ever to have accused her of bad temper. He was more apt to think himself, not her, in need of forgiveness.

She read the sentence again. The previous paragraph had been teasing in tone. Perhaps Lord Daniel meant to roast her? Turning back to the previous page she reread it, puzzling over his meaning, then gave up with a sigh and went on with the second page.

Now he begged her pardon. He was stupidly sensitive about his right arm and ought not to have ripped up at her when she asked about it. The explanation was simple: it was an old injury. The nerves had been damaged and had not grown back properly. Most of the time he had full use of the arm but sometimes, without warning, it failed him as she had seen. Usually, he added—she imagined the wry look on his face—at an awkward moment.

Once more he begged her pardon, this time for burdening her with an explanation of what must have been at most a matter of passing interest to her. He remained her most obedient servant, Daniel Winterborne.

For several minutes Amaryllis gazed blindly at the paper. She felt his explanation to be less a burden than an honour, a mark of confidence. He trusted her enough to expose his weakness before her, the weakness of which he was so unnecessarily ashamed.

What cruelty had made him ashamed of his injury? Had she discovered the reason for his melancholy, for his shunning of the world?

The letter was precious now. She folded it carefully and put it in her pocket to take up to her chamber. Expecting to see him on Sunday, she did not write to him. However, when his carriage arrived to pick up Isabel, it was Grayson who came to the door.

"The master's up at the castle," the coachman explained. "Seems Mr. Majendie's right clever at drainage, the which is an odd sort o' thing fer a gentleman, to my way o' thinking."

"Yes," said Amaryllis, who had come down with Isabel. "I believe he drained the marshes all along the Colne."

"The master's a-goin' to drain some bottomland round us, I reckon. He sent me for to fetch Miss Isabel up."

The child put her small white hand confidingly into his large brown one and they went off together. Isabel came back in the same way, saying that her Papa had been invited for dinner and to spend the night at the castle, or rather the mansion on the hill. Drainage was a very complicated thing, she revealed to Louise, and though Papa and Mr. Majendie had talked about it all afternoon they had not exhausted the subject when it was time for her to leave.

"What did you do while they were talking?" enquired Louise. "Never say they let you explore the castle on your own!"

"I sat with Papa in Mr. Majendie's study and looked at books. I often used to sit in his lap when he had business when I lived at home."

Louise looked awed at the thought. She could not remember ever sitting in her father's lap, and when he had visitors or his steward in on business everyone had strict orders to stay far away and creep about silently.

Amaryllis, overhearing this conversation, tried to imagine what it would be like to try to conduct business with the lively Louise in one's lap. The notion almost raised a smile, but she was feeling inexplicably blue-devilled that evening. When she went up to her chamber to change for dinner, she tore up Lord Daniel's letter and burned the bits.

The letter had been in a drawer, under a pile of handkerchiefs. In taking it out she had disarranged the pile, so she lifted it out to straighten it. A square of linen fell open, exposing an embroidered rose. She had heard nothing of the sinister Spaniard for weeks, and had almost forgotten him. Whatever his mysterious mission, presumably he had accomplished it and departed, and it had had nothing to do with her after all. She was glad she had not alarmed Tizzy and Aunt Eugenia by telling them of her frightening encounter in the dark garden.

No sense in throwing out a perfectly good handkerchief. She folded it neatly and put it back in her drawer.

Lord Daniel did not appear the following Sunday. Isabel said he had gone to London on business and would come back just in time to fetch her home for the Christmas holiday.

Damp November gave way to a frosty December. Queen Caroline, the case against her abandoned, drove in state to St. Paul's to give thanks, surrounded by cheering multitudes. The King, still uncrowned, returned to London from Brighton where he had retired with Lady Conyngham to sulk throughout the trial. He began to make plans for a magnificent coronation from which his infuriatingly popular wife would be excluded.

Isabel received several letters from her father in London. Amaryllis received one from Bertram, a brief scrawl to say that he would be in Castle Hedingham on the Friday before the party, but would have to leave on Sunday to take Louise home. He had to spend Christmas at Tatenhill with his parents. His sister Caroline, he added in a postscript, was delighted that her daughter was proving useful as an excuse for reuniting her brother with his beloved. She sent her best regards and looked forward to welcoming Amaryllis into the family.

Amaryllis wished she had written to Lord Daniel as soon as she had read his letter. Her lack of response must have offended, even hurt him. It was too late now, she decided sadly. After the long silence it might look as if she was setting her cap at him, and that was the last thing she wanted him to think.

The last week of the school term finally arrived. The young ladies fidgeted through their lessons, whispering about their plans for the holiday. There were usually one or two who stayed at school, but this year the cold, dry weather had left the roads in excellent condition for travel. Those who lived at a distance had all been invited to visit friends. Miss Hartwell, Mrs. Vaux, and Miss Tisdale looked forward to three weeks of peace even more than to the ball at the castle.

Most of the girls were to leave on Saturday, though a few, including Louise Carfax, would not go till Sunday. Fortunately one of these was a senior pupil well respected by the younger girls, so she could be left in charge on Saturday evening. The three schoolmistresses took their new gowns from the presses and hung them out to air.

Friday afternoon was devoted to packing trunks and boxes. Cook had prepared a festive dinner, with roast goose and plum pudding taking pride of place. After dinner they all retired to the common-room, decorated with branches of fir and scarlet-berried holly, to play round games and sing carols.

The servants were enjoying their own celebration down in the kitchen. Their merriment was interrupted by the arrival of Lord Pomeroy's groom, with a message for Miss Hartwell. As the only male in the household was old Ned, the young man was made most welcome and sat down with a glass of rum punch while Daisy went up to the common-room.

Lord Pomeroy's compliments, and he would do himself the honour of calling on Miss Hartwell at eleven o'clock tomorrow if convenient. Miss Hartwell, laughingly losing a game of speculation, would be happy to receive his lordship at the stated hour. Daisy went straight back to the kitchen with the response, but it was a good two hours before the groom, now slightly wobbly on his feet, wended his way back through the village and up the hill to the castle mansion.

Saturday morning, as Amaryllis had foreseen, was a chaos of arriving and departing carriages, emotional farewells and joyful greetings, servants running upstairs and staggering down again under the weight of their young mistresses' possessions. When Bertram arrived she simply left Tizzy to keep order and took him to her study.

He took off his multicaped greatcoat. As always his dress was plain but fastidious, not a speck of dust on his Hessians, his cravat a perfect Waterfall. He took both her hands and looked her up and down.

"Beautiful as ever," he said.

Amaryllis smiled and shook her head. She knew she was tired, untidy, even a little grubby from rushing about since five this morning, but he would never tell her she was looking less than perfect.

"I know you are busy," he went on, "so I will not stay long. I hope you will manage to rest for a while before this evening, for I mean to take as many dances with you as country propriety permits."

"Two," she said, laughing, "just the same as in town."

"Then I shall not push my luck by demanding more than three. Including supper. Does Mr. Majendie provide a supper?"

"Yes, and a very abundant one, though no one does it justice because we are so well fed at dinner."

"Supper, then, and three dances. I have brought you something." He picked up his greatcoat and delved into a pocket, withdrawing a square leather box.

With great trepidation she opened it, and gasped. A magnificent necklace of emeralds set in gold winked and gleamed at her.

"No!" she said, and snapped it shut. Bertram looked surprised and hurt. "I beg your pardon, but I cannot wear it tonight."

"You said your gown was green."

"It would go beautifully with my gown, my dear, but only think what everyone would say to see me decked in finery so far above my station. Half the guests would cut me dead, I daresay."

"Do you like it?"

She opened the box and studied it. She had scarcely seen it before. She had been too dazzled and shocked by its glittering extravagance. A closer look revealed the delicate workmanship, the deep, glowing perfection of the gems, the elegant setting. She coveted it.

"It is superb," she said honestly. "I should like above all things to wear it tonight and have all the condescending squires and their plump wives gape at me. But I must not. Do not tempt me. Keep it for me, Bertram, until we are married."

She held it out to him, but he ignored it.

"Then you will marry me?" he demanded eagerly. When she did not answer at once, he read her face. "No, you are still undecided. I cannot understand, but I accept it, for now. I shall come back next month, Amaryllis, and then I must have an answer. My father is weakening daily. If we are not betrothed before he dies, I shall have to wait out a year of mourning before we can marry."

"And I have already tried your patience beyond belief. I give you my word, I shall tell you in January. You are too good to me, my dear."

"I should not dream of contradicting a lady," he said, and with these paradoxical words he took his leave.

He had scarcely gone and Amaryllis, having taken a moment to regain her composure, was about to leave the office, when a pair of messengers arrived. The first, Lord Daniel's groom, brought word that his lordship was at the castle, consulting Mr. Majendie. He had been invited to stay for the assembly and hoped that Isabel would not be too disappointed at postponing her return home until the morrow.

Amaryllis was a little surprised that Bertram had not mentioned Lord Daniel's presence. It could only mean that he considered it insignificant. Isabel was perfectly happy to spend the evening with Louise, but both girls were thrown into a flurry of confusion by the communication of the second messenger.

Lady Caroline Carfax wrote in haste to say that two of Louise's brothers had come home from school with scarlet fever. On no account was Louise to venture near her home until the quarantine was over. Her ladyship relied on Miss Hartwell to make arrangements for her daughter's accommodation over the holiday, for which she would gladly pay. Louise's face crumpled. To have to stay alone at school over Christmas was more than even her intrepid spirit could face with equanimity. Isabel ran to her and flung her arms about her.

"Don't cry!" she said urgently. "You must come and stay with me. I shall ask Papa, but I know he will say yes. Don't cry, Louise, pray don't!"

Two little faces, one tear-stained, looked pleadingly up at Miss Hartwell.

"An excellent idea," she said slowly, "but one to which I cannot consent without consulting your family, Louise. It is most fortunate that your uncle is in the village."

Lady Caroline's servant was dispatched to the castle with two letters in round, childish hands whose inkblots lent force to their urgency, and two in calmer vein. Lord Daniel, reading Miss Hartwell's composition, could not have guessed that she had torn up three previous efforts before producing a missive that was a model of brevity.

He was in Mr. Majendie's drawing-room when he read it, taking a glass of sherry before luncheon. There were several other guests, members of the local gentry, who, like himself, lived too far off to return home comfortably after the ball and had been invited to stay the night. Lord Pomeroy was also present.

Until this moment, the two gentlemen had succeeded in avoiding any communication beyond polite greetings. Now Lord Daniel looked up and saw in his lordship's hands two letters like the two in his own. With visible reluctance, Lord Pomeroy approached him.

"Well, Winterborne, what do you think?"

"With your concurrence, I shall be happy to receive your niece," he said stiffly.

"I don't like it," said Lord Pomeroy frankly, with a frown. "It is not as if you are a relative, or even a friend of the family. And you have no wife to take care of the chit."

Lord Daniel crimsoned with anger. "I believe Isabel has not suffered for that reason." His voice was sarcastic. "My influence is scarce malignant enough to harm Miss Carfax in three short weeks. She and Isabel are bosom-bows, you know, and she has visited Wimbish thrice already. Incidentally, my brother will be spending Christmas with us, if that makes your mind easier. He, at least, is thoroughly respectable."

"George? I saw him in town not a week since, and he

mentioned going north. I had assumed he meant into Northumberland, to Bellingham."

"My father goes to Bellingham, I believe. He has been at the trial of course. George has business in London next month and does not care to travel so far."

"I wish I might take the child to Tatenhill, but my father is not well enough to have grandchildren running about, especially one like Louise. Are you aware of what you would be taking on?"

"I have heard of her exploits," Lord Daniel admitted, his face lightening somewhat.

"She's a little devil. Tell me, why are you so willing to invite her?"

"It will greatly distress Isabel if I do not."

"Ho, has you under the cat's paw, does she? Well, I cannot like it, but I would not condemn even that little wretch to spending Christmas at school, even under Amaryllis's care. If you are quite certain it will not inconvenience you, I must thank you for your kindness and give my consent."

Lord Daniel, who had been relaxing, pokered up at the mention of Amaryllis's name. He nodded curtly.

"I shall write to Miss Hartwell at once," he said.

"And I after lunch."

They bowed to each other and parted with relief.

Reading between the lines, Amaryllis guessed at once that Bertram and Lord Daniel were not exactly enamoured of each other's company, and that Bertram's consent had been given unwillingly. It made not the least difference to the joy that shone in Isabel's and Louise's faces at the news.

"My uncle George is coming for Christmas," said Isabel. "You will like Uncle George."

"I like everyone," her friend assured her.

"Even my Papa?"

"Of course!" Louise was astonished. "He's nicer than *my* Papa, and I *love* my Papa!"

Isabel absorbed this in silence.

By midafternoon the stream of carriages had slowed to a

trickle. All three ladies managed to snatch a couple of hours on their beds before dressing for the ball. Daisy had ironed their gowns, not entrusting them to the other maids' careless hands. She scurried from chamber to chamber helping with hooks and eyes here, pinning a reluctant curl there, gasping with admiration at delicate gauze and intricate lace.

There was a pier-glass on the top landing for the use of pupils and teachers alike. Amaryllis emerged from her room and went to look in it, to see that her dress was in order. A figure from the past gazed back at her.

The underskirt and bodice were of shimmering deep green *crêpe lisse*, cut very simply and without the now fashionable flounces and rouleaux. From the high waist fell an overdress of Honiton lace, open in front, and an inset of the same lace raised the low neckline to a respectable level. Clasped about her throat, where Bertram's emeralds would have looked so well, was a gold chain with a locket containing miniatures of her mother and father. Her hair, gathered in a silk band on the crown of her head, fell in a cascade of red-gold ringlets to her white shoulders.

Six years ago the lace would have been from Brussels, the *décolleté* unabridged, the hair cut in a modish crop. It was the ghost of a young girl she saw in the mirror, a creature of dreams, now gone forever. She sighed and turned to admire Tizzy and Aunt Eugenia in their lavender and blue.

They went down to the common-room to give the remaining girls a glimpse of their finery. Though the others were unimpressed, having seen mothers and older sisters in ball gowns often enough, Isabel stared, wide-eyed.

"You are beautiful!" she whispered to Amaryllis, then ran up and stood on tiptoe to kiss her cheek. "I hope you dance every dance."

They heard the front doorbell ring below.

"Lord Pomeroy's carriage is at the gate," announced Daisy.

$=14=$

THE OLD BRICK bridge over the dry moat was illuminated by
lanterns, and a pair of footmen stood by to point out the
way. The ground was already white with frost. The castle
towered more tall and grim than ever, black against the
star-filled sky. Additional lanterns bordered the steps up to
the door, along with footmen to lend an arm to nervous
ladies. Amaryllis glanced down into the oubliette on her left
and shuddered. Even Louise would not have dared that dismal pit at night.

The Guard Room was brightly lit by lamps and candles.
Amaryllis had heard the story of one year when Mr. Majendie had used rush torches to give his party a mediaeval at-
mosphere. He succeeded only too well. The smoke and stink
had greatly offended delicate modern nostrils, and the experiment was not repeated.

A colourfully dressed crowd stood chatting in groups
about the hall. There were clear divisions between gentry,
burghers, and yeoman farmers, but Amaryllis knew that
after a few glasses of Mr. Majendie's mediaeval mead the
groups would mingle merrily.

The first person who caught her eye was Mr. Raeburn,
sober in black. As a clergyman he was naturally welcomed
by all. The footman announced their names in a ringing
voice and the vicar looked towards them.

Amaryllis saw his jaw drop, and she followed his gaze
towards Miss Tisdale. Her choice of the lavender silk gown
had been excellent, Amaryllis thought smugly. She had paid
somewhat extra for ruching about the bosom and a num-

150

ber of flounces on the skirt, and the result did wonders for her governess's spare figure. Besides, Tizzy had been persuaded to do away with her cap, and on her neatly braided pepper-and-salt hair reposed a charming confection of Urling's net and lavender silk bows. Perhaps, nothing could make her what most consider pretty, but she looked unexpectedly elegant and matronly. The vicar scarcely spared a glance for Amaryllis and her aunt as he rushed up to greet Miss Tisdale.

Bertram was not far behind. He made his leg to Mrs. Vaux, who greeted him absently and went off to try to wipe the expression of outrage from Miss Augusta Raeburn's face.

Bertram looked at Amaryllis with a satisfied smile. "This is more like the woman I fell in love with," he said, "though if I had not vowed not to mention them, I would say that it is a pity you are not wearing the emeralds. They are pretty enough in the box but they need your beauty to set them off."

Amaryllis was not entirely pleased by this speech. However, she was determined to enjoy herself so she ignored it. She also had to ignore the sniffs and stares of the squire's wives and daughters when they realised that not only had the schoolmistress dressed herself up fine as fivepence, she had snabbled the most eligible man in the room as well.

She could not, and had no desire to, ignore the dazed look in Lord Daniel's eyes when he saw her. He was talking to a farmer and turned as she stopped to speak to an acquaintance nearby. Unlike Bertram, he had never seen her in anything but drab duns and greys. She thought he hardly recognised her, but he moved towards her like a sleepwalker and bowed over her offered hand without taking his eyes from her face.

"Miss Hartwell!"

"How do you do, my lord?" She felt stupidly breathless and found it impossible to break their locked gaze. "I trust your business in London prospered?"

"Very well, thank you, ma'am."

"We . . . Isabel missed you."

She became aware that her hand was still in his and withdrew it. The other was tucked into Bertram's arm. For a moment she had forgotten his presence.

"There is our host," said Bertram firmly. "Come and make your curtsey, Amaryllis."

He led her away. She glanced back to find Lord Daniel watching her with a look of yearning despair that left her shaken. After speaking to Mr. Majendie, Amaryllis glanced round again, but Lord Daniel was gone.

She and Bertram continued round the room, greeting acquaintances here and there. They were back near the door when an elderly couple entered, followed by a dark man of about Bertram's age, narrow-faced, mustached, and dressed like a Tulip of the Ton. The shoulders of his green coat were grotesquely padded, the waist pinched in, the waistcoat liberally embroidered in gold thread. Oddest of all, he wore a sword, a fashion outdated for a decade or more.

The footman leaned forwards to catch their names. An expression of puzzlement crossed his face, and he asked something. The dark young man, appearing irritated, pulled a card case from his pocket and handed over a square of pasteboard.

"Sir Peter and Lady Hoyle," the footman announced stolidly. "Monsewer Donald Migyuwel Rodridges dee la Rosa."

"Don Miguel Rodrigues de la Rosa," translated Bertram, his diplomatic training standing him in good stead. "And that, if I am not mistaken, is the gentleman I saw at the inn some months since, making enquiries about your school."

"De la Rosa," repeated Amaryllis, troubled. "I suppose Rosa means rose? I believe I have a handkerchief of his in my dresser drawer."

Bertram demanded an explanation so she described her encounter with the silent stranger in the garden. He was shocked and distressed that she had not told him before.

"The next time I saw you was when we toured the castle," she said. "The girls were with us, and besides, you had already moved from Halstead with the excuse of protecting me from the Spaniard. Then when nothing further happened I forgot."

"It's devilish peculiar. However, I can hardly challenge him to explain his actions when we cannot even be sure it was him."

"He came with the Hoyles. I know Sir Peter slightly so I will see if I can winkle any information out of him." She was moving towards the knight and his wife when dinner was announced.

On Bertram's arm, Amaryllis joined the slow procession up the spiral stair to the Banqueting Hall. With some adroit dodging she managed to seat herself between her escort and Sir Peter at one of the long, white-draped trestle tables. Fortunately, Mr. Majendie did not stand on ceremony at his assemblies, or Lord Pomeroy would have been sitting at the high table between Lady Dawson, deaf relict of a baronet, and the enormous Mrs. Bailey, whose husband was fourth son of a baron.

Mr. Raeburn had a place on the dais, and Amaryllis was delighted to see that Tizzy was beside him. He delivered a brief grace on the text, "Then I commended mirth, because a man hath no better thing under the sun, than to eat, and to drink, and to be merry." Head bowed, Amaryllis peeped through her lowered eyelashes and saw Tizzy's lips move. Without a doubt she was quoting chapter and verse.

Mrs. Vaux and Miss Raeburn sat together at the far side of the hall, the latter rigid with disapproval. The Spaniard was near them, next to the pretty daughter of a local farmer. Judging by her trilling laugh, he was making himself pleasant in reasonably good English. Of Lord Daniel there was no sign, and Amaryllis did not care to crane her neck to see if he was seated farther down on the same side of the table out of her view.

Half the population of the village had been pressed into service. They scurried about the tables bearing dishes of roast sirloin, goose, hams, pheasants dressed up in their own tail feathers. With much ceremony a pair of suckling pigs was borne in, apples in their mouths and bedecked with thyme and rosemarie, being the closest Mr. Majendie could come in these degenerate days to the traditional Boar's Head. Tankards of heady mead appeared, with small beer and cider for those with weak heads or stomachs. A group of wassailers filed into the gallery opposite the high table and serenaded the diners with rounds and carols, and the huge hall echoed with the merry sound.

Amaryllis turned to Sir Peter. A neat, elderly gentleman with a white goatee, he remembered her at once and asked politely after the school. After an exchange of commonplaces, she said, "I noticed that you brought a young gentleman with you. What a shocking mishmash the footman made of his name."

"Was it not? Don Miguel was not best pleased, but he assures me he is grown used to it. He has been several months in this country."

"Is he a friend of the family?" asked Amaryllis brightly, hoping she did not appear grossly impertinent.

"Yes," said Sir Peter, looking vague. "In a way. My son fought in the Peninsula War, you know. Are you acquainted with Thomas, ma'am?"

"I believe not."

"He is still in the army. Major by now. Stationed in Ireland at present. We have not seen him in over a year, which distresses Lady Hoyle no end."

"I am sure it must, sir." Amaryllis steered him gently back to the subject that interested her. "Thomas—Major Hoyle—met Don Miguel in Spain then?"

"So Don Miguel says. I do not recall that Thomas ever mentioned him, but doubtless he met any number of Spaniards. I do not care to question the Don—proud, fiery sort of chap he is."

"Does he stay with you indefinitely?"

Sir Peter shrugged helplessly. "He has been here for several months. He was ill for some time—our wretched

154

climate, I daresay—and he's been off for the odd week now and then, but he always comes back. Fact is, don't know how to get rid of the fellow. But I must not bore on, Miss Hartwell. It is kind of you to listen to the problems of an old man."

"It is fascinating, my dear sir," gushed Amaryllis. "The customs of foreigners are vastly odd, are they not? Does the major know he is with you?"

"Lady Hoyle wrote of his arrival, and Thomas replied that he hoped we would offer him our hospitality for the Spanish *guerilleros* were no end good fellows whatever anyone may say of their regular troops."

"I suppose you do not know why he chooses to remain in this corner of Essex?"

"He has not seen fit to inform us, but he and his servant ride out in all directions and at all hours. I would not have you think he is a difficult guest, ma'am. He fits himself to our little household ways most graciously."

"Indeed," Amaryllis murmured.

She could think of no more questions, so she looked up at the subject of their conversation. He was glaring across the room, she could not tell at whom, with a look of such animosity on his face that she was excessively glad it was not directed at her.

Bertram claimed her attention at that moment, and she was glad to turn to a comparison of the present jolly occasion with the elegant dinner parties they had both attended in the past. Geniality versus insipidity were the words that sprang to her lips, vulgarity and propriety to his. They argued their cases good-humouredly, careful not to be overheard by their fellow guests.

The first course was removed. In its place appeared pies and jellies, mince tarts and syllabubs, crisp, sweet russet apples, and nuts of all kinds. Bertram cracked a mixture of hazelnuts, almonds, and brazils for Amaryllis, while she glanced around the hall again. Tizzy, her cheeks pink with animation, was deep in conversation with the vicar. Aunt Eugenia, looking every inch grande dame in her blue-striped lutestring and matching toque, was holding forth to Miss Augusta, who looked overawed and had no attention to spare for her brother's misdeeds.

At last the banquet came to an end. The ladies were invited to step upstairs where the upper floor, with its myriad alcoves and niches, had been transformed into a dressing room for their convenience. The gentlemen went back down to the Guard Room, while the trestle tables were removed and the Banqueting Hall prepared for dancing. Amaryllis and Tizzy went up together. At the top of the stair a maid curtseyed and handed them each a card with a column of numbers and a pencil attached by a ribbon. Miss Tisdale turned hers over curiously.

"It's a dance programme," Amaryllis whispered. "The gentlemen write their names against the numbers so that you know which dance you have given to whom."

"Oh, but I shall not dance." She tried to give it back to the maid.

Amaryllis snatched it. "If Mr. Raeburn asks you, you most certainly will," she hissed, "if I have to drag you onto the floor myself."

"He . . . he did mention the cotillion. But he is a clergyman, surely he will not dance?"

"Remember his text, Tizzy dear. Mirth and merriment. Our vicar is no preacher of hellfire."

Miss Tisdale flushed. "Oh dear, I gave him that text. He had forgot he would be expected to pronounce grace, you see."

Amaryllis laughed so loud that several people stared at her. She hugged her governess and kissed her. "Let me see," she said, consulting the back of the card. "The cotillion is number four. I shall write in Mr. Raeburn's name."

"You shall not! If he cares to sign it himself, I . . . I shall stand up with him."

Amaryllis clapped, and they went to tidy their hair. Soon the sound of an orchestra tuning its instruments floated up the winding stairs from the gallery below. A young lady scarce out of the schoolroom tiptoed down and returned breathless to report that the gentlemen were already entering the Banqueting Hall. As if blown on a steady breeze, the ladies began to drift towards the stair.

Bertram pounced on Amaryllis as she emerged at the bottom. "Let's see," he said, "the first is a country dance. I'll take that. And then the waltz, there seems to be just one, and whatever is just before supper. Are you sure you will not give me more than three?"

"I never said I should give you more than two, and indeed I ought not."

"Gammon! No one will notice."

He scrawled his name three times on her program.

Amaryllis gave in, though she knew very well that everyone in the room would notice. As heir to an earl, Lord Pomeroy was by far the highest-ranking person present. It was not in his character to put on airs of self-consequence. By the time the orchestra struck up "Strip the Willow," only two dances remained unclaimed on her card. Bertram swore that rather than let her remain a wallflower he would stand up with her willy-nilly, if no one forestalled him. They took their places in the set.

Skirts swirled primrose, cherry, celestial blue, and demure white. Gentlemen bowed to their partners and swung them right and left. When Amaryllis's turn came she danced up the row, returning breathless after swinging with each gentleman to link arms with Bertram in the middle and swing the other way. He danced back down the row of ladies and together they formed an arch for the other couples to promenade through.

Catching her breath as the next lady made her way up the set, Amaryllis glanced up at the gallery. Two of the arches were filled with musicians, scraping and bowing and blowing with a will. Beneath the next arch, nearest the stair, a solitary figure caught her eye. Lord Daniel leaned on the balustrade, watching the dancers broodingly. He noticed at once that she had seen him, sketched a salute, and stepped back into the shadows. She thought he was still there, but at that moment it was her turn to spin and she lost sight of him. When the dance ended, she moved from the floor in the direction of the stairs.

"Go and find your next partner," she ordered Bertram. "Yes, I daresay you have not signed any other cards, but there are plenty of young ladies, and not so young, who are in need of partners."

"I shall dance with Mrs. Vaux," he said obediently, grinning. "I've no intention of raising hopes in any maidenly breast but yours."

"Coxcomb!" she snorted as he went off. She hurried up the stairs.

Lord Daniel was leaning against a pillar, gazing at nothing. He started as she appeared, then bowed to her with a sardonic look.

"You do not appear to be enjoying yourself, my lord," she commented.

"I do not dance, Miss Hartwell."

"Do you mean you cannot dance, or you will not dance?"

His mouth was grim, almost sneering. "You know my disability. What do you suppose would happen if I swung my partner with my right arm at the wrong moment?"

"She would fly off across the room." Amaryllis giggled, and unwillingly his face relaxed a little. "No, you are quite right, I cannot advise you to join the country dances. But I see no reason why you should not waltz. Do you waltz?"

"My sisters taught me when they learned," he said guardedly. "That was a decade ago, and I have never tried it in a ballroom."

"It is very easy," she assured him. "The music practically tells your feet what to do. I shall put you down for the waltz."

"I have not asked you, ma'am."

"No, I have asked you. Think of it as a challenge. Surely you will not cry craven. I depend on you. There!" Ruthlessly she scratched out Bertram's name and wrote in Lord Daniel's. As an afterthought she put Bertram's in one of the empty spaces, which happened to be the last. "I must go, my next partner will be looking for me." She flashed him a dazzling smile and hurried down the stairs.

=15=

As THE SECOND dance ended, Sir Peter approached Amaryllis and begged leave to present the Spaniard. Don Miguel bowed with a flourish and requested the honour of standing up with her. Uneasily, she agreed and allowed him to sign the one remaining space on her programme, only because she thought she might be able to find out his purpose in visiting Essex.

In the meantime, she had the felicity of seeing Miss Tisdale and Mr. Raeburn leading the cotillion, performing the intricate figures with amazing expertise and grace. Concentrating on her own steps, she had no time to try to discover what Miss Augusta thought of their performance. She told Bertram she had substituted the last dance for his waltz. He raised his eyebrows, but as she expected he was by far too gentlemanly to protest.

Her next partner was Don Miguel. To her relief the dance was a polonaise. She had not watched him during the country dances, but it seemed unlikely that he had mastered the Gay Gordons and the Eightsome Reel during his brief sojourn in Britain. The polonaise was sufficiently international that even the Spanish might be expected to know it. As it consisted mainly of a stately promenade, there would be plenty of opportunity to interrogate him.

He opened the conversation with a succession of fulsome and elaborate compliments. They made her want to giggle. She decided to reciprocate and spent some time admiring his waistcoat and his sword, which was quite appropriate to this particular dance but must have been a decided hazard at times. The gold embroidery on his waistcoat depicted a pattern of intertwined roses. She enquired whether this was significant, in view of his name, and was told that it was his family emblem.

"Is mark on many of my possessions," he said, confirming her guess that she had met him before under very different circumstances. Before she could think what to ask him next, he took the initiative. "Sir Peter say you have *una escuela*—a school, no? The English ladies are *muy independientes*. You teach the young ladies?"

"Yes, I do." As you are very well aware, she thought. "You are particularly interested in schools, sir?"

"*De ningún modo*—not at all," he said airily, but he went on, "Your pupils are gone now to the houses, the homes, for *la Natividad*, as I believe?"

"La Natibithath?"

"The Christmas. Until when áre gone?"

"Pray do not think you must entertain me with conversation about my school when you are not interested in it, sir," said Amaryllis firmly.

She was disturbed at the evidence that he actually was interested. She still did not know how to find out his business without asking straight out, which seemed unwise, so she turned the conversation to the castle. Don Miguel was properly impressed by its romantic reminder of past glories. In fact, he seemed unnaturally drawn to its bloody history, deeply regretting that England's days of chivalry and honour had ended,

"It is not so in *la España*," he told her. "We *hidalgos* hold up the honour of the family to the death."

Amaryllis paled as she wondered whether this was a direct reference to her father and the ambassador's daughter. However, at that moment Don Miguel caught sight of someone over her shoulder and the look of sneering malevolence that she had noticed before crossed his face. She was sure it was not directed at her. She would have liked to warn the Spaniard's prospective victim, but she still could not tell who it was. Shortly thereafter the dance came to an end.

As Don Miguel bowed to her, he patted the hilt of his sword. "This weapon that you admired, señorita," he said significantly, "rest assured that it is no ornament. At the *duelo* I am expert."

With this alarming farewell, he stalked off.

Amaryllis's next dance with Bertram was a welcome relief after her battle of wits with Don Miguel Rodrigues de la Rosa. The figures of the dance did not allow for conversation so she could not immediately tell Bertram what she had learned. Meanwhile, it was soothing to exchange smiles and cheerful remarks with someone who had no ulterior motive in seeking her company. As the dance ended, an announcement was made that supper had been set out in the Guard Room below and they joined the general movement towards the stairs.

Amaryllis looked out for Lord Daniel. There was no sign of him, and she hoped he would turn up for the waltz. She had no objection to a brief stint as a wallflower. She'd had a partner for every dance so far, and people would probably think she considered the waltz too fast for a schoolmistress. However, Bertram had not been pleased when asked to relinquish his prior claim, and she did not care to have distressed him for nothing.

The trestle tables had been moved down from the Banqueting Hall and were loaded with delicacies. In spite of her energetic evening, Amaryllis was not hungry. Bertram had danced with Mrs. Vaux, Miss Tisdale, and a number of young ladies whose plainness made it unlikely that they would refine too much upon his politeness, so he was ravenous. He munched his way through a heaped plateful while Amaryllis toyed with a Chantilly cream and told him about Don Miguel's mysterious inquisition and final threat.

"It sounds to me as if he is more interested in the school than in you," he said finally. "I'd wager all the schools for young ladies in Spain are convents, so perhaps he expected you to be a nun."

"He did comment that English ladies are very independent. At least that was what I understood him to say."

"Even so, he can scarce expect to challenge you to a duel. I am sure his last words were a boast, not a threat. Judging by what you tell me of his opinion of English decadence, he probably thinks Englishmen cannot handle a sword. His contemptuous scowl was undoubtedly directed at British manhood in general."

"And can you handle a sword?" asked Amaryllis laughing, reassured.

"I used to fence at Cambridge," said his lordship sheepishly, "but I have not touched one since."

After supper there was one dance before the waltz. As it drew to a close, Amaryllis saw Lord Daniel standing at the end of the room, watching her. Her partner, a young lawyer, regretfully delivered her to Lord Daniel's side.

Unfortunately, his expression was not one of pleasurable anticipation. He bowed to her awkwardly and asked in a tight voice if she was enjoying herself.

Suspecting that he was nervous, she did her best to put him at ease. She chattered about the task he was taking on by inviting Louise to his home and even surprised a laugh out of him by recounting one of the child's exploits that he had not yet heard. However, when the musicians finished tuning and couples began to take their places on the floor, he squared his shoulders as if bracing for an ordeal before he led her out.

After the first few stumbling steps, when she wondered if she had been mad to persuade him, he caught the rhythm. As they swirled about the hall, she was conscious only of his hand at her waist, hers on his arm, her right hand clasped in his left and his dark eyes burning down into hers. She felt the oddest sensation, as if flames raced along every nerve from the points where they touched.

Suddenly he stiffened, his face paled, and his hand began to slip from her waist. She realised at once what had happened and managed to link her arm beneath his to support it. There was a sheen of sweat on his forehead. He missed two or three steps until he felt her strength and resolved to rely on it. They circled the floor more slowly now and with care.

Amaryllis concentrated on her left arm, willing all her strength into it and trusting him to guide her. Just when she was afraid she would have to suggest that they sit out the rest of the dance, she felt his hand firm at her back again. She looked up and was surprised to see a gaze of such fervent gratitude that she blushed and lowered her eyes.

They went on dancing without further mishap, but she was uneasy with him now. It was nothing to do with his weakness. The intensity of his emotion frightened her a little, and she withdrew, conscious of the crowd about them, unable and unwilling to abandon herself once more to her own feelings. As they moved to the side of the room, she was glad to see Bertram waiting for his last dance. She turned to thank Lord Daniel. He bowed silently and walked away.

It was immediately apparent that Bertram was displeased with her. "I should never have given up my waltz had I known with whom you meant to dance it," he said severely. She raised her eyebrows in haughty interrogation. "To visit Winterborne's house as chaperone for his daughter was one thing," he went on. "To take to the floor in what the highest sticklers still consider an improper romp is quite another."

"Oh don't be Gothic, Bertram," she said impatiently. "Just because he is the father of one of my pupils. May I remind you that you are the uncle of another?"

He calmed down. "I forgot that I never told you," he apologised. "The man is divorced and, for all anyone knows, his wife is still living."

Amaryllis did not go so far as to feign surprise, nor did she admit that she already knew of the scandal.

"Whether his wife be living or no, he is not married to her. And if he were—well, I have danced with married men before without provoking the least frown on the face of the stuffiest tabbies. Pray do not be making a Cheltenham tragedy out of nothing."

His lordship looked as offended as his good-natured face allowed, but said quietly, "Let us not quarrel, if you please. This is our dance."

"I am tired, Bertram, and I'll wager Tizzy and Aunt Eugenia are equally so. We are not used to burning the candle at both ends, remember. I hope you will not mind if we go home now."

"I shall order my carriage at once," he said, disgruntled but obliging to the last.

He could hardly argue with her. The company had thinned out since supper. Mrs. Vaux was clearly visible nodding in her chair, while Miss Tisdale had lost her anchor some time since, as Mr. Raeburn had to be up for early service on the morrow. With punctilious courtesy Lord Pomeroy walked the ladies down to the carriage and handed them in. The air was icily refreshing, and Amaryllis was touched to find that he had ordered hot bricks for their brief journey down the hill.

She was glad when, as he bowed over her hand, he murmured, "I shall call in the morning before I leave."

They rumbled down the hill and through the quiet village. Here and there lights shone in windows where those who had served at the party were expected home. A lantern glowed on their own front porch, and in the vestibule stood three candles and a lighted lamp. The house was silent.

Mrs. Vaux yawned a delicate yawn as she lit the candles. "I don't know when I have enjoyed myself more," she declared. "Pray let me not be wakened in the morning."

They started up the stairs. Miss Tisdale's mouth was curved in a secret smile, and her usually shrewd eyes were dreamy.

" 'He giveth his beloved sleep.' Psalm one hundred and twenty-seven," she said vaguely when they parted on the top landing. "Goodnight."

"Goodnight," echoed Amaryllis and went to her chamber to indulge in a fit of the dismals before falling asleep.

After retiring in the small hours of the morning, she was not surprised to see the sun high in the sky when she woke. She dressed quickly, suddenly remembering that not only was Bertram coming to see her, but Lord Daniel was to pick up the girls. She hurried downstairs. The house was so quiet that she heard Daisy humming to herself in the dining room. The maid turned with a smile as she entered.

"Musta been a grand ball, miss, and all of you sleeping in so late. Shall I fetch you some breakfast?"

"Some tea and toast will do very well, Daisy. Where is everyone?"

"The young ladies is all gone, miss. There's a couple o' letters for you in the common-room. I'll bring 'em down."

She bustled out, and Amaryllis sat down at the table. She was facing a window that looked out on the front garden, and suddenly she noticed that the flowerbeds appeared to have burst into bloom overnight. Curious, she went to the window. Around the brown stubs of the pruned rosebushes spread a riot of colour. Purple and orange and peacock blue, scarlet, primrose, lavender, and peach, two score curly ostrich feathers nodded their heads in the breeze.

"Louise!" exclaimed Miss Hartwell, not for a moment at a loss to know who to blame.

"Isn't it downright pretty?" said Daisy, coming back with a tray. "That there sourpuss Ned wanted to pull 'em all up, but me and Cook assuaded him to leave 'em till you seen 'em."

"Very pretty," agreed her mistress, "but we shall be the laughing stock of the village if it gets about that we grow feathers in our garden!"

"Let 'em be till the miss and the madam's seen 'em," begged the maid. " 'Sides, 'tis market day and all the world'll know by now."

The accuracy of her prediction became obvious as a group of small boys ran up to peer over and through the fence, laughing and pointing. With a sigh and a shake of the head, Amaryllis turned to her breakfast.

There were two folded notes beside her plate, each carefully inscribed "To Miss Hartwell." She opened the one in Isabel's writing first.

"Dearest Miss Hartwell," it said, "Thank you for letting Louise come to my house. I hope you have a happy Christmas. I shall miss you. Love, Isabel."

Louise's was longer, though her writing was more laborious. "Dear ma'am, Please forgive me I skipped Scripcher last week to go to the market to buy the Osterch Fethers. Mr. Raybern is to good to scold or tell tails. I hope you think they are pretty. I do. They will remind you of Me and you may scold when I return. Your obed't servant, Louise Carfax. PS They are Artifishul so did not cost to much."

Amaryllis was still laughing when Bertram strolled into the dining room.

"Is your gardener run mad?" he demanded.

She handed him Louise's letter and, while he was reading it, pocketed Isabel's.

"I might have guessed," he groaned. "That child will be the death of me."

"I doubt it. Her pranks are never harmful or malicious. I suspect she saw this one in the light of a farewell gift, for she hopes that I may find the feathers pretty."

"You are very forgiving, my dear." He sat down beside her. "May I hope that you will forgive me for my carping last night? I had no excuse to find fault. I must confess that I was jealous."

"How can I not forgive when it arose from such a flattering cause?" She avoided telling him he had no reason for jealousy. "But I must ask your pardon too, for I ought not to have responded with such heat, and it was excessively rude of me to leave before the last dance."

"You were tired, I could see it. And I gather Mrs. Vaux and Miss Tisdale are still abed? When we are married I shall dance every dance with you."

"Now that will in truth create a scandal," said Amaryllis with a smile.

He took her hand. "I wish I might stay," he said, "but I

am expected at Tatenhill tomorrow and must not delay. I shall be back in January. You will have an answer for me then?"

"I shall," she promised.

=16=

HAVING MISSED THE morning services, the three ladies all went to Evensong at St. Nicholas's. Mrs. Vaux had a lifelong habit of regular churchgoing. Amaryllis felt it necessary to counteract the frivolous impression her behaviour of the previous evening must have produced on the local populace, and Miss Tisdale needed no reason beyond the stars in her eyes.

Mr. Raeburn insisted on escorting them back along the dark street. Amaryllis and her aunt dawdled a little exclaiming loudly over the brilliance of the stars. They caught up with the others at the gate, in time to overhear the vicar bemoaning the fact that the school holiday would deprive him of his usual Monday visit.

"It is dreadfully lowering to sit down only three to dinner when one is used to a crowd," said Amaryllis mendaciously. "Perhaps you and Miss Raeburn would dine with us tomorrow?"

The vicar brightened. "That will be delightful," he assured her. "At least, I must enquire whether Augusta has any prior engagement, but I believe we are free."

"Then we shall expect you unless we hear from you. Do not stand about out here too long, Tizzy, or you will catch a chill," added Amaryllis in governess-like tones as she and Mrs. Vaux went on into the house.

Having taken off her pelisse, Mrs. Vaux hovered at the window, peeking between the curtains. "He is holding her hand," she reported. "Oh, he has kissed her cheek! Amaryllis, I do believe they have come to an understanding at last."

from the window, do, Aunt Eugenia. They will see you. Come and tell me how to seat five people, four of them female, about a table intended for thirty."

Distracted by this question of polite usage, Mrs. Vaux followed her upstairs to the drawing-room.

"I have known great houses," she said, "where ceremony prevailed to the extent that one or two people might have the whole of one side of a lengthy table to themselves while host and hostess sat at either end. I consider it a shocking want of propriety, for naturally conversation is impossible and surely one's duty to entertain one's guests should come first. I believe I shall ask dear Mr. Raeburn to take the head. I shall sit on his left, with Augusta beside me, and dear Miss Tisdale shall sit on his right, with you next to her. Yes, that will be most satisfactory. If Augusta decides to be difficult, she will not find it easy to be rude crosswise across the table. Perhaps Ned might find some tall flowers to set between them?"

"In December, in this weather? I hardly think so. Do you expect Miss Raeburn to cause trouble?"

"She has been very good recently," said Mrs. Vaux, looking worried. "I had quite cowed her with my chatter of the Fashionable World, as I told you, but last night she was excessively shocked to see her brother on such intimate terms with Tizzy. I had some ado to stop her making a spectacle of herself."

"You seem very well able to control her, dear Aunt."

"Yes indeed," said the widow with pardonable complacence. "One must be sympathetic to her fears but not allow oneself to be ruled by her vapours. Of course, it is a great help that she is so much in awe of the Haut Ton. I believe that if she knew my brother to be a viscount, she would eat out of my hand."

"So long as you did not reveal that he is also an ironmonger. Well, you may tell her if you will, for I daresay I shall soon be married to Bertram, and no one will care then that the village schoolmistress can lay claim to an Honourable before her name."

"You know, she is quite sensible and good-natured if she is not permitted to dwell upon her megrims," Mrs. Vaux said thoughtfully. "I wonder whether . . ."

At that moment Miss Tisdale came in, her cheeks pink with excitement, nose red with cold.

"Matthew has proposed," she announced, trying to be solemn as befitted one about to embark upon the holy sacrament of matrimony, but unable to suppress a smile of diffident joy.

"And of course you have accepted." Amaryllis jumped up and ran to hug her. "Dearest Tizzy, I am so happy for you."

"I had to tell you, but it is not to be generally known until Matthew can make provision for Miss Raeburn. And, of course, we shall not be married until the end of the school year. Matthew understands that I cannot desert you."

"That is more than Bertram does," exclaimed Amaryllis. "But you are frozen. Come to the fire."

Mrs. Vaux embraced her more decorously, and wished her happy. "Does the vicar mean to tell Augusta at once?" she enquired. "I shall willingly take it upon myself to do so, if you wish."

"Matthew is afraid she will be displeased," said Tizzy, looking worried.

"And he is positively hen-hearted where she is concerned. She is bound to cut up stiff, but never fear, I can turn her up sweet," said Mrs. Vaux confidently.

"Aunt, such unladylike language!" Amaryllis laughed.

"Augusta suffers from such an excess of underbred gentility that it makes me quite long to shock her, and I find all the dreadful things Henry used to say returning to me," she retorted. "Just leave her to me, dear Miss Tisdale."

" 'A faithful friend is a strong defence: and he that hath found such an one hath found a treasure.' Ecclesiasticus I, verse 14." Tizzy sounded unwontedly emotional, but she soon regained her usual dry manner. "Now I must write to my brother. I hope his delight that I am to marry a fellow student of Magdalene will overcome his astonishment that I am to marry at all!"

The dinner party on Monday night began inauspiciously. Miss Raeburn, a sharp-faced female of middle years, studiously ignored Miss Tisdale and confined her remarks to her next-door neighbour, Mrs. Vaux. In a larger company this would have been correct, but with only five at the table conversation might have been expected to become general.

The vicar, nervous but valiant, attempted to entertain his betrothed and Miss Hartwell with a description of his youthful travels in Scotland, which neither lady had visited. He was also enthusiastic in his praise of the food, and indeed Cook had outdone herself. A fricassee of veal and mutton-and-oyster-hot-pot were accompanied by Brussels sprouts in a Bechamel sauce and carrots with lemon butter. The second course consisted of a galantine of chicken, an almond pudding, treacle tart, and poached pears with custard. Amaryllis suspected that somehow the servants knew of the betrothal, even if Miss Raeburn did not.

After dinner they all went up to the drawing-room. The vicar's sister glanced about it and pronounced it a tolerable good sort of sitting-room, though not so fine as the one at the vicarage. She then cornered Amaryllis and proceeded to interrogate her about her acquaintance with Lord Pomeroy.

"I was greatly shocked to see you stand up with him a second time," she said condescendingly. "It looked most *particular*."

Amaryllis threw a harassed look at her aunt. "Lord Pomeroy is a *particular* friend of mine," she retorted. "I have known him forever. I believe he was introduced to me by my father, the Viscount Hartwell, who never objected to us standing up together more than once at Almack's."

Miss Raeburn was momentarily startled, but made a quick recovery. "I am sure manners are different in Town. In the country, you know, my dear Miss Hartwell, we are sadly Old-Fashioned. Lord Hartwell is your father? I wonder Eugenia never mentioned it." She sounded suspicious.

Amaryllis put her hand to her mouth in feigned alarm.

"Oh dear," she exclaimed, "I have let it out. Papa has emigrated to America, on account of his democratic principles, and he does not wish anyone there to know that he is a peer."

"I assure you not a word of this shall pass my lips." Miss Raeburn was drinking it in, apparently not wondering how the revelation might flow from her lips to the population of America. "I do not quite follow . . . That is, I expect it is your Democratic Principles that have caused you to open this school?"

"Not at all." Amaryllis spoke with great disdain. "I despise the very idea. I am dedicated to the Education of Women. I hope I do not greatly shock you, Miss Raeburn?"

"No, no," she gasped. "Lord Hartwell . . . Lord Pomeroy . . ."

"Pray do not mention either of those gentlemen again," said Amaryllis firmly, tiring of the sport. She saw her victim eyeing Tizzy speculatively and considered declaring that lady to be the daughter of a duke, also devoted to the Education of Women. However, such a rapper was not to be compared with the taradiddles she had already indulged in, and it seemed likely to land her in the briars. The rest must be left to her aunt. "I believe I shall ring for the tea tray," she said with a sigh. "Do you care to drink tea?"

After their guests left, and Tizzy had retired to her chamber, Mrs. Vaux took her niece to task. "I did not care to hear you making a May game of Augusta," she said with gentle severity.

"It was not well done of me, perhaps, but she was being odiously condescending. She will not try to come the high and mighty over me again. I only wish I could do something about her rudeness to Tizzy."

"She is afraid of Miss Tisdale, my love, afraid of losing her brother and her home."

"Why, I believe you begin to like the woman, Aunt Eugenia."

"I sympathise with her position, which is not easy."

"Forgive me, dear Aunt. Of course it not unlike yours,

before Godmama offered you an allowance on my marriage. But you must have known I should never abandon you."

"No, dear, but I should not have liked to be a poor relation in Lord Pomeroy's house, any more than she cares to be dependent on her brother after his marriage."

"Then what are we to do? I shall not let her spoil the match."

"No, we cannot allow that. Do not worry, I have an ace up my sleeve."

"And you always abhorred cards. Very well, I shall not worry, but I hope you will have the matter settled before Bertram returns next month."

"You are going to marry him, are you not, Amaryllis?"

"Undoubtedly. He insists on an answer when he comes, so perhaps we shall have a double wedding in June."

"I am so glad he will not let you dither any longer."

"So am I," muttered Amaryllis. She went up to bed dissatisfied with herself and the world.

The weather continued cold but fine. Every day Amaryllis went for long walks through the frosty fields, returning hungry and rosey-cheeked but still discontented. On Saturday, the day before Christmas Eve, she found herself shortly after noon on the outskirts of Finchingfield. Usually she turned back before she had gone so far, and she doubted her ability to walk all the long way home before dark.

Passing the duck pond on the green, its water glinting icily, she went into an inn near the guildhall. She ordered a bowl of soup and a carriage. The landlord was happy to oblige, boasting of his wife's pea soup, a local speciality, while apologising that the only vehicle he had available was a gig.

"We've rugs a-plenty to wrap about 'ee, miss," he assured her, showing her to a seat near the fire in the coffee-room.

"So it gets me there, it will suffice," she told him.

As promised, the soup was delicious. Its soothing warmth spread through her, making her reluctant to face the cold air outside. At last she could postpone her departure no longer. She went to stand in the window while the gig was brought to the front of the inn. She was halfway to Wimbish. It would be as easy to go there as back to Castle Hedingham, she thought. If she were not a gently bred young lady, she would bid her driver go west, not east. What would Lord Daniel say? Would he scowl and demand to know her business or would he . . .

The sound of hooves broke in upon her musing. It was not the expected gig but a coach and four, coming up the hill from the green. With a shock, she recognised the driver. It was Grayson. Inside the carriage, through the misted windows, she saw the silhouettes of a gentleman and two small girls.

"Stop!" she whispered.

The carriage drove on past the inn, out of sight.

"The gig, miss," announced the landlord, and she went outside to be helped up onto the seat and bundled in rugs.

"Thank you," she said numbly. "I shall be quite warm."

The innkeeper looked at the frozen misery on her face and wondered, but he bade his ostler whip up the single horse and they clattered down the hill.

The brief winter day had faded by the time she reached home. The lights in the windows looked warm and welcoming. She paid the ostler and hurried into the house. Mrs. Vaux was trotting down the stairs as Amaryllis entered the vestibule.

"It is you, Amaryllis," she cried. "I heard a carriage. I have been in quite a worry for it has been dark at least half an hour, and you are not used to be so late."

"I went farther afield than I had intended, and had to hire a gig to bring me home."

"A gig! You must be chilled to the bone. Come up to the fire quickly. I have such a deal to tell you."

Amaryllis obediently followed her up to the drawing-room. "Where is Tizzy?" she asked listlessly, standing before the fire and holding out her hands to the flames.

"If you had spent more time at home this week, you

would know that she has been meeting Mr. Raeburn in the church. A shocking place for a vicar and a vicar's daughter to rendezvous, is it not? But I am very nearly ready to break the news to Augusta. I have been visiting her every day, preparing the ground, as Ned would say, and today—you will never guess—today she invited us to dinner on Christmas Day."

"All of us?"

"I had to be very firm with her. She invited you and me, and I told her that we could not possibly accept any invitation that did not include Miss Tisdale. She realised how excessively improper it would be to withdraw the invitation, so we are all to go. It seems to me that Christmas Day, being the season of goodwill and peace on earth to all men, it ought to be to all women also. Is it not odd how the Bible talks of men all the time and mentions women so rarely?"

"Very odd. You think, I collect, that on Christmas Day even Augusta Raeburn must be charitable enough to accept without hysterics the news that her brother is to marry Tizzy."

"Yes, but I have another string to my bow."

"I understood you to have an ace up your sleeve, but a second string to your bow will do very well. You are not cooking up another Bedlam tale, I trust?"

"No. It would not answer, besides being quite untrue. Are you sure you are going to marry Bertram?"

"Yes," said Amaryllis drearily. "I believe I shall go and lie down for an hour or two before dinner."

"Daisy shall bring up a hot brick for your feet and a cup of tea, my love. You will soon feel quite the thing."

More than willing to let her aunt believe that her low spirits were the result of freezing in the open gig, Amaryllis plodded upstairs to her chamber.

The weather changed overnight. The rising sun was a pallid circle scarcely visible through a grey haze, and by the time the ladies set out for Church it had disappeared behind a pall of clouds. Though it was warmer outside, the stone-flagged church was bitterly cold. Villagers and farmers filed into their pews, their holiday clothes hidden under warm wraps.

St. Nicholas's was gay with holly and mistletoe and branches of evergreens. Mr. Raeburn abandoned his usual Christmas text of "On earth peace, goodwill towards men" and preached instead a heartfelt sermon on "It is not good that man should be alone." Miss Tisdale hid her scarlet cheeks under her bonnet.

That afternoon, Amaryllis went over her accounts and then, feeling a little cheered, wrote a long letter to her father. She told him of Tizzy's betrothal and that she expected soon to be married herself, and asked for his blessing. Only when she reread her words did she realise that she had not mentioned whom she meant to wed. To save her father's purse she had written small and close. There was no room for insertions. She sealed and addressed it as it was, wondering what conclusions Lord Hartwell would draw about his future son-in-law from her omission.

Miss Tisdale insisted on going to church again on Christmas morning, just because she liked to sing carols, she claimed. Afterwards they hurried home to dress. Mrs. Vaux had decreed that the new gowns were to be worn to the vicarage.

"They are much too fine for such an occasion," she said privately to Amaryllis, a martial glint in her eye, "but it will impress Augusta, and Tizzy's spirits will be supported by knowing she is dressed to the nines."

On the short walk to the vicarage, Miss Tisdale's spirits showed no signs of needing support. Amaryllis was amazed at the jaunty bounce in the steps of her staid governess. The smile that had rarely been seen, even when she was amused, now rarely left her face. And all this had been wrought by the knowledge that one gentleman at least found her attractive enough to marry. Amaryllis had never lacked for suitors. She knew her aunt, in her day, had also been much sought after. Amaryllis had never considered how utterly lowering it must be to be ignored by the male sex.

Impulsively she slipped her arm through Tizzy's and whispered, "I am so happy for you!"

As soon as they were shown into the vicarage's parlour, Mrs. Vaux sat down beside Augusta Raeburn and engaged her in serious conversation. Amaryllis exerted herself to ensure that their tête-à-tête was not interrupted, not a difficult task since Mr. Raeburn and Miss Tisdale showed no interest in anything but each other. If she had not been so fond of Tizzy, she would have found it amusing to see the plump vicar and the lean governess smelling of April and May like any youthfully handsome couple. At last dinner was announced. With a smug smirk on her face, Mrs. Vaux accepted Mr. Raeburn's arm to lead her into the dining room. She stood on tiptoe to whisper in his ear, and he beamed.

The meal went better than Amaryllis had imagined possible. The conversation was cheerful and Miss Augusta actually addressed a remark or two to Tizzy. The golden-brown turkey was stuffed with fragrant herbs; the plum pudding ignited in a satisfactory blue blaze of brandy. As the parlour-maid bore off its remains to the kitchen, the vicar rose to his feet and proposed a toast to his betrothed. Without a murmur of protest, Miss Raeburn joined in raising her glass to the health and happiness of the beaming Miss Tisdale.

When Mr. Raeburn sat down, Mrs. Vaux stood up. "I have an announcement to make too," she said. "Augusta has agreed that when I retire from the school, she will come and live with me."

Amaryllis looked at her aunt in surprise. There was not the least shadow of uneasiness on her face, so it must be that she was now perfectly in charity with the vicar's sister. If it was really what she wanted, it was certainly a perfect solution to a number of problems, and vastly easier than turning the school into a Bedlam.

Amaryllis had her own good news to impart, but decided

to save it until they had returned home through the dark, quiet streets. As they reached the top landing on their way to their bedchambers, she stopped them.

"Tizzy, Aunt Eugenia, wait a moment," she said. "I have something to add to your sweet dreams. I brought the accounts up to date yesterday. By June, if we do not suffer some dreadful calamity in the meantime, there will be over two thousand pounds in the emergency fund. Tizzy shall have a dowry of seven or eight hundred, and Aunt Eugenia the same to set up her new home in luxury.

With bright eyes and vowing they should not sleep for planning how to spend such a windfall, they trotted off to bed. Amaryllis went wearily to hers, smiling at their pleasure. Half her own share would be her wedding gift to Tizzy, the other half a housewarming present for her aunt.

When she married Bertram, such a paltry sum would be neither here nor there.

=17=

FOR A WEEK it rained, and then the weather turned cold again and it snowed. Confined to the house, Amaryllis thought with longing of the library at Wimbish as she tried to concentrate on next term's lesson plans.

At last the sun came out, pale in a sky of the palest blue. Even at noon it had no warmth to melt the white carpet that scrunched under Amaryllis's boots as she walked briskly into the village, enveloped in her warmest cloak. Small boys with red cheeks and noses were throwing snowballs in the streets, and a snowman was under construction in the churchyard.

She went into the Bell to see if there was any post. A mail coach had gone into a ditch on the Braintree to Cambridge road the day before, but today it had come through. There was a letter from America. A sense of déjà-vu seized her and she turned, half expecting to see Lord Daniel waiting impatiently for the innkeeper to finish serving her. The long, low room, lit up by sunlight reflected from the snow outside, was empty but for a couple of old men in the chimney nook, warming gnarled hands at the fire.

She paid the landlord the postage due, put her father's letter and a couple of others in her pocket, and stepped out into the white street. Though she was eager to see what Lord Hartwell had to say, there was nothing like the emotion that had overwhelmed her upon receipt of his first communication in six years. He could not have received her most recent letter yet, so he would have no comment on her prospective marriage.

She went on to the draper's to purchase some ribbon and thread for her aunt before turning back towards home. As she passed the churchyard, she noticed that the snowman was now adorned with a red and white muffler. It looked suspiciously like one she had recently seen about the vicar's neck, and she was not surprised when Mr. Raeburn waved to her from the church porch.

"Good day," she called, waving back, and pointed to the snowman, adding, "I see you take seriously your duty to clothe the naked."

He nodded sheepishly as he joined her and begged her not to tell either his sister or his betrothed.

"Though it was much too gaudy for a clergyman," he pointed out. "I found it in a box of clothes given me for the poor, and, bless my soul, I could not resist it."

When she reached home, Amaryllis went up to the drawing-room to read her letter. There was a fire there, and she would be alone since Tizzy and Aunt Eugenia were spending a great deal of time at the vicarage these days.

Lord Hartwell was proud of his daughter's enterprising spirit in opening a seminary for young ladies. He had known that whatever she chose to do, she would do it well. However, there was no need any longer for her to struggle to make a living. His hardware emporium was so successful that if she joined him she might lead a life of leisure. There was no stigma, he assured her, in having a tradesman for a father. The Americans were much more sensible about such things, and she would be able to enter such society as Philadelphia provided without a qualm.

She was tempted. To run away from her uncertainties, to discover a new land, new customs, new faces, to be reunited with her irresponsible but beloved Papa—was this what she wanted? Experiencing a confusion of thought and feeling, she sat gazing into the fire until Mrs. Vaux bustled in, full of chatter and bearing an invitation to dine at the vicarage.

There was no opportunity that evening for Amaryllis to consider her father's offer. When they came home from the vicarage, she bade her aunt and Tizzy good-night and went into the drawing-room to find his letter. Daisy had built up the fire in expectation of a cold night, so Amaryllis sat down by the banked grate and pored over his words, trying to read between the lines whether he really wanted her to join him. The house fell silent and still she sat there musing.

She was half asleep when a sudden dull thud roused her. For a moment she thought she was dreaming, then there was another thump, and another. The sound came from the direction of the window. She opened the curtains a crack and looked out. There was a full moon. Trees and bushes stood out in sharp relief against the white snow, and shadows showed blackest black in contrast.

Beneath the window, two of the shadows were dancing. As she looked down, puzzled, one of the dancing shadows stooped, straightened, and threw something towards her. Snow splattered against the glass, startling her. Pulling her shawl close about her, she opened the casement a few inches.

"Miss Hartwell! Help! Oh please, ma'am, come down and let us in!"

Louise! And no doubt the other shivering shadow was Isabel, dragged into who knew what scrape by her madcap friend.

"I'm coming," she called, then closed the window, and ran down.

Louise was excited, Isabel weeping, both girls shaking too violently with cold to be able to explain their presence. Amaryllis hurried them to the kitchen, opened the stove to let out a glow of warmth, and set a kettle on top to heat water for chocolate. She helped them out of their pelisses and hugging them to her pulled them close to the fire.

"It's Papa!" blurted Isabel as soon as her teeth stopped chattering for long enough. "Up at the castle. Please, you must help him!"

"At the castle?"

"We were kidnapped," announced Louise in portentous tones. "It was the first time we'd been out in ages, because of the weather, and we were riding through a spinney and two men jumped out and pulled us off the ponies."

"They wrapped rugs round our heads so we could not call for help, and they put us in a carriage."

"I could not breathe so I fainted." Louise sounded as proud of herself as if she had done it deliberately. "So did Isabel. When we woke up we were in the castle, in the Minstrel's Gallery, all tied up. We shouted and shouted but no one came."

"Mr. Majendie is away," said Amaryllis, unable to think of any sensible comment to make. "Have you any idea who the men were?"

"They talked some funny language," Isabel said. "It wasn't French. They came back after a while and we heard them talking but the only word I understood was Winterborne. Then they went away again and it got dark."

"Isabel was frightened," said Louise, "but I told her it was only an adventure and her Papa would come and rescue us, and he did."

"Not for ages. And now he is stuck there instead of us," wailed Isabel.

"He came creeping up the stairs and he cut the ropes and we were just going to escape, only when we got down to the hall we heard the men talking down by the front door. Lord Daniel told us to hide in a corner and to come to you if we managed to get away, then he went up the stairs again, only noisily this time, and when he got right to the top of the castle he shouted out and the men came running up and as soon as they went past us we dashed down and ran all the way down the hill and through the village till we got here."

"No one answered the door, but Louise is so clever, she thought of throwing snowballs when we saw a light in a window. Oh please, will you help Papa?"

"Of course," said Amaryllis, her mouth dry, "though I expect he is perfectly all right." She did not believe her own words. The kidnappers could only be the Spaniard and his servant, and remembering the ugly look on Don Miguel's face and his obscure threats, she trembled for Lord Daniel.

"You must go up and wake Miss Tisdale," she went on steadily, though her mind was in a whirl. "She will take care of you, see that beds are made up." She kissed Isabel. "Don't worry, my dear. I'm sure it is all a misunderstanding, but I had better hurry all the same."

Pulling on boots and cloak, she rushed out into the icy street and ran towards the village. She thought of trying to wake some of the village men to help her. It would take time, and more time to persuade them of her need. She dared not wait.

The hill up to the castle was slippery. She felt as if she were in one of those nightmares where one slides two steps back for every step forward, but urged on by dread she struggled up the slope.

The moonlit keep towered over her, indifferent to her fears as it had been indifferent to the men who died bloodily in its shadow centuries ago. She turned the corner, raced up the stair, and, heart in mouth, stepped through the arched doorway and into the darkness of the Guard Room.

Another stair was on her left. Was it her imagination, or was the faintest of faint lights emerging from the stairwell? Straining her eyes she moved towards it, feeling for the wall.

She stiffened at a sound behind her. Before she could turn something hard poked her in the back, and a threatening voice spoke words she could not understand. Under the relentless pressure of what she assumed to be the barrel of a gun, she mounted the spiral on shaky legs and emerged into the Banqueting Hall.

Don Miguel was pacing the floor, his excited voice and the click of his heels covering the sound of her arrival. He held a pistol in one hand. In his gaudy clothes he reminded her of a beautiful but deadly snake she had seen once in an illustrated book about India. The pistol was pointed at Lord Daniel. Seated on an upturned basket, he lounged against the wall. He wore a look of boredom, but his face was pale. She could see the strain about his eyes, fixed on the

Spaniard.

The servant behind her spoke and both gentlemen gaped at Amaryllis with identical expressions of horror as she moved towards Lord Daniel.

"Isabel?" he asked, his voice unnaturally loud in the sudden silence.

"She is perfectly safe."

"Thank God. You should not have come."

"I hoped I might help." She shrugged helplessly and tried to smile. "I am ill prepared to deal with such an emergency." Feeling her lower lip quiver, she bit down on it fiercely.

He stood up and took a step towards her.

"Stop!" barked Don Miguel.

Lord Daniel threw him a look of distaste. Then he bowed to Amaryllis and indicated the basket.

"Pray be seated, Miss Hartwell."

She sat down with what dignity she could manage. He stood beside her, leaning against the wall, his left hand on her shoulder. She felt warmth and strength flowing into her from the contact and glanced up at him, but he was looking at the Spaniard.

"Well?" Lord Daniel asked sardonically.

Don Miguel had recovered from the shock of her appearance. His pistol as well as that of his manservant were pointed unwaveringly.

His first words were in Spanish. The servant nodded and went back down the stairs. Then Don Miguel addressed his prisoners with a sneer.

"So the independent Miss Hartwell interferes. She wishes, perhaps, to learn that which passes here. Who am I that I deny a beautiful señorita? We will begin again the story."

"That is not necessary," said Lord Daniel roughly. "I have heard your tale and . . ."

"*Silencio*, milord! If you wish that the lady leaves unhurt, you will not speak."

Amaryllis felt his hand tense on her shoulder and put up

her own to cover it warningly. She did not believe for a moment that the Spaniard would dare to harm her, but what he might do to his lordship was another matter. Besides, she had to confess to a certain curiosity as to what had engendered the bitter hatred in Don Miguel's eyes.

"I had a cousin, Miss Hartwell." Don Miguel resumed his pacing. "Doña Francisca Cortés, a most beautiful young lady, gently bred, as you English say, of a modesty *impecable*. Her I loved with all my heart. She was older than me, a year or two, and I awaited *con pasión* the moment when I should be of an age to wed her. We were promised, you understand, betrothed since childhood.

"Then the French invade *la España*. The family is dispersed, scattered. For five years we fight in the mountains, we fight in the plains. At last we drive them back across *los Pirineos*. My brother is dead. My cousin, Don Emilio Cortés, is dead and of Doña Francisca there is no word. My uncle dies of grief.

"For seven years there is no word of Doña Francisca. Then comes to my house in Zaragoza a woman. Is ill, is dressed in rags, is old of face—is my Francisca!

"I take her in. She is dying, but before she dies she tells me all. She tells me of fleeing from the French army, of a fine young Englishman who seduces her, who marries her in a church in Coruña and takes her to England as his wife. She tells how he grows tired of her, abandons her in a foreign land. These heretical English do not believe in the sacred Catholic marriage. He divorces her in the Parliament, though in the eyes of the Church she is still his wife."

Amaryllis was distantly aware that Lord Daniel had removed his hand from her shoulder. She did not dare look up at him, could not tear her eyes from the face of the Spaniard who so clearly believed every word he spoke.

"Francisca turned for help to another officer," he went on. "Innocent, trusting, again she is betrayed. He takes her to Vienna, where he dies of a fever. Alone again in a foreign country, what is she to do? I leave you to imagine, señorita, the horrors of her life and how she came at last home to

Zaragoza to die."

He called out to his servant, who came up the stairs bearing a sword.

"So, milord," he said, his hand on the pommel of his own sword, "I am the only one left to avenge the honour of Doña Francisca Winterborne. We fight with the swords, to the death!"

"I will not," said Lord Daniel, his voice cold and calm. "Francisca has woven a clever tissue of half truths, and I am not surprised she deceived you, but I assure you that before I met her your cousin had lost any honour worth fighting for."

"It is easy for a coward to speak ill of the dead," snarled Don Miguel. Whipping a glove from his belt, he strode forwards and struck Lord Daniel in the face with it.

Amaryllis jumped up. Lord Daniel's eyes were blazing, but he maintained his rigid calm.

"I cannot meet you with swords," he said, "but with pistols I should have a fair chance."

"Gentlemen do not duel with pistols," sneered the Spaniard. "It is as I supposed, the gentlemen of England are *afeminados y decadentes*. It is beneath me to fight with such a one, but there are other forms of vengeance. Milord will kindly disrobe."

Lord Daniel and Amaryllis both stared at him.

"I have the wrong word?" he asked, negligently waving his pistol. "Undress. Take off the clothes."

"Are you mad, man?" demanded Lord Daniel. "I will do no such thing."

Don Miguel said something in rapid Spanish to the servant and gestured towards Amaryllis. Before she realised what was happening, the man had seized her from behind and twisted her arm up behind her back.

"Undress," repeated Don Miguel.

His eyes on her face, Lord Daniel put his hand up to his cravat and began slowly to untie it.

"Faster!"

The servant jerked on her arm, and Amaryllis could not

suppress a gasp of pain. Lord Daniel quickly stripped off neckcloth, coat, waistcoat, and shirt. She tried not to look but her gaze was drawn to his broad, pale chest, every rib distinct.

He does not eat enough, she thought irrelevantly, and then she saw his arm. A jagged white line ran down from his shoulder. Just above the elbow it spread into a twisted knot of scar tissue. She raised her eyes, full of horror and pity, and met his questioning look.

The servant decided things were not moving quickly enough, and again she gasped in pain. Lord Daniel sat down on the floor and pulled off his boots and hose. Standing again, he began to unfasten his riding breeches. She kept her eyes fixed on his, willing herself to faint if by fainting she might spare him this humiliation. The pain in her arm was excruciating, but her head was clear as ever.

"*Y los calzoncillos*," said Don Miguel's inexorable, contemptuous voice, "The drawers, milord." A moment later he gestured with his pistol. "And now, down the stairs."

Lord Daniel's head was held high, his back straight as he led the little procession down. Next came Don Miguel, pistol in one hand, lantern in the other. Amaryllis was surprised to find that her legs did not work properly. The manservant half carried, half dragged her after them.

They went out onto the landing. Prodded by the pistol, Lord Daniel climbed onto the rail. In the moment before he fell, he looked like an enormous plucked goose. Amaryllis closed her eyes, a hysterical giggle rising in her throat. She felt herself lifted up, then she landed beside him in the oubliette with an impact that drove the breath from her body.

=18=

THE FULL MOON sailed across a cloudless sky. Its light shone pitilessly down into the roofless dungeon, reflecting from the snow on the floor and leaving no place of concealment. By the time Amaryllis recovered her breath, the Spaniards' lanterns were gone from the stair and the sound of horses' hooves told of their escape. Lord Daniel crouched beside her, reaching towards her tentatively with his left arm, his right hanging useless at his side.

"Are you all right, Miss Hartwell?" he asked anxiously.

Amaryllis sat up with the greatest caution.

"I believe so, though doubtless I shall ache tomorrow. No bones broken, at least."

"Thank God."

"And you, my lord?" She began undoing the fastenings of her cloak.

"I landed on my bad arm, and have not been able to move it since." He spoke with attempted nonchalance, but she sensed the fear behind his words. "I shall not be able to help you climb out."

Looking up at the sheer twelve-foot walls, she grimaced. "I'd wager I could not manage it if you did." She stood up, took off the cloak and held it out to him. "Here, put this on."

"No, you will need it. I daresay you feel warm now from agitation, but, believe me, by morning it will be devilish cold down here."

"My gown is warm. Come, surely you will not deny that you need it more than I."

She looked down at his crouched, shivering form, pale in the moonlight.

He made no move to take it, so she draped it about his shoulders.

"There. I shall turn my back while you arrange it as decently as may be."

She moved towards the wall under the stair, where a strip of dirt-covered floor was free of snow. After a moment, she heard his voice close beside her.

"Miss Hartwell."

She turned to face him. The cloak covered him down to mid-shin. He had not fastened it but held it awkwardly closed with his left hand.

"Your feet," she said helplessly. "What shall we do about your feet?"

"My feet are the least of my worries," he said with a crooked grin. "I suppose it is of no use to shout for help until the morning?"

"No. Mr. Majendie is away, so the servants will have retired. It must be past midnight. And besides, the bulk of the castle is between us and the house."

"Then I must make a suggestion that may shock you."

"My lord, if you think anything can shock me after the events of this evening, then you are a . . ."

"A mooncalf?" he offered. "I wish you will stop calling me my lord. Our present situation hardly calls for formality. My name is Daniel."

"And mine is Amaryllis. If you think to shock me by calling me by it, you are fair and far off."

"That is not the suggestion to which I referred. Our main problem is going to be to stay warm until morning. Two bodies will conserve heat better than one." He stepped forwards and embraced her with his left arm, holding her close.

"Daniel! My lord!" She pushed against his chest with all her strength.

"Pray do not turn missish on me now," he snapped. He looked down at her, his eyes gleaming. She felt his heart beating, felt the warmth of his body slowly seep through her clothing. For a moment she thought he was going to kiss her, but he released her and moved away. "You noticed the difference?" he asked.

She laughed shakily. "A number of differences. Yes, i would be warmer thus, but we cannot stand here all night!"

"That's my brave girl. No, we shall lie down, here where there is no snow." He knelt, then lowered himself to lie on his right side. With his left hand he spread the right side of the cloak across the ground, then beckoned to her. "Come."

She knelt on the edge of the cloak, trying to read his expression, but in the shadow of the stair it was impossible She had no choice but to trust him. She turned her back to him and lay down. His left arm pulled her closer, wrapped the left side of the cloak about her. There was nothing between them but the silk of her dress, the fine linen of her shift.

For a few minutes she lay stiffly stretched. Then, with a little sigh, she relaxed, pillowed her head on her hands and curled up against him. His lean body formed itself to hers His left arm held her close, his hand resting between her breasts. His heart sounded like thunder in her ears, or was it her own?

"Amaryllis," he whispered into her hair.

He said nothing more and did not attempt to caress her It seemed like forever she lay there in drowsy contentment, scarcely aware of the cold nibbling at her hands and feet.

"Miss Hartwell!" It was the vicar's voice, and not far distant. "Miss Hartwell, are you there? Halloa, Miss Hartwell!"

"Mr. Raeburn!" She jumped to her feet, stepped out from under the stair, and looked up. A dark shape was climbing the steps, a lantern bobbing above it.

"Miss Hartwell? Where are you!"

"Down here, in the dungeon. Lord Daniel is with me. Thank heaven you are come!"

Lord Daniel stood up, staggering, supporting himself against the wall.

"Bless my soul!" said the vicar, peering over the railing.

"Well, this is no time to ask how you came to be in such a fix. Just tell me if you have any suggestions as to how I may extract you without rousing half the village."

Amaryllis had never thought to be glad of Louise's venture into the depths of the oubliette, but now she remembered where the ladder was kept that had rescued her pupil. She described it to Mr. Raeburn, watched him trot down the steps, and turned to her companion. He had sat down again, leaning against the wall.

"Tizzy must have sent him. He is the very person I would have hoped for to save us."

"I am not sure I shall be able to climb the ladder," said his lordship wryly.

"Your arm?"

"No, Miss Hartwell, my feet, if I still have any. They are completely numb."

Amaryllis bent over him anxiously. If they had to call for more help, there would be no hiding his nakedness. Then she remembered how she warmed her hands in bed on a cold night.

She knelt before him. "Give them to me," she ordered, hoping he could not see her fiery face in the moonlight.

She pressed his icy feet between her thighs, massaging his ankles with her hands to make the blood flow. He did not speak. She kept her eyes fixed on her task, but she felt as if his gaze was burning into the top of her head. By the time they heard the vicar returning, banging the ladder against the castle wall as he turned the corner, she at least was surprisingly warm. She stood up quickly and held out her hand to Lord Daniel. He took it in a firm clasp, but rose without assistance.

"Thank you," he murmured, and there was a tremour of laughter in his voice. "My feet are reborn."

She was sure her cheeks were crimson by now, but the tension was released and she could not help a giggle as she responded, "That is very clever, my lord, and highly improper."

Mr. Raeburn was panting as he struggled up the stair

with the ladder.

"I'm back," he announced as he reached the top. "Stand clear and I shall lower it."

With much thumping and muttering he lifted it over the side.

"You go first," whispered Lord Daniel, "and explain my situation to him before I come up."

Her skirts were very much in the way, but she negotiated the ladder successfully. In a low voice she told the vicar that his lordship was dressed only in her cloak, and begged him not to demand an explanation at this point.

"Bless my soul!" he exclaimed, peering over the rail at Lord Daniel, who was having even more difficulty climbing than Amaryllis since the cloak was equally in the way, and he only had the use of one arm. "Bless my soul! Bare feet, too! Well, that is soon remedied. I saw a pair of galoshes in the toolshed where I found the ladder. Wait here." He scurried off.

Lord Daniel reached the top, only to find that the most difficult part of the climb was the descent from the railing. With Amaryllis's help he managed it, though ungracefully.

"Let us wait inside the keep," she suggested, shivering. "It may be a little warmer."

The door was locked. Don Miguel must have stolen a key when he stayed with Mr. Majendie after the Christmas ball. They decided it was best to keep moving, and started down the stairs. Before they reached the bottom, Mr. Raeburn reappeared with a large and dilapidated pair of galoshes.

"I ought to take the ladder back," he said as Lord Daniel put them on.

"Leave it," advised Amaryllis. "It will only start another ghost story."

They met no one on the way down the hill and through the dark, snowy village. When they reached the vicarage, Mr. Raeburn let Lord Daniel in and told him to wait by the fire while he escorted Miss Hartwell home.

"I will do myself the honour of calling on you in the morning, Miss Hartwell," said his lordship stiffly, his teeth chattering.

"It is morning now. You had best wait till afternoon," said the vicar kindly. "Come now, ma'am, Miss Tisdale is waiting up for you."

Tizzy took one look at her white, exhausted face, her shivering cloakless form, and rushed her upstairs.

"Into bed quickly," she ordered, asking no questions. "I have already put hot bricks in to warm it, and there is soup on the stove which I shall fetch up to you at once. Here, let me undo those buttons, your hands are shaking."

In five minutes Amaryllis was in bed, curled up between the warm sheets. Fits of shuddering still shook her, from the cold that had crept into her bones and from remembered fear. When she closed her eyes Lord Daniel's shocked face appeared before her, so she kept them open.

A fine revenge the Spaniard had attempted. If they had stayed in the oubliette till morning, if they had survived the bitter night, the news of his lordship's nakedness would have been all over the county within days. For her interference, she would have been disgraced along with him.

A timid tapping at her door distracted her from the horrid contemplation of the ruin she had so narrowly avoided. Isabel entered, tripping over the hem of a nightgown twice her size.

"I heard you come in," she said in a quavering voice. "Miss Tisdale said I could see you. Is Papa . . . is he all right?"

"Yes, my dear. He is spending the night at the vicarage with Mr. Raeburn."

With a sob, the child ran to her and hugged her, burying her face in her shoulder.

"I thought those men would kill him," she wept.

Amaryllis put her arms round the thin, trembling body and stroked her hair.

"It's all right, love, it's all right," she murmured. "Hush now. Come, creep under the covers with me, or your feet will freeze."

Miss Tisdale brought in the hot soup and found them

asleep in each other's arms.

When Amaryllis woke, it was past noon, and Isabel was gone. Recalling at once that Lord Daniel was coming to see her that afternoon, Amaryllis dressed quickly and hurried downstairs. Miss Tisdale, Mrs. Vaux, Isabel, and Louise were in the dining-room. The girls seemed none the worse for their adventure. In their presence Tizzy and Aunt Eugenia restrained their curiosity, though Amaryllis could see that a hundred questions hovered on their lips.

Agitated at the thought of the coming interview, she ate little, though Louise reminded her that for her the meal was both breakfast and luncheon. Afterwards, Amaryllis went to her office and sat down at the desk. She took out some correspondence but was unable to concentrate, starting up at every sound to look out of the window.

It was not long before Lord Daniel appeared. At first she did not recognise him as he limped down the path. Though his dress was always casual, he was now dressed in a strange assortment of ill-fitting clothes that must, she realised, have come from the vicar's supply of castoffs for the poor. His hat was an old-fashioned three-cornered creation that he wore at a rakish angle that made him look almost piratical. Judging by his awkward stride, either his shoes were as ill-fitting as the rest or his feet were still sore from being frozen and then forced into the gardener's galoshes.

His right arm swung slightly as he walked, though less than his left. Amaryllis hoped that was a sign of returning strength. She flexed her own arm, the one the Spanish servant had mistreated. She had not noticed before, her thoughts elsewhere, but it was sore at shoulder and elbow, and her back ached from her landing in the dungeon.

In the dungeon—where she had lain in Lord Daniel's naked embrace, quietly, without protest and without shame. She felt the colour rising in her face. What was she to say to him when he walked through that door? What would he say?

She retreated behind her desk, sat down, and put on her spectacles. They made her feel much safer. Straining her ears, she heard the front door open and a murmur of voices. She listened for his step in the passage, but it did not come.

She wondered at the delay, and was beginning to grow angry when it dawned on her that Lord Daniel had gone to see Isabel first.

Waiting was unbearable. She was halfway to the door when it opened and he came in. She stepped backwards until she was leaning against the desk. He appeared as ill at ease as she felt. He stood there, twisting his hat in his hands, his wrists protruding from the sleeves of the too-short coat. He mumbled something that she took to be a greeting.

"Good day, my lord," she answered with tolerable composure.

"Are you . . . I trust you are not much bruised?" he blurted out.

"Not seriously, thank you. How is your arm?"

"Improving."

She wanted to ask about his feet. The memory of how she had warmed them back to life stopped her. The impropriety of her action appalled her, but she seemed to feel again the icy touch between her thighs, bringing a shiver of excitement she had not felt the night before.

"Miss Hartwell," he broke the silence that had fallen between them, "your vicar has urged me to ask you to marry me, as soon as may be."

His voice sounded strange, half-strangled, and a flush stained his thin face as she looked at him in outrage.

"Mr. Raeburn has Gothic notions of propriety," she said coldly. "I should not dream of following his advice."

"But indeed, I had every intention of asking you anyway." He stepped forward eagerly.

She put up her hands as if to ward him off.

"I assure you it is unnecessary. I do not consider myself compromised in any way, nor need you fear that Mr. Raeburn will spread the story. He is a clergyman and a true gentleman."

"I *want* to marry you. It is the only honourable thing to do."

"Honourable! And was it honourable to abandon your wife in a foreign country?" The Spaniard's narrative, lost in the terror of the night, flooded back to her. "Was it honourable to leave her in a position where her only alternatives were death or dishonour? Yes, I heard Don Miguel's words, my lord. Would God I might have closed my ears to them, but I heard them. Little wonder that you shut yourself away in the country, ashamed to see family or neighbours. And you want to marry me? Do you suppose that by treating me well you will wipe out your mistreatment of your first wife? Why should I marry you?" Because I love you, her heart cried out, but the words did not reach her lips.

His face was white now, the dark brows drawn together in a scowl.

"If you wish to believe de la Rosa's words, I cannot prevent it," he said with a sneer.

"If it is not true, why do you hide from society like a craven?"

"Are you not in hiding yourself, Miss Hartwell? George has told me the sorry tale of your own little scandal. Why did you not face society and fight it out, instead of retreating to a life of drudgery?"

"At least I earn an honest living."

"If you marry me, you will escape the drudgery."

"I do not need to marry you to escape. I am going to marry Lord Pomeroy, and I have no conceivable need of you. I beg you will leave at once, my lord, and I pray we may never meet again."

In two strides he was at her side. He swept her into his arms and kissed her savagely. She fought him with all her strength and suddenly he released her. His arm hanging useless at his side he left, without a word, without a backward glance.

Amaryllis sank into the nearest chair, buried her face in her hands, and wept.

=19=

FOR TWO DAYS, Miss Tisdale and Mrs. Vaux treated Amaryllis like a fragile porcelain doll. They asked no questions. She did not know how much they guessed or had been told by the vicar, but she was grateful for their forbearance. Often, in silent misery, she embraced them and was comforted as if she were eight years old again.

Early on the third day, a note arrived from Bertram. He was back at the castle and longed to see her. Unless he heard to the contrary, he would pick her up at eleven and take her driving. She sent the groom back bearing her acceptance and turned to the anxious ladies with a calm smile.

"I have been behaving like a spoiled child," she confessed wryly. "You are too good to me, dear Aunt, dear Tizzy. I shall marry Bertram and do my best to make him a good wife."

They smiled and sighed with relief and reminded her of his faithfulness, his kindness and generosity, his indulgence of her waywardness.

"Shall we have a double wedding, Tizzy?" she asked, then added teasingly, "No, you shall have your day of glory, for I want to be married by Mr. Raeburn, and he cannot officiate at his own wedding."

Mrs. Vaux decided it was not the moment to point out that Lord Pomeroy would undoubtedly expect to be married at Tatenhill, since his father was ailing. The fewer disadvantages Amaryllis saw to the marriage, the less likely she was to be overcome by one of her distempered freaks and to risk losing so eminently satisfactory a bridegroom as his lordship.

Bertram picked her up promptly. It was a still, cold, sunny day. Much of the snow had melted, but the air was wintery chill. He was driving his curricle, so she wrapped herself in her warm cloak, refusing to think of the last time it had been used. Bertram tucked a fur rug about her knees. He looked particularly handsome as he grinned down at her, asking solicitously if she thought she would be warm enough. His many-caped driving coat fitted to perfection. His hat was set at a jaunty angle, and his boots gleamed with blacking as his team of chestnuts gleamed with much currying.

She smiled with a rush of affection and assured him she would do very well. He gave the chestnuts the office, and they set out towards Halstead and Colchester. She asked after the earl and his mother and told him about Miss Tisdale's betrothal and Mrs. Vaux's plans for finding a small house. Not unnaturally he found this encouraging, but he waited until they had passed through the busy streets of Halstead before he broached the subject on the tip of his tongue.

"Amaryllis, have you made your decision? Will you marry me, my darling?"

"I must tell you something first. I ought to have told you long ago. When you hear it, you may wish to cry off."

He looked at her in alarm.

"It is my father. I told you he is in America. Bertram, he has opened a shop. A hardware store, he calls it. He is an ironmonger."

His lordship shouted with laughter, making the horses twitch their ears and shake their heads.

"Viscount Hartwell an ironmonger!" he exclaimed. "What an excessively respectable occupation for the old reprobate. Oh, I beg your pardon, Amaryllis, but I never for a moment thought he would come to so honest an end."

"But you cannot wish to be married to the daughter of an ironmonger," she said, with a glance of reproach for his levity.

"If he opened up shop in Leeds I might be concerned for my father's sake. With the Atlantic Ocean between us, I have not the least qualm in the world about begging yet again for your hand."

Amaryllis's heart sank. She realised that unconsciously she had hoped he would cry off. He was not particularly high in the instep, but he would soon be Earl of Tatenhill. He had a duty to his family. Society might forgive her for having been a schoolmistress. They might forgive the viscount for running off with the daughter of the Spanish Ambassador. They might even forgive one of their own for turning to trade to keep body and soul together, but they would certainly look askance at a countess with all three instances of bad Ton against her.

Bertram did not care. For a moment the thought cheered her. She looked up at him and met blue eyes full of self-confident hope and a trace of amusement. The words trembled on her lips, the words that would make her his forever.

"I cannot!" A vision of dark eyes filled with pain and anger hid him from her. "I cannot. I love someone else."

She leaned forwards, head bowed, curling around the agony in her heart. He pulled up the horses, put his arm round her shoulders, and held her against him.

"Winterborne?" he asked gently.

She nodded, not trusting her voice.

"Does he know?"

"No. I don't know. We quarrelled most dreadfully. How can I love a man who is so impossible? I do not know if he even likes me."

Bertram offered her his handkerchief, but her eyes were dry. He turned the curricle and drove back through Halstead in a thoughtful silence. After a while, hoping to distract her, he began to tell her about the latest ghost to haunt Hedingham Castle. He described the ladder found in the oubliette, the missing galoshes, the clothes discovered mysteriously inside the locked keep. Every word stabbed her with memories of that horrifying night, with fear that someone might unravel the mystery.

"There is no clue as to whom the clothes belong to?" she asked with heightened colour.

"They are very ordinary gentleman's apparel, of good quality but in no way distinguishable from any others. No fancy waistcoat, no monograms, no card case in the coat pocket."

She could not suppress a sigh of relief and he turned on her instantly.

"Amaryllis, you know something of this. Do not deny it. I hope I can tell by now when you are gammoning me. What happened?"

She lowered her eyes, but she knew that her flushed cheeks were giving her away.

" 'Fore God," he said savagely, "if he has hurt you I shall make him pay for it, whether you love him or not."

Shaking her head, she laid her hand on his arm and forced herself to speak. "No, he was badly hurt himself. Not physically, at least not seriously, but . . . I cannot tell you, Bertram. It is not my story."

His jaw was clenched, and she saw a muscle jumping in his cheek. He kept his eyes on the road and presently spoke in a deliberately calm voice.

"I hope I have said nothing to mislead you. I have learned something more of him since last I saw you, and I must believe him more sinned against than sinning."

She did not dare ask him to elaborate, especially when it occurred to her that he might be speaking from kindness, not knowledge. She wished passionately that she was in love with him. The curricle drew up in front of the school, and he handed her down.

"I'm sorry," she said. "You must think I have been playing fast and loose. I did indeed intend to accept. You know I hold you in the greatest affection, and I would have tried to make you happy."

"Hush, love. How could I be happy, knowing that your heart was given to another? I wish you every happiness with . . . him."

"Can we be friends?"

"One day. Yes, one day. It is too much to ask of me now." He bowed and swung himself up into the carriage.

"You are the most perfect gentleman I have ever known," she said in a soft voice.

His eyes were on his horses. "Yes," he agreed bitterly, "I am a gentleman." He drove off.

Amaryllis went into the house and up to her chamber without seeing anything on the way. She sat down on her bed, stiff and straight, staring blankly at the wall. She had driven Lord Daniel away. She had refused Bertram. Tizzy was to be married, and Aunt Eugenia was making plans with her new friend that did not include her niece.

Only Papa was left to her. When Amaryllis went down to dinner, some hours later, she announced in a cool, calm, and decided tone that come June she would be going to Philadelphia. Miss Tisdale and Mrs. Vaux exchanged glances and did not argue.

It was only two days until the school reopened for the spring term. Amaryllis rose early the next morning to complete her preparations. There was a cold, empty place inside her. She ignored it and concentrated on her work, defying the ghosts that wandered through her office.

At a little after eleven Daisy knocked on her open door. "There's a gentleman to see you, miss. Here's his card."

Not Lord Daniel, then, nor Bertram. The maid knew them both by name. She looked at the card.

George, Lord Winterborne.

"Show him in, please, Daisy."

When she heard his steps in the passage, she rose and went round the desk to greet him. He closed the door behind him and stood looking at her in silence. She returned his gaze.

George Winterborne: tall, dark, and handsome; gazetted flirt; breaker of hearts though he had never broken hers; something of a rake if rumour spoke true; heir to the Marquis of Bellingham and as such one of the most eligible gentlemen in the kingdom. Yet, careful Mamas had warned away susceptible debutantes. Lord Winterborne was not hanging out for a wife.

At six and thirty, George's waistline had thickened a little. There were a few grey hairs at his temples, adding to the thoughtful maturity of his face—that face, so like his brother's. She closed her eyes to avoid the sight.

"Miss Hartwell." He bowed.

"George." She tried to collect her wits. "Will you not be seated?" She sat down, and he followed suit. "I did not expect a visit from you."

"You know I have been staying at Wimbish?" he asked guardedly.

"Isabel mentioned it. She is very fond of you."

"And of you. Miss Hartwell, it is going to be difficult explaining my errand. I hope you will be patient with me."

She nodded. She did not remember ever seeing the self-assured Corinthian looking so uncertain.

"Three days ago, I went to visit friends," he began. "I did not return to Wimbish until afternoon the next day, when I discovered the house in an uproar and Daniel and the girls missing. Before I could decide what to do, they returned. I ought perhaps to say that these past few weeks I have thought that at last, after eleven years, Daniel was beginning to forget the past. He has been in better spirits than I can remember since he was a boy, and I have had intimations of your responsibility for the change."

She made a gesture of denial.

"Do not demur," he said quickly. "It is in all respects a change for the better. But when he came home that day, he looked hag-ridden and ill. He told me what had happened, and that you had believed the Spaniard's tale. He had not talked so openly to me since . . . since he told me a story that I should like to repeat to you, if you are interested."

"What makes you think I might be interested?"

"Pomeroy came to Wimbish yesterday. He did not see my brother, but he asked me to tell him that you had refused his offer of marriage. That is all." He looked at her enquiringly.

She sent a silent blessing after Bertram and asked, "Did you tell him? Lord Daniel?"

"No. I thought it best to speak to you first. God knows I do not want to raise any false hopes. Danny has been through hell, and I want to explain that hell to you."

"I am willing to listen."

"It began in 1808. Danny had always been mad for a pair of colours and when Wellington—Wellesley he was then—was ordered to Portugal, my father allowed him to join the army. He went out to the Peninsula in November, just in time to march with Sir John Moore into Spain. I have talked to others who were on the retreat to Corunna, as well as to Danny, and I will try to make you understand what it was like. Picture the scene, Amaryllis—the Spanish mountains in winter . . ."

The pallid youth clasped his right arm, with its bloodstained bandage, closer to his chest as the cart hit a particularly vicious pothole. Shifting his legs, he tried to ease the position of the man lying in his lap. He scarcely noticed the major's constant moaning now. More disturbing were the occasional groans and whimpers of the others in the cart, but worst of all were the cries for help, the savage cursing, of those for whom there was no room. Wounded, frostbitten, or simply too tired to move, they would lie in the trampled snow by the stony mountain road till death or the French caught up with them.

The young man shivered convulsively. A cheerful voice hailed as Lieutenant Gerald Fox rode up beside the cart, his mare stiff-legged with fatigue.

"Danny, can you make room for a lady? The wheel came off a carriage full of Spanish refugees back there."

Perched on the mare's crupper, a slight figure swathed in black gazed pleadingly at the passengers. Her eyes, black as her clothes, glowed huge in a pretty face now pinched with cold. The men moved uneasily, trying to make room where there was none. Then one spoke in a hoarse voice.

"Looks like Jem's bought it, sir. 'E won't mind now if the Frogs get 'im."

The driver glanced over his shoulder, then hauled on the reins to bring his plodding mules to a halt. Lieutenant Fox summoned a pair of nearby dragoons, and while they unloaded Jem's stiff body, Fox made the introductions.

"This is Lieutenant Lord Daniel Winterborne, ma'am. He'll take care of you. Danny, the Doña Francisca Cortés. She speaks a few words of French."

"Pleased to meet you, ma'am." muttered Lord Daniel, blushing a fiery red and looking down quickly as his eyes met hers. He tried to smooth down his unruly, dark hair. "Gerald," he added desperately as his friend dismounted and swung the lady down, "my French ain't exactly fluent."

"Nor is hers," the lieutenant assured him blithely and deposited Doña Francisca beside him. "How's the arm, old boy? The guides say we're nearly through these confounded mountains. If we can just beat Soult to Corunna we'll be home in a week." With a salute that was more of a wave, he rode off.

Napoleon's marshal on his heels, Sir John Moore marched his diminishing army northwest towards the Bay of Biscay. Six thousand men he lost, to skirmishes, cold, and exhaustion. When at last the demoralised column straggled into the port of Corunna, the promised transports had not yet arrived.

"They had no time to set up hospitals in Corunna," said George. "Think of it, Amaryllis. Danny was just nineteen, reduced from dashing cavalry officer to semi-invalid, feverish too, for all I know. And there's this pretty young woman with languishing black eyes looking up to him as the hero who can save her from the ravishing Frenchmen. Is it surprising that he married her as soon as he found a willing priest? As his wife she could count on a place on the transports."

Two days passed before the fleet sailed into the harbour. As the ships dropped anchor, Marshal Soult's corps was sighted in the hills south of the town. While the wounded and sick were hurried onto the transports, the general led his troops out to battle. The French were repulsed, but there were no songs of victory. Sir John Moore was dead. They buried him hastily in the citadel. Next day the army sailed for England.

When they reached Portsmouth, Lord Daniel took rooms for his bride and commended her to the care of his brother officers. He wrote a brief and shaky note to his parents to inform them of his return and his marriage, and then submitted himself to the knives of the army surgeons. The bullet they removed from his upper arm had smashed against the bone and fragmented. By the time they had finished, muscle, nerve, and tendon were mangled. Full recovery of the use of the arm was doubtful.

"I arrived a week later," Lord Winterborne went on. "By that time Doña Francisca—she never wanted to be called Lady Winterborne—was no helpless waif. Danny's friends had rallied round, taken her shopping, encouraged her to learn English. She visited Danny every day, Gerald Fox saw to that, and spent the rest of her time holding court in that little room or gadding about the town with the officers. Oh, she was an attractive minx, with an enchanting giggle and a way of looking at a man as if he was the only one in her universe. If she had saved that for Danny . . ."

The colonel went to see Lord Daniel. By that time he was clearheaded, able to sit up in a chair, and he accepted with equanimity the news that his military career was at an end. He had already planned to sell out for Francisca's sake. She could not, like other officers' wives, retreat to the bosom of her family while her husband was occupied.

He left the hospital, rejoined his bride, proudly accepting compliments and congratulations on his marriage. He adored his pretty wife with her engaging ways. His brother, staying in a nearby hotel, tactfully left the newlywed couple to themselves until he discovered that the constant entertaining was continuing. After three days, Danny was no stronger and when he suggested a peaceful day without visitors Doña Francisca pouted and declared she could imagine nothing duller. However, Major Tomlin had invited her to drive with him, so Danny could rest while she was out.

"Major Tomlin was a notorious libertine," George said, frowning down at his linked hands. "A handsome, dashing, redheaded Irishman, who had been in Portugal with Wellesley since the beginning. Danny asked her not to go, and she sulked all day. That was when he decided he was well enough to travel to Bellingham."

"What did Lord Bellingham think of the marriage?" asked Amaryllis.

"He was not happy. Danny was nineteen. A foreign bride, a Papist marriage, no acquaintance with her family. But there was no fear of him disinheriting my brother. He gave him the manor at Wimbish. My mother was shocked at the news, of course, but far more concerned about his health. She wanted him under her care. We took the long journey into Northumberland in easy stages, but it exhausted him, and drove Doña Francisca wild with impatience. Perhaps we should have waited. It seemed more important to remove Doña Francisca from Major Tomlin's influence, especially when Gerald Fox told me of hearing a rumour that they had met in Lisbon, before ever Danny went out there."

THE VISIT TO Bellingham was not a success. At first Francisca was impressed and a little overawed by the vast mansion, but within a few days she was bored with it and its inhabitants. She made no effort to hide her boredom. She found the wintry moors about Bellingham dreary, the Tyne a rivulet compared to the Ebro, the neighbours who came to pay bride visits as dull as their surroundings. She was impatient with Danny when his arm failed him. An attempt at flirtation with George led to general embarrassment, and George escaped to his Dorset estate. Lord Daniel found himself defending her against unvoiced criticisms at every turn.

"I rarely saw them after that," George told Amaryllis. "How could I visit my brother when his wife gave every appearance of setting her cap at me? They came down to Wimbish in February. Danny intended to spend the Season in London, showing off his prize to the world, but in March I heard from mama that Doña Francisca was increasing. She was brought to bed in June and delivered of a fine child, my niece Isabel, not six months after their marriage."

"A fine redheaded child," said Amaryllis, horrified.

"You recall the major. Francisca and Daniel were both dark, and Daniel did not even arrive in the Peninsula until late November. It is possible, but unlikely, that Isabel is his daughter."

Daniel sent a curt announcement of the birth to his parents, now in London. On their way north to spend the summer in Bellingham, the marchioness made a detour to see her granddaughter. She burst into tears at the sight of the baby, embraced her brooding son, and refused to speak to his wife. Within a quarter of an hour, she was gone.

Francisca recovered quickly from the birth. She had no interest in her child, and the charms of domesticity had palled. She wanted to go to London and refused to believe Daniel when he told her that the Ton shunned the city in the summer. She sulked, until she discovered by chance that his old regiment was recently garrisoned at Colchester. Within a few days a group of officers rode over, and from then on the house was rarely without a uniform or two.

"I paid a brief visit in August. Already Danny had withdrawn into himself," he said. "He doted on the baby and divided his time between the nursery and his estate, leaving Francisca to entertain the callers. He would not talk to me, not the way he used to when he was wont to bring all his problems to his big brother. And one of the most frequent visitors was a dashing Irish major. I did not stay long. In October the regiment was sent back to Spain. Doña Francisca went with it.

"She was faithful to Tomlin, I will give her that. She followed him through Spain and into France. He went to Vienna with Wellington in '14 and I saw them there. She had aged. She must have been older than Danny, though God knows he aged too. He is five years younger than I, and I do not flatter myself when I say that he looks as much older. It was in Vienna that Tomlin abandoned her, after all those years, and went off in pursuit of an Austrian heiress. He was killed in a duel. The next time I saw her was in Italy. I paid her fare to Barcelona."

"And Daniel?" asked Amaryllis, her throat tight with unshed tears.

"Daniel became a hermit. He would not see the family. My father pushed the divorce through the House of Lords with as little fuss as possible. My mother died soon after, and I took the news to Daniel. After that he let me visit, and Mary, too, on the rare occasions when she can get away from her family, but he has never welcomed us. He adores his daughter, though she bears none of his blood."

"I know. That was what made me first look beyond his shocking manners. Only then I learned about the divorce, and then Don Miguel said . . . He said that Daniel . . ."

"Daniel told me. He thought you had not listened, and then you threw the whole business in his face the next day."

"He could have explained. He could have told me the true story."

"No, he could not. He had been humiliated before you; would you expect him to humiliate himself further? The deserted husband, cuckolded even before marriage. That is a fine tale to use as a plea for sympathy."

"Don't speak of him like that," cried Amaryllis, furious. "Why should he care what I think, anyway? He only asked me to marry him because the vicar said he ought."

"Now there you are fair and far out," said George with an appraising look. "Is that what he told you? It's my belief the young fool was in no condition to consider his words, and he certainly did not remember them. He told me only that you had refused his offer."

"He offered because he thought he had compromised me."

"He may have thought it, but that is not why he proposed. Devil take it, Amaryllis, a man don't fall into black despair unless the woman he loves turns him down."

"Black despair?"

"He came home and told me everything, and since then he's scarce spoken nor eaten nor slept. He looks like a scarecrow. Do you think I'd have come here and embarrassed you with all this if he'd been a little blue-devilled? He was like this just after she left."

Amaryllis paled. In George's dark eyes, so like his brother's she read worry, and hope. She stood up in sudden decision.

"You brought a carriage? I shall go back with you. Pray let us leave at once."

He laughed as he rose and seized her hands.

"You have not changed. But I'm damned if I'll starve, even

for Danny, and breakfast was long ago. Find me a crust and a rind of cheese and we'll be off."

She ordered cold meat and bread and ale for him, then ran to find her aunt and Tizzy.

"I'm going to Wimbish," she announced.

" 'The wicked flee when no man pursueth; but the righteous are bold as a lion,' " said Miss Tisdale, encouraging though confusing.

"You will never be able to return before dark," said Mrs. Vaux in alarm. "You must take one of the maids."

Amaryllis shook her head determinedly. "No, one way or the other it will not matter. I must go now." She kissed her aunt and hugged Tizzy and sped downstairs again to bundle Lord Winterborne into his carriage with his mouth full. He finished his sandwich as they crossed the River Colne, took two wrinkled russet apples from the capacious pocket of his greatcoat and offered her one.

"I suspected I might not be allowed to eat in peace," he said drily as she impatiently waved it away.

She was much too agitated to make conversation. She sat bolt upright on the edge of the seat, clutching the tasselled cord hanging there for that purpose and peering out of the window as if watching the scenery could make it pass faster. George watched her with amusement as he crunched his apples, then laid his hand on her arm and made her sit back.

"You will be exhausted long before we arrive," he pointed out, his voice gentle. "I think perhaps that like Daniel you have slept little for a couple of days. Try to relax."

She leaned back against the squabs and looked at him affectionately. "When I knew you in London, I never guessed you were such a sensitive and considerate person," she said, to his embarrassment. "I should be perfectly willing to fall in love with you if I were not already in love with Daniel. He is lucky to have such a brother."

"Spare my blushes, ma'am." he growled with heightened colour.

"You would make an excellent husband," she said, teasing him. "How is it you have never married?"

"With my brother's example before me, I could not screw my courage to the sticking point," he answered grimly. "Now if you were to provide a pattern-card of domestic felicity, I might change my mind and stick my head into parson's mousetrap after all."

"I shall do my best," she promised with a joyful smile, but by the time they passed through Finchingfield her apprehension had returned. "Are you sure he wishes to marry me?" she asked, painfully anxious.

He took her hand between his. "No man can read another's mind," he said, "but I'd wager my last farthing on it and I'm no gamester."

With that she had to be content. She sighed and leaned back again, wondering whether she could bear to be married to Daniel if he did not love her. Meanwhile, Lord Winterborne, who was not a praying man, raised a fervent prayer that he had read his brother's feelings aright.

At last they pulled up in front of the manor. Its red brick looked warm and inviting in the pale winter sunshine. Amaryllis stepped down from the carriage and smoothed her skirts. She was wearing one of her shabbier brown woolen gowns, not having spared a thought for her appearance when she left home. Suddenly she wished she had changed into her green silk, inappropriate as it was for afternoon wear, or at least into her Sunday best. With nervous hands she poked at her hair, until George impatiently urged her up the steps.

"You shall go upstairs to tidy yourself before you see him, if you wish," he said, "though I doubt he will notice your hairstyle. You are a beautiful woman, my dear, and not one of those whose beauty is dependent upon her dress."

Amaryllis blushed and gave him a speaking glance of gratitude. Nonetheless, she went up to Isabel's chamber and borrowed a comb. She had just let down her copper braids and was wondering indecisively what to do with them, when Isabel and Louise bounced in.

"Miss Hartwell," cried Louise in astonishment. "We did

not know you were coming." She hurriedly followed her friend's lead and curtseyed. "We came up to get our coats and boots to go out in the snow."

"It's mostly melted." Isabel looked at her gravely. "Are you come to see Papa? He is very unhappy."

"Yes." Amaryllis found herself at a loss to explain her unexpected arrival. "Yes, your uncle George brought me."

"Let me help you do your hair," offered Louise eagerly. "Mama often wears it braided at home. I'll show you how she does it."

With amazingly nimble, clever fingers she created a double loop on either side of Amaryllis's face, then she teased down a few curls to soften the brow. She examined her handiwork with delight. Amaryllis regarded her image in the mirror. It looked somewhat Quakerish, but charming. She smiled at her young coiffeuse and thanked her. There was no more excuse for postponing her meeting with Lord Daniel. She pinched her cheeks in a vain effort to give them a little colour.

"You look very pretty," said Isabel reassuringly, and hugged her in her loving, impulsive way. "Papa will be glad to see you."

"I am going to marry him," she whispered, then bit her lip and hurried from the room before she should say anything else she might regret.

She went slowly down the stairs. No one was about, no servants, and no sign of Lord Winterborne. Of course, she could ring for someone to tell her where to find Lord Daniel, but she did not want to. With uncertain steps she went to the library. The door was closed firmly. She raised her hand to knock, then took a deep breath and opened it without announcing her presence. She stepped through and closed it behind her.

Lord Daniel was slouched in a chair by the fire, hands in his pockets, staring at the flames. "George?" he said, not raising his head.

"No, it is not George," she said softly.

He sat up, looking round incredulously, then jumped to

his feet.

"Miss Hartwell! What the devil . . . I beg your pardon won't you be seated?"

She moved towards him, noting the pallor of his frown ing face. She sat down, and he stood scowling at her.

"What brings you here, ma'am?" he asked abruptly.

"Pray sit down, my lord," she answered with composure "I cannot speak to you while you loom over me like the castle keep."

He resumed his seat.

"Aha, I have it," he said after a moment's silence, sneer ing. His eyes were hard. "Pomeroy did not come up to scratch. In spite of my cruelty to my wife, you have recon sidered my offer to rescue you from your life of drudgery."

"How dare you!"

"You cannot expect me to hold open an offer of marriage indefinitely, but I daresay we can come to some arrange ment."

"How *dare* you!" Eyes blazing, fists clenched, Amaryllis jumped up and stalked to the window, where she stood with her back to him. "Lord Pomeroy did come up to scratch. In fact, he held open an offer of marriage for over eight years, until after much heart-searching I refused him yesterday. Bertram was a very dear friend. I shall never for give you if I have lost his friendship for nothing."

"Forgive me? What have I to do with your refusal?"

His tone was contemptuous, but she thought she heard yearning in it. Resolutely she kept her back to him.

"I told him I loved you, and it was true in spite of the dreadful things you let me believe about you."

He was silent. She swung round and met a look of such misery she was startled. He was standing by the fire. When he met her eyes he turned and leaned his left arm against the mantel, resting his bowed head on it.

"You loved me." His voice was so low she moved nearer to hear him. "It was half-true what Don Miguel said, a clever mixture of truth and lies. I am sure he believed it himself. Yet you loved me in spite of it. Have I driven you away,

Amaryllis, with my curst temper?"

Unable to speak, she took his right hand and raised it to her cheek. He looked at her in dawning wonder. His arm went round her, and he held her tight, his cheek against her hair.

"*She* would not touch that hand," he said, and Amaryllis realised he was weeping.

Gently she led him to a sofa. They sat down, and she put her arms about him, waiting for the tears to stop. At last he raised his head, his dark eyes devouring her. She smiled at him lovingly.

"You are one of those lucky souls who can weep without reddening your eyes," she said. "If I indulged in a like bout of tears, I should have to hide away for an hour before I was presentable. But we women are fortunate in being permitted to cry. I think that was long overdue, was it not?"

His face was younger, as if ten years of unbearable tension had washed away. She smoothed his ruffled hair, conscious of its crisp, springy texture. He took her face in both hands and kissed her lips with the utmost gentleness. "Amaryllis," he murmured.

A shiver went through her and she moved into his arms.

They sat in silence for a while, heart to heart, then he said, "I can tell you now. I can tell you all about it."

"There is no need, my love. Your brother has explained everything."

"He told you about Francisca? About Isabel?"

"Yes. Bertram came here to inform him that we were not to be married after all, and he went to Castle Hedingham to . . . to discover my feelings, I suppose, and to tell me the truth about Francisca. Bertram is as good a friend to me as George is brother to you."

"You do not mind that Isabel is not my child?"

"She is your child, Daniel. Have you not loved her and watched over her all her life? You have been both parents to her, and I see a great deal of you in her, not of looks but of character."

"Not of my temper, I trust."

She laughed. "No, but then, I suspect she rarely sees your temper."

"Nor shall you see it henceforth," he said seriously.

"Make no promises you cannot keep. I shall be vastly surprised if we do not come to cuffs now and then, for I have a temper of my own."

"Once I knew you, I was only angry when I thought you did not care for me. Do you care for me, Amaryllis?"

She looked up at him, suddenly shy. The tenderness and hunger in his eyes made her heart beat faster.

"I love you so much it hurts. And you, Daniel?"

"I adore you. You are the light of my life. That may sound trite but it is true, so do not giggle, my darling. You have led me out of the darkness where I thought to lie entombed forever. I adore you."

That highly satisfactory answer called for a kiss, so she supplied one. His response left her breathless.

"There is one little thing you have forgotten," she said when she could speak again. "A mere formality, but I must insist that it be observed."

He looked alarmed and puzzled, till he saw that she was teasing.

"What is it, love?" he asked indulgently. "Have you some guardian hidden away of whom I ought to ask permission to address you?"

She laughed, eyes sparkling. "Yes, there is, though I had quite forgot him. You told me you are aware of my scandalous past, but what you cannot know is that Papa is now an ironmonger in Philadelphia, and a highly successful one by his own account."

"I'm sorry, but if it means waiting for a reply from America, I must respectfully decline to approach Viscount Hartwell."

"You do not mind that he is in trade?"

"You need not fear that I mean to cry off only because your Papa chooses to make his fortune selling nails and . . . whatever else ironmongers sell."

"You cannot cry off," she pointed out severely, "for we

are not yet betrothed. The proposal is the formality to which I referred."

It was his turn to laugh. "How remiss of me, my darling. Now I come to think of it, all I have done is to offer you carte blanche. Under the circumstances it is most improper in you to have encouraged me to kiss you, but I assure you I do not mean to cavil." His eager mouth swiftly approached hers.

She dodged. "How excessively ungentlemanly!" she said with great indignation.

He slid from the sofa to kneel at her feet, and took her hand in his.

"My dear Miss Hartwell, you must know how greatly I admire you. Will you do me the inestimable honour of accepting my hand and heart in marriage?"

"That is much better." Amaryllis fluttered her eyelids at him coyly. "My lord, I am sensible of the honour you do me, and I confess that your sentiments are reciprocated. I will."

With ceremony, his heart in his eyes, he raised her hand to his lips. At the last second his bad arm gave way. Calmly he caught her hand with his left and continued the gesture, touching his lips to the back in gentlemanly fashion and then turning it over and pressing a passionate kiss on the palm.

"There," he said, "now we are properly betrothed, and you are permitted to encourage me to kiss you."

She was about to do so when the door burst open. Isabel ran in, out of breath, the spaniels gambolling at her heels.

"Papa, Mama, pray come quick," she gasped. "I *told* her there was not enough snow left."

Amaryllis blushed as Lord Daniel looked at her with raised eyebrows, grinning. He turned back to his daughter.

"What's to do?" he asked.

"Oh do come quick! Louise was sliding off the stable roof into a drift of snow and I think she has broke her arm!"

217

If you have enjoyed this book and would like to receive details of other Walker Regency romances, please write to:

Regency Editor
Walker and Company
720 Fifth Avenue
New York, NY 10019